Late Night Boyfriends

TALES OF THE GAY VAMPIRE

EDITED BY ETHAN KILBURN

KORHUGGTANDER PRESS

Kilburn, Ethan
    Late Night Boyfriends: Tales of the gay vampire / edited by
    Ethan Kilburn.
    ISBN-10: 09813416–0–8
    ISBN-13: 978-0-9813416-0-6
    1. Vampires—Fiction. 2. Gay men—Fiction

First Korhuggtander Press edition: September 2009

Contents

Slave
RYAN BRIXTON · 4

All in your head
EPHRAM GREEN · 24

Brotherhood
VICTOR HARROW · 38

Immortality found in a laundry mat
PERRIN LATIMER · 54

Campus coverup
IAN RICHMOND · 76

Rescue
LUC RUISLIP · 88

Attack
ADAM SHEPARD · 100

A happy accident
OLIVER SLOANE · 114

Secrets
MATT CAMDEN · 124

The ex-boyfriend
ISSAC HOLLAND · 150

Skater boys
VIAN WATFORD · 164

The new boy
SPENCER TERREAN · 182

Second chance
ETHAN KILBURN · 202

Slave

BY RYAN BRIXTON

Snow had started to fall when I walked through the part of boys town where a casual glance was an invitation. Since I was looking for trouble, I found it quickly.

He came round a corner emerging out of a dark alley and I was completely mesmerized by his good looks. The tails of the long wool coat he wore flew behind him in the wind. Though it was buttoned loosely with the collar turned up, he didn't look cold. In fact, even at the current fridged temperature he wore only a black t-shirt and nothing on his head, revealing closely shaved black hair. Tight leather pants clung to his legs and I could see the silver of two zippers sparkle against the black on each side of his bulging crotch. His face was dark and hidden in shadows.

When I smiled as he approached, he regarded me with hunger. He stopped and opened my jacket, feeling my body with his cold bare hands. Finally he leaned his head to my neck and inhaled sharply then whispered, "you will do."

With no other word I followed him to a converted warehouse several blocks away. Boys town was still in the rougher part of the city, but slowly the brick warehouses were being converted and the neighborhood gentrified. But his building was still on the edge between the renovated lofts and the rough industrial factories and warehouses.

He led me up two floors and into a large open double-height loft. His coat was on a hook before he'd locked the door behind me. I slipped mine off and hung it next to his while he disappeared up a set of steel stairs a few feet away.

I followed him up the stairs, passing through a small seating area in the upper loft that might normally have been the bedroom. A door tucked around a corner led passed a bathroom deep into the actual bedroom, a large windowless room. The man stood by the bed, his feet bare and t-shirt removed to reveal a muscular upper body covered with a light dusting of short black hair mainly over his belly and descending into his pants.

He moved to me quickly, pulling my sweater and shirt off in one move. Soon he was undoing my jeans. Pushing me onto the large bed, he removed my jeans and socks. I slid myself further onto the bed and he knelt down, his leather sheathed legs straddling mine.

Before I could blink he had opened his mouth, and pulled back his lips in a wicked grin. I watched in shock as he canine teeth grew into two sharp fangs. I suddenly felt the teeth roughly pierce my neck, not realizing how quickly he had lowered his face to my throat. I felt his lips as they pressed against my skin and he sucked at my blood.

Quickly I came to me senses and acted. "Turn me," I whispered, almost pleading. I had seen many a vampire film and a few porns to know I'd rather be undead then really dead. He pulled away from my neck and smiled, licking my blood from his lips.

"You want to be like me?"

"Yes," I moaned, "please make me immortal." I begged further.

The expression on his face was serene, thoughtful and yet somehow devious. Maybe it was the addition of his fangs, which he showed again when his lips parted. Only the tips protruded passed his upper lip, but my eyes were still focused on them.

"I have made my decision," his smile was warm yet wicked as he spoke.

"You will live to be my," he paused and closed his eyes, took a breath and tried to look sexy. "...slave," he finished enunciating the final word with a sudden viciousness to his smooth voice.

"What?"

"I don't make a habit of turning every boy who asks and I see no reason to make an exception for someone as plain as you. But you are lucky, my last servant got a little cheeky and I drained him. Now I have an opening."

I must have looked skeptical, when deep inside I was fearful. His eyes swept across me.

"You were only meant to be a meal, and you will still be one if you disobey me. I shall allow you three days to clear up your former life and move in here," he chuckled. "Well into the servant's quarters, not my bed," he added, shoving me off the bed. I hit the floor, landing on my back.

Grabbing me roughly the vampire dragged me out of his room and down the stairs. The double height living room zoomed by at the bottom of the stairs, as did the kitchen and dining area under the loft. A narrow hallway led passed an office and the laundry room to a small bedroom directly underneath his.

"This will be your room. You can keep or throw away the last servant's possessions as you see fit. Don't bring much of your former life, I do not like a mess."

I drew up some courage and spoke lightly, "what is stopping me from running away?"

The vampire smiled, again showing his sharp teeth, "I have your scent and I can find you anywhere. If you run or attempt to go to the authorities, you will be lucky if I let you meet your death quickly. Also," he paused and glared at me. Unknowingly a lowered myself and kneeled in front of him. He continued, "why did you kneel?"

"I don't know, I just had this desire to do it."

"No, I made you do it. When I choose, I can control you. You may or may not know I am controlling you. For example," he stopped and smiled but I heard his voice rang out inside my mind, *"stand up slave!"*

I stood slowly, shaking with fear. The vampire advanced on me slowly, forcing me against the bedroom wall. He bared his fangs and looked down at me.

"You belong to me now. And you will serve me with whatever I need." He pressed his face to my neck and inhaled deeply. The second bite was rougher but as I winced in pain, I held back the whimper.

When he withdrew his sharp teeth his hand gripped my balls like a vice. I collapsed to the floor when he finally released them. Lying on the cold concrete in agony, I watched him disappear at super-human speed and return a few seconds later. He throw my clothes on the floor, then knelt down beside me. "That is just a taste of what you can expect if you cross me. Now go."

I dressed in a rush and went to leave, but as I touched the door, he stopped me and stared into my eyes, gently caressing my face.

"I can be nice too, if you behave. Now, go but know that I will be watching you. Return at sunset tomorrow." He unlocked the door and allowed me to leave.

I hurried back to my place and began to form a plan, hoping to return before the next evening when the sun was still out. Around midnight he came through my apartment window, seeming to have scaled the nine stories. I cowered in the corner of my small studio, frightened he'd changed my mind.

"This is the part where I show up and remind you not to come up with any plans to kill me."

"I wasn't," I lied.

"Come now, don't lie, I can hear your heart beat faster. You probably thought you would return during the day. Be honest with me now and spare yourself the pain."

"Okay, you're right."

He crossed the room in one stride and smacked me.

"You have one day to clean up your life. Take what you can, leave the rest to be thrown out. Tomorrow you will end any employment you have. Tie up loose ends so people do not come looking for you. Then return to my place at 3," he smiled wickedly, "that's right, before sunset."

Then he vanished out the window.

I obeyed the orders and called into my crappy job, telling them I was moving suddenly. I packed what I could, which was not much and called my friend Ashton, who happened to be my apartment building manager. I explained I was leaving to deal with a family emergency and needed to give notice. He came by and helped me put most of my things, minus the cheap furniture in a spare storage locker in the basement.

Ashton and I had flirted on many occasion, and I had hoped to get him into bed, though he had a steady boy friend now. He made the vampire look ugly, a young cherub of a boy, just 22 with bright blue eyes, a sculpted face, thousand watt but alluring smile and gorgeous blond hair. Ashton was everything I was not; built, good looking and well hung, but as I had heard from friends, we were a match in the bedroom. He seemed concerned for me, and wanted me to keep in touch.

We moved my furniture to a common storage area where other tenants could take what they wanted. Finally I gathered two suitcases and went to leave. Ashton gave me a long kiss goodbye and again told me to call him.

A few minutes before 3pm I found myself knocking on the vampire's door. He opened the door and stood as I'd seen him in his bedroom, wearing only tight leather pants. I had hoped to get inside those pants the night before but found a nightmare instead. The sunlight bathed his sculpted upper body.

I discovered then that he could move through daylight, but lived nocturnally. He warned me over time that he could not be killed, though eventually I discovered another vampire could do him in. On that first afternoon, we finally exchanged names, though he rarely addressed me as Zac.

My life was now to serve Caleb, and run his errands. Amazingly he gave me the freedom to move about, though he warned me to avoid my former life. From time to time he would bring other men back to the apartment, sometimes having sex before feeding from them. Some, those who didn't know they'd been fed from, were allowed to leave, but most were drained. I was always shown the boys so that I could get a sense of Caleb's type. Twice he allowed me pick up guys saying I could play with them for a bit, instead he took both for himself.

The first few weeks had been the hardest. For the first two months, I was a captive inside his loft. Groceries were delivered once a week.

Caleb did not require food, only human blood, but he purchased a small amount to keep me fed. A stocked kitchen seemed mostly for display should any guests wonder into the kitchen or require food themselves. The fridge was well-stocked with wine, beer and other alcoholic drinks, again primarily for guests though Caleb did drink regularly.

Every night, Caleb would venture outside the apartment, locking the heavy steel door as he went. The deadbolt required a lock on both sides and only Caleb held the key. On his third or fourth night out, once I could guess the lengths of his prowls, I searched the loft determined to find the key. I had been extremely careful to search without disturbing the exact placement of everything. When he returned with his dinner, Caleb quickly scanned his eyes across the apartment and knew.

My search had reached the office when he sent a message directly to my mind. *"Go to your room, slave,"* he commanded. At first I jumped with fright, his voice sending an icy chill down my spine. I tidied the office and dove into my room, silently closing my bedroom door as I heard his key in the door.

I stilled my breathing and listened as Caleb brought in his prey, the sound of their feet fading to nothing as they ascended the stairs. I sat on my bed and fidgeted, unsure what to do. This was the first time he brought a guy home since I'd moved in. The same scene from my first night played in my head. I wondered if he planned to feed, kill or have sex.

My thoughts were shattered when he came gently through the door in a rage, his fangs descended. Caleb pushed me into the bed, forcing his weight against my body. He clamped one hand over my mouth, while another crushed my balls. He sank his sharp teeth into my neck viciously. Instead of piecing the skin, his tore into it. I heard his heavy gulps as he drank back my blood before he seemed to calm down. After a long minute, he stopped drinking.

He whispered in my ear. "Don't you ever go looking through my things again. What were you hoping to find, be honest and I might go easy on you?" He loosened the pressure over my mouth, but did not remove the hand.

"Keys," I whispered back, weak and scared.

"You will not find another key, there is only one and it is always with me." He sat up straight, the hand removed from my mouth, but the other still crushing the balls. Unfortunately I was getting hard. He smiled as my cock swelled. "I have a guest and don't wish to be disturbed. You will remain in your room and silent as a corpse. Make a sound and you will become one."

A smile spread across Caleb's face and his sigh sounded erotic. "Hm, I was hungry but I think your blood will hold me over while I fuck that delicious morsel upstairs." He stood and walked into the hall, leaving the door open. At first I figured he had left it open so I might hear the sounds of sex from upstairs but instead I heard something slide, followed by a thump and the click of a lock.

Causally I leaned across the bed and peered out the door, a surge of pain reminding me that my balls were tender. A pocket door blocked the hallway, locked from the outside and keeping me trapped but able to use the bathroom. I hadn't noticed the hidden door before, and I found with further snooping over time that door was well camouflaged, recessed flush and designed to create the appearance of a wall from the other side. Should this or another guest wonder through the apartment, he would not discover anything beyond the laundry room.

I learned that night to keep some food stored in my room as this guest remained for two nights, while I remained behind the wall. After the second night and another morning, Caleb unlocked the door and showed me his victim. I recognized him from the clubs. He was about my age, muscular but toned and lean, his ass two firm globes. There were bite marks on his neck, thighs and dick. Caleb had dumped the body on the living room floor and returned to his bed.

As I devoured whatever food I could find in the fridge, I stared out at the corpse, fearing that someday I would be there too. Worst, I worried the day away in fear that Caleb would fly into another rage if I didn't remove the body.

Late that evening he came down the stairs, scooped the young man into a body bag and left. Eventually when I was allowed out on my own, I snuck a visit to a internet cafe and researched several of Caleb's victims. All were found in their own apartments, never any evidence of foul play and no clues to how they died. I wanted to tip off the authorities but knew better.

More often than not, Caleb simply drank a small amount from his prey and allowed them to live, usually if they hadn't discovered his secret. He fed on me at least once a week and brought a guest home also about once a week, or not at all if he'd fed on me twice that week.

Even when the weeks dragged by and I became used to my new life, I found Caleb's violent mood swings unpredictable. In the beginning I thought he was more vicious if he hadn't fed, but he soon proved that theory wrong. I made every attempt to tread carefully but the smallest and most random actions would bring Caleb to my throat.

I knew he was setting the boundaries and laying down the law, but on one evening without any provocation he sprang on me. He had fed the night before and barely fed from this time, choosing instead to assault me. But his assaults were never sexual and I longed for the moment he would impale me with his cock. The moment never came.

One evening I was stocking the fridge with several cases of beer Caleb had brought home. I had spent the entire day fulfilling a growing list of chores as he kept adding more tasks to do. Nearly done the fridge stocking, Caleb came into the kitchen and lifted me up and threw me against the wall. The bottle I was holding slipped and smashed on the tile floor. He looked even more discussed then tore his fangs into my throat but didn't feed. The bites continued across my body as Caleb ripped and torn my clothes off, finally leaving me in my underwear covered in cuts.

The wounds healed quickly every time, thanks to his special saliva, but he'd soon create new ones at a whim.

I lived in fear. Constant fear that he would disapprove of a single action. But at other times he would be kind and gentle, which made him all the more unpredictable. Eventually I was allowed to make myself more at home and he allowed me to have free time when my chores were done and there were no visitors. I was even permitted to use the tv on occasion. One evening I had just begun to watch an old black and white movie when Caleb wandered over at sat on the couch next to me. Soon his was cuddling against me.

The next night his demeanor was again cold and distant. When I delivered fresh towels to Caleb's bathroom, he knocked me to floor and knelt with his knees pressing against my chest. He again crushed my balls in his hand while he glared at me. Almost for show he slid his fangs down and licked his lips. I wondered then if he wanted to feed or was contemplating finally killing me. But as quickly as the attack came, he stood and left.

After nine months as his servant, my has birthday arrived. It is the first holiday I have suddenly felt a pang of nostalgia for. In the early evening my cellphone rang. I was shocked as few people knew I'd kept the number and it had not rung much as a result. I was delighted to see that it was Ashton calling me.

"Hey," I answered eagerly.

"Zac, is that you?"

"Yeah Ashton, it's me."

"I'm amazed you still have this number."

"Oh, you know, um, I needed a connection to my real home," I said awkwardly.

"I just wanted to try calling to wish you happy birthday!"

"You remembered, that's so sweet. Thank you," I turned and found Caleb sitting next to me.

He started to speak and I told Ashton to hold on.

"Who are you talking with?"

"An old friend," I pointed to a photo among a sea of snapshots on my wall next to the bed. "He called to wish me a happy birthday."

Caleb looked at the photo briefly and smiled, "I didn't realize it was your birthday, I am sure you were uncomfortable raising the topic," he paused, then smiled warmly showing a new kindness. "Tell him you're back in town and go for drinks with him. It is your birthday and you've done your chores."

Although I was taken aback by Caleb's pleasant behavior, he had recently been showing me less distain. I took Ashton off hold and continued the conversation.

"Look Ashton, I just arrived in town, are you free to meet up for a drink?"

"Really, that's great. Yeah I'm totally free tonight. How about the Eagle at 10pm?"

"Perfect, see you then."

"Bye," he hung up.

Caleb smiled and stood up, "come to my bedroom, I have something for you that I think you can wear tonight."

Surprised I followed him to his room where he presented me with a black gift box containing a pair of the same leather pants he often wore.

"I need my servant to dress a little better, and I've seen the way you look at my legs when I wear my."

"Thank you, I don't know what to say."

"You just did. Now you'd better get ready."

"Thank you," I moved to embrace him but stopped. His cold glare reminded me of my place.

Minutes before ten I arrived at the Eagle wearing my new pants, combat boots and a black hoodie. Ashton was already drinking a beer at the bar and smiled when I came in. He was wearing leather pants too, only the popular 501 style topped with a simple tight short sleeve v-neck leather shirt, finished with a band around his left wrist. I had never seen him in leather and he looked good, hotter than ever. Then again I hadn't seen him in nine months.

He pulled me into a hug and gave me a quick kiss.

"Wow Zac, I can't believe you're here, and you look good," he said smacking my ass. "Leather fits you."

"You too, I didn't know you were into leather?" I stated as a question.

"Oh yes, I never worn them when I was with Kevin, it wasn't his thing. That's the problem with liking twinkies, so few are into leather." He looked me over with hunger in his eyes then opened my hoodie to reveal my smooth chest. I had begun to use the tiny gym in Caleb's building and was finally starting to show a little definition. "Better," he said simply, then leaned over and kissed my neck.

His lips sent shivers down my back, for him to kiss me, it was sexy, but he reminded me of the times Caleb would feed off me.

"So how's Kevin?"

He inhaled deeply and smiled, "gone. Left me for another twink last summer."

"Oh, I'm sorry."

He shrugged, "I'm not. Oh, gawd. Check out the guy at the end of the bar."

I turned and searched the crowd until my eyes fell on Caleb. He smiled, but not at me.

"Hmm, he's looking at us," Ashton whispered in my ear.

"No, probably just you."

Caleb motioned us over.

"Hey, he wants us, do you want to go, we don't have to if you're uncomfortable?" he asked, sounding eager but aware this was our time together.

"We'd better," knowing full well I'd be punished for keeping Ashton from Caleb. I hadn't tried to hide my plans, but Caleb had superior hearing and obviously heard when and where I'd be. After all, he knew enough to gift me the pants.

"Hi there," Ashton said seductively to Caleb, "I'm Ashton."

"Hello," Caleb purred, taking and kissing Ashton's hand, "I'm Caleb." He smiled and locked eyes with Ashton who broke the stare first and turned to me.

"This is Zac," introducing me.

Caleb caught my eyes but didn't smile, "hello." Apparently he wasn't going to let on I knew him.

"So, Caleb, I don't see you in here much?" Ashton asked.

"I'm a regular, but I haven't been in a few months. Actually to me you seem new."

"Well I was attached for a while, must not have crossed each other's paths."

I wondered if Caleb had heard my conversation with Ashton.

"True. Well since you aren't now attached, I assume, why don't you both come back to my place."

Shit, I thought, there went my chance with Ashton.

"Um," Ashton looked at me, "what do you say, it's your birthday?"

Caleb stared at me, fully intending for the stare to mean saying yes was an order. He confirmed as much inside my mind, *"say yes, slave."*

"I'd love to."

"Shall we then," Caleb put down his bottle and moved for the door.

Surprisingly Ashton took my hand in his and walked me out. When we entered the loft, Ashton was full of praise.

"You have a very nice home."

"Thank you, if would you a drink, you are more than welcome to help yourself."

"I'd be happy with another beer," he turned to me and asked still holding my hand, "yeah, a beer would be nice, I didn't get to have one at the Eagle."

Caleb gave me a look, not for the comment but suggesting that as the servant, I should get the drinks.

"Why don't I get them," I walked into the kitchen and as I opened the fridge Caleb took care of Ashton.

"Ashton, why don't you have a seat? Zac, while you're there, bring me a beer too."

I returned with three beers, the tops already removed, to find Caleb had straddled Ashton on the couch, their lips locked together passionately. This was getting awkward and I wasn't sure where to go.

"Sit down here," Caleb finally said, taking the beer and pointing to the couch opposite Ashton and himself. But when I handed Ashton the beer, he hooked his hand in the my waist of my pants and sat me next to him.

"Sit next to me." Before he took a sip from his bottle, Ashton leaned over and gave me a kiss. I watched Caleb as he glared at me, a wicked smile beginning to form on his face.

Continuing to ignore me, Caleb returned his attention to Ashton, who used one hand to unzip and grab my member while using his other hand to do the same with Caleb. Ashton was finally touching me and I had a hungry vampire between us. He contined to pump both Caleb's cock and mine.

Caleb finally sat straight up and regarded Ashton with lust, his hard cock slipping from Ashton's hand stood proud.

"Let's say you and I continue this is the bedroom," Caleb stated.

Ashton turned his head to me and raked his eyes across my body. It was obvious he wanted both of us, but I didn't know which one he wanted the most.

"Sure, but I want to fuck Zac, and," he paused holding his mouth open seductively, "I'm hoping you'll be fucking me when I did him."

Caleb regarded me cooly then smiled when he looked back at Ashton. "If that would make you happy, it would be my pleasure. I especially want Zac there for the climax," he added mostly toward me. He took Ashton's hand and began to walk him to the bedroom. Ashton quickly grabbed mine and pulled me along, smiling back at me with a wick. Fear was creeping into my mind; I wondered what Caleb was planning on doing now that I was going to be there. He had never fucked me, choosing only to fed instead. Allowing me to join in would allow me pleasure, but maybe he just wanted me to watch.

When we entered the bedroom, Caleb wrapped his arms tightly around Ashton and began kissing him all down his neck until his shirt prevented Caleb from kissing the blond's chest. Completely in control, the vampire pulled Ashton's leather shirt off while he gave me a push onto the bed. With a final hand motion he instructed me to turn round the moment Ashton had his head covered. Gently Caleb led him to the bed so he could begin removing his pants. Ashton made a move to further undo Caleb's own pants, but he took hold of Ashton's hand and held it before leaning closer and kissing him. Their kiss was long and passionate, but Ashton's hands still groped around the bed to find me.

When Caleb finally pulled away and stood to remove his pants, Ashton turned around to kiss me. He fumbled for the zippers on my pants. Now naked, his stiff cock ready for attention, Caleb knelt on the bed and pulled Ashton's pants away, throwing them against the far wall. My pants had been freed from my legs and we were all naked. Ashton leaned in and kissed me, but was soon pulled away by the greedy vampire who directed the blond's mouth to his hard cock.

I was soon jealous, seeing the expression on Caleb's face as he enjoyed being sucked—clearly Ashton's mouth was indeed working its magic.

After several minutes, the blond finally moved his mouth to my dick, unaware that Caleb gave me a dirty look for attracting Ashton's mouth away from his needs. His voice rang out in my head, *"he's mine, slave."* I quickly pushed Ashton off my cock and repositioned my own mouth around his cock while he returned to Caleb's eager member.

I enjoyed and worshipped Ashton's cock, after nine celibate months and countless more pining for this particular penis. All too soon, Ashton pulled away from Caleb and turned to me, holding his dick in his hand, giving me a knowing look. I pressed myself against the sheets and allowed him to slide into me. I feltw Caleb stand over me and soon heard Ashton's sucking resume while he fucked me. When Caleb became bored, he withdrew his cock, but didn't disturb Ashton's thrusts.

We repositioned our bodies, this time into a three-way. Caleb had mounted Ashton from behind forcefully. The blond had moaned loudly when Caleb's large cock had impaled him.

I faced back toward the two men with Ashton's cock still inside me. He pushed into me with every plunge Caleb made into him. Ashton became an extension of Caleb and for the first time he was in giving me pleasure. But it was Ash I had always wanted inside me. Even my master could not say no to the sweet beautiful blond. I wanted Ashton's gentle thrusts to go on forever. My stiff member bounced off my stomach with every forward advance, oozing pre-cum. I held my legs back for Ashton which made it impossible for me to touch my own cock. I wanted it back inside the blond's warm mouth.

Ashton's eyes remained tightly closed, his facial expression modulating between slack and tensed matched with each heavy pant or moan caused by another push from the vampire.

Slowly Caleb's mouth opened and I watched as he unsheathed his fangs. His tongue crawled across his lips and he focused his sight on Ashton's neck; his pounding into his ass never ceasing. I knew then that Ash's life was in danger.

I was terrified for my beautiful blond, yet seeing Caleb's fangs nearing Ash's neck was turning me on. The vampire had made me watch him feed several times, but this was the first time it caused me excitement in my groin. I could feel myself getting close, but I didn't want to finish too early.

Caleb locked eyes with mine. His grin was chilling. Continuing to bore his eyes into me he lowered his sharp fangs to Ashton's neck. He held his fangs against the skin, applying ever increasing pressure as he rammed his cock in and out of Ashton. Finally Ashton let out a sudden moan and I felt the heat as he came inside me. At the same moment Caleb's sharp teeth broke Ashton's soft skin. The forceful thrusts in and out of the blond continued as he gulped back Ashton's blood. I couldn't hold back any longer. With Ashton's release I felt ready to finish, but it was Caleb's feeding that sent me finally over the edge. The cum shot across my chest.

Ashton opened his eyes and smirked lazily, his orgasm making him unaware of the vampire feeding from his neck. He held my gaze and continued to gently thrust into me, buffering the harder onslaught delivered by Caleb. I watched Ash's face begin to register the sensation on his neck just as Caleb pulled his fangs away with a quick lick of his tongue across the twin punctures. A grunt escaped his lips as he climaxed inside Ashton. He immediately pulled his cock from the blond's ass while he licked the blood from his lips, a great look of satisfaction still across his face.

I suddenly felt alone and empty when Ashton slid his member from my ass. He turned to look at Caleb and unconsciously wiped a hand across his neck. Ashton glanced at his palm and saw the streak of blood. The confused expression across his face dissolved when his sight focused on Caleb's fangs.

The vampire smiled seductively at the blond, then turned and for a split second gave me a stare that conveyed menace and spite. Without a word Caleb raised his wrist and sank his sharp teeth into the flesh. He slid closer to Ashton and extended his arm, offering the blood flowing from the torn wrist.

"Drink from me Ashton, and live forever."

"What? You're a vam... a... shit," Ashton said, too shocked to find the right words.

"A vampire, and you will be one too. I have lived a long time Ashton. I seldom bestow this gift on a human, but you are a beautiful young man and you can stay as you are forever. You will have power beyond your reckoning. It's not something I would give to a weak human such as this worthless servant you pleasured," he finished, gesturing to me.

Ashton turned and looked into my eyes. They had begun to fill with tears. I loved Ashton and didn't want him to be another meal for Caleb, but the tears had increased when I was relieved to know Ash would become a vampire and not die.

"Servant?"

"Yes. Zac has been my servant for several months now. He was meant to be a meal and die the night I picked him, but he begged to be turned. I took pity and delayed his death by giving his life purpose in serving me."

"Will you turn him someday?"

"No, this offer is for you, and you only."

"But," Ashton seemed drawn to me, not just as he inched closer, but because he seemed to want me. "I will accept if you turn him too."

"Never. He has another purpose soon enough."

"Then I won't. Kill me then."

"I won't kill you, I am going to set you free."

"Really?"

"Yes, Ashton," he paused and placed his hand on Ashton's face, gently caressing it. "You are so beautiful, and you would make an even better vampire by my side."

"Why are you doing this, you don't love me or think I'm a reincarnated lover do you?"

Caleb laughed, "you are right, I don't love you. No, love or romance has nothing to do with this. Honestly, I just feel like it. I see you and I see your potential. And it would give me no greater pleasure then to turn you in front of this servant."

Ashton's voice was steady as he shot back angrily, "so he begs for it and instead you give it to me to torture him. You're twisted."

The vampire looked enraged by the words. Caleb moved too quickly for me to see, one second he was staring at us with menace, then the next Ashton was lying on his back beside me, Caleb pinning him to the bed, the blood smeared wrist forced against his surprised mouth.

"This will set you free," he said finally. "Ahh yes, it will take very little, but you can have more," he cooed as his blood was smeared across Ashton's lips.

I watched Ashton struggle against the wrist for a few seconds, but it was too late, he had tasted the blood. The effort to repel the wrist shifted suddenly and Ash was pulling the wrist closer, sucking greedily for the blood. But soon enough Caleb pulled the wrist away and gave it a lick to close the wound.

"Good, am I not?"

Ashton lay motionless, a slight erotic moan building deep inside him. His muscles tightened and flexed, then grew noticeably more developed and firm. He balled his fists and arched his back while he rode the change. I watched his cock harden again and grow longer and thicker than before, even bigger than Caleb's. He pushed his head back further into the bed and opened his mouth wide. A moan of ecstasy reverberated through his body as his canines grew longer, sharper.

"There you go," Caleb said smoothly. "How do you feel?"

The new blond vampire was panting but quickly caught his breath. He rolled around to face Caleb, making sure to catch my eye and give me a smile before answering.

"It's amazing. My senses are, they're so alive. Ohhhh," he groaned sensually, "I feel like I'm having an amazing orgasm."

"Yes, that's a good description," Caleb chuckled. "And it will only get better when you feed." He immediately caught my eye, but continued speaking to Ash, "Ashton?"

Ash, still enjoying his new gift, focused and locked eyes with Caleb.

"You must feed to survive. The sooner you feed the easier it will be to control," Caleb stopped and smirked wickedly. "That is why Zac is here, to be your first kill."

The blond vampire was upright before I saw him move. "NO!"

"You will do as you are told."

"I am not your servant."

"But you are, just an immortal one," Caleb paused and let his words sink in. "I am done with Zac. Feed."

Ashton turned and faced me. Tears were flowing from his eyes, but he smiled. He opened his mouth wide showing his pointed fangs. I thought he was resisting as he drew nearer.

"Ashton," I sobbed, "I'd rather die to let you live than him. Please do it," I pleaded. His face hovered over mine and gently he kissed me. He winked at me unseen by Caleb and swung his mouth around to my neck. I could feel the prick as his fangs broke the skin. It was a gentle bite, a love bite.

I heard the sucking sound and I slowly began to feel weak. He brought his face to my and smiled.

"One more kiss goodnight. Thanks Zac, for the gift," he said at normal timbre loud enough for Caleb to hear. But before he pressed his lips to my, I saw him sink his fangs into his lower lip. The blood began to fill his mouth. The kiss was passionate as Ashton fed me from his bleeding mouth.

"Enough, finish feeding," Caleb yelled with impatience.

Ashton gave me another wink when he pulled his mouth from my. I felt him press his lips to my neck again and heard the sucking sound, but no blood was being drawn. With one exhale I dramatically closed my eyes as if falling asleep. I slowed my breathing as much as possible and waited. Ashton gave my body a shove and limply I fell to the floor. Stealing a peek, I could tell I was unseen by the vampires.

"You have done well newborn," Caleb said softly.

"Thank you master, for the gift."

I listened and as quietly as possible I held back the orgasmic moan I wanted to release during my oncoming transformation.

"You are most welcome. For now you may share my bed until I grow tired of you. Do not disobey me or you will find death after all?"

"But how can we die, we are immortal?"

"Refrain your questions for now. As I am stronger than you, it would be easy for me to end your existence."

My muscles had grown and hardened, my cock now twice it's original size, and the fangs were just coming into place. I grinned and waited. The bed shifted as the two laid down properly. A moment later Ashton's hand reached over the edge searching for mine. I took hold and he pulled me up.

Moving at a speed I had only dreamed of, I flew through the air and descended on Caleb. His eyes closed, he didn't see me coming. I sank my sharp fangs into his neck and drank greedily. Beside me Ashton bit down on the other side and we both drank. At first Caleb struggled fiercely, but together we just had the advantage. Eventually Caleb ceased struggling and his veins ran dry. Ashton pulled me away from the corpse forcefully.

"It's done," he said.

"We must take precautions. Cut off his head and burn the remains," I instructed, but mostly to myself. I ran unseen and returned with the largest kitchen knife.

Caleb had been moved to the floor. His head came off easily and together Ashton and I dressed ourselves and carried the corpse to a dumpster on a nearby construction site. The steel box burst into flames and turned its' contents quickly to ash, including the corpse.

I was free.

Ashton took my hand and we walked, at a human pace back to the loft. For the second time that night, he pulled my leather pants off and took my dick into his mouth. But this time, he spread his legs and allowed me to impale him.

We finished hours after sunrise and lay still in the bed, wrapped in each other's arms.

"Thank you," I finally said.

"For what?"

"For the gift."

"I wasn't going to be immortal without you. Besides, he only turned me to spite you, I couldn't let you die without getting him back."

"Are you okay with this?"

"Yes, it's confusing, but I have you."

I grinned, showing my fangs, before kissing him. He smiled, a look of hunger across his face.

"Do we have to wait until sunset before feeding?" he asked, confused and unsure.

"No, the sun won't hurt us, but it's just easier to live by night."

"I'm starving, but I don't want to kill."

"Oh babe, we don't have to kill to survive. A little taken from a confused victim is all it takes."

"Good, then I have an idea. Let's go find my ex and his boyfriend. He'll think we're up for a foursome."

"Hmm, I'm hard just thinking about it."

Ashton found his clothes and dressed. I returned from my old bedroom in jeans and a sweater and accompanied him back to his apartment. He changed into a similarly casual outfit before we went searching for our first meal together.

I realized, walking down the street holding his hand, Caleb was right, Ashton did make a beautiful vampire.

All in your head

BY EPHRAM GREEN

"Owww! You bit me."

"What?"

"You're playing too rough."

"Sorry. Are you enjoying this or what?"

"Pfff. It's all good."

"I think you're a little drunk."

"We're all a little drunk."

Was it my imagination or did I hear him laugh to himself and mutter, "I'm not." I opened my eyes but found my room a blur. "Hold on, I have to pee."

"I can wait."

"But I can't. Just a sec." I got up and felt my way into my bathroom. I didn't trust the room from spinning too much. The door clicked shut and I flicked the lock, which wasn't something I normally did. The toilet filled as I thought about why I'd locked the door behind me. Oh yeah, so I wasn't interrupted by the next person. I think I need a moment to regain my composure, maybe if I sit down I'll feel better. I sat down and rested against the door.

The ring of my phone made me jump. I fumbled around in my pocket until the phone was in my hand. The display lit the darkness but I couldn't focus on the number.

"Hi," I said, my voice rough.

"Nik, how was the rest of your night with Mr Hot?"

Harris was being his usual chirper self. "I don't know. What time is it?"

"It's almost 2. You missed brunch so I figured you were still having sex."

Harris had a habit of confusing me. "I just woke up."

"That good then, good boy."

"What are you talking about?"

"The sex you've had with that hot guy you left with last night. Mind you, you seemed more drunk than usual."

"Wait a sec," I pulled the phone away from my ear and opened my bathroom door. My bed was empty. "Um, I think I screwed up."

"What'd you this time?" Harris said with his overly sarcastic mocking tone.

"I think I fell asleep in my bathroom. He must have left, but I don't remember bring someone here. Are you making this shit up, 'cause I don't remember a guy at all?"

"You know, seriously, you need to drink less. You spent the entire night with the hottest guy. I took a picture on my cellphone and damn he was fit. Wait, stupid phone. Camera cut him out of the picture."

Harris rambled on about his new camera phone while I walked over to the window and pushed one of the curtains aside. Instantly I was blinded. "Fuck," I yelled and pulled the curtain shut. "Why is it so bright out?"

I had said the question more to myself, but Harris thought it was directed at him, "because you have a serious hangover."

"Harris, this girl doesn't get hangovers."

"Whatever. So, do you want to do coffee?"

"Sure, but later, like after the sun sets."

"Baby. Fine, I'm going for a walk down at the beach. Really, you know we don't get many sunny days here, you should get outside."

I pinched the curtain and let a sliver of sunlight in but it seared my eyes. "That's okay, I'll call you later."

"Ok, bye," Harris made his kiss-kiss sound and hung up.

My vision was still clouded by spots which made it hard to see my way back to my bed. I was suddenly thankful for sparing no expense for the black out curtains. The city might be grey and rainy all the time, but the city lights still made it hard to sleep without these curtains. When my vision had cleared I could make out the details of my bedroom again. The light seeping in under the door was the only source of light and seemed more than enough for me to make out every detail.

Grabbing my wrap-around sunglasses, I went back into the bathroom and flicked on the dimmest set of lights, the tiny accent lights above the sink. My reflection stared back at me pale through my squinted eyes. I started to wonder why I was having such a rough day, I didn't usually get hangovers. Old age, that's it, I'm finally getting old. I hated being 25.

Even with the sunglasses, dim light and barely open eyes I could just see the fading bite mark. I leaned over and held my neck close to the mirror. The two marks were faint, but I was certain he had bitten me. A slight problem, I realized. I suddenly remembered he had bitten me, but I could not recall meeting that someone or bringing him home.

I returned to the comfort of my bed after first throwing my blanket across the floor in front of my bedroom door. Obviously I hadn't had enough sleep on the floor of my bathroom. I needed a proper rest.

My head felt better when I opened my eyes again. I stared around my bright bedroom searching for the light, but one wasn't on. When I slowly pulled the curtains aside, I found it was twilight, but the sky still seemed bright. I pulled off the sunglasses and squinted my eyes. "Shit," I said aloud. The glasses went back on and I wandered over to the bathroom to have a pee. I stood at the mirror again and examined my neck, it was bare and unblemished.

"What the hell!" I yelled. The twin marks were gone, or maybe they had never been there at all. I rolled my eyes and decided I must have still been seeing spots when I thought I'd seen the bite.

I was feeling better, but there were still odd side effects of the hangover

I wasn't used to, such as the photosensitivity. My mouth dry, I crept to the kitchen, hoping the light wouldn't bother me.

After gulping back a large bottle of water, I started searching for something to eat in the fridge, my finger pressing the fridge's light switch down. The smells made me nauseous though and I slammed the door shut. Maybe it was too soon.

I grabbed my phone and called Harris.

"Oh, finally up?" he said after one ring and no hello.

"Yeah, just woke up."

"Seriously? I was joking. Maybe you have something more than just a hangover."

"I feel better, except it's really bright right now."

"Huh? I don't know, I'm not a doctor."

"Only if that were true."

"Okay, but I don't diagnose over the phone. Come over before we go out. It's sort of late for coffee."

I fixed my eyes on the microwave clock, 8:45pm. "Nah, I haven't had any all day, I could use some."

"Are you decent or do you need time to fresh up?"

"Yeah, give me 30."

"I'll be waiting," he hung up.

The spray from the shower was refreshing and I felt even better. My mood was decidedly down though, so I made the shower short and got dressed. I threw on a pair of black jeans with a black polo. I throw a different pair of sunglasses on and left.

Since Harris lived in the same condo building, the trip was short, except he had a townhouse with his own outside entrance off the third floor court yard behind the main building. He came to the door quickly with a stethoscope around his neck.

"Harris," I whined and played up my sickness.

"Come in, let the doctor take care of you."

He led me up to his spare bedroom and made me sit on his examining table. This was actually his play room, not an office, and the stirrups had another use.

"You do look pale, although you're skin is amazingly clear. What the hell are you using for ache 'cause it's working, and faster than medically possible?"

"Nothing, I didn't even wash my face until 15 minutes ago."

"Well last night you had a bunch of pimples. Let me check your heart rate," he pressed the warm stethoscope to my chest and felt my wrist for a pulse. "Well it's nice and low." He shrugged.

"Harris, where were you keeping the stethoscope?"

"I put it down my pants when you called. Wanted it warm for my little patient."

"Gross. I should report you to the medical board," I kidded.

He smiled, the sick pervert.

"Are you going to take off your sunglasses?"

"Are you going to turn out the light?

"It'll kinda make it hard for me to see the patient," he responded, a bitchy tone in his voice, before his expression changed to serious and worried. "Is the light bothering you that much?"

"Yeah, it's like bright as day in here with the shades."

"Odd," he paused and started chewing his bottom lip. When Harris the doctor was puzzled with a diagnosis, he chewed his lip.

"Give it to me straight doc, do I have long to live?"

"Shut it," he shook his head and rolled his eyes. "Do you have a headache?"

"No, I felt like shit this afternoon, but not really a headache."

"Any nausea?" he asked while placing his palm on my forehead. "Odd."

"No. What was odd?"

"Oh, you're a little cold. At least you're not running a fever. How is your vision?"

"Fine, except for the brightness. I'm a little photosensitive right now."

"No, you're photophobic." Harris dug around a drawer in the examining table. He pulled out a pair of handcuffs and a dildo, which he set aside, then pulled a small flashlight. The light was first focused on my arm then he flicked it passed my eyes.

"Ouch, SHIT!" I yelled when the light hit my eyes.

"Did that bother you?"

"Yes!"

He snapped his fingers near my ear.

"Hey, not so loud!"

He exhaled then left the room, returning after a minute with a digital thermometer which he stuck in my ear.

"Well?" I asked.

"Nik, you know us doctors, we don't causally give out diagnoses without all the facts."

"And yet you're an opinionated bitch."

"True. Have you ever had migraines?"

I shook my head. "I've had headaches, but nothing serious."

"No, migraines are worse. Photophobia and phonophobia are two symptoms, which you're exhibiting."

"Phono-what?"

"Increased sensitivity to sound." The thermometer beeped and Harris quickly checked it. "I was leaning toward measles but now I'm going with a migraine. Your temperature is lower than normal, do you feel cold?"

"No. Apart from the lack of appetite, the phono-whatsit and the photosensitivity, er I mean photo-pho-be-ah," I said slowly pronouncing the last condition, "I feel pretty good."

"Which is why I'm perplexed. Are you sure you're still up for some coffee, 'cause maybe you should go back to bed."

"No, I could use a coffee, but one last thing."

"Sure."

"You were being absolutely serious about me leaving with a guy last night?"

"Totally. A really hottie. You basically ignored Todd and I when he first started flirting with you."

"I don't remember meeting anyone or taking him home, but I had the strangest memory of being bitten. I checked my neck when you first called and I swear there were two bite marks here," I placed my finger near the spot.

Harris looked at my throat then laughed. "Well I don't see anything. You certainly found yourself someone kinky."

"I didn't say he was kinky, I said he bit me and left two marks like a vampire."

"Seriously Nik, there's no such thing as vampires."

"Don't dismiss it so soon. You said you didn't get a picture on him on your phone, and I'm photophobic. And look how pale I am."

"First off, I saw your guy's reflection in several mirrors last night and there was lint on the lens of my camera," he said, pulling the phone out and showing me several photos from the night before, all with a blur over the left side of the photo. "If you wouldn't mind turning around for a moment, you'll clearly see your reflection."

I turned and stared at myself in the mirror that covered one entire wall on the playroom. "But look how pale I am," I said, raising my arm in the mirror.

"Yes, well you drank a lot last night. You're feeling under the weather."

"I'm not."

"Also, there isn't a scratch on your neck."

"Well don't bites heal quickly."

Harris was getting annoyed, "oh come on, in movies sure, but not in real life. Would you like me to prove it?"

"Okay!"

He started chewing his lip for a moment.

"Now what, I thought you were going to prove it."

"Sure, but I'm just trying to remember if I've got a sterilized scalpel or lance in the house."

"Nothing in the sex kit," I kicked the table.

"No, I don't break skin. Hold on." He disappeared again and returned with a sealed package of disposable razor blades. "Not exactly the best medical practice here."

"Oh just give me that," I pulled the bag from his hands, ripped it open and removed one razor, tossing the bag aside. Razors scattered across the floor. I flicked the cap off with my thumb and dug the blades into my forearm.

"Shit, careful."

"I'm going to prove I can heal quickly."

"Why, because you think you're becoming a vampire?"

"That's right. Just watch."

I held my arm up and we silently watched the wound bleed. I licked the blood away and presented the arm again. The cut welled up with blood again but didn't heal.

"Should I get the garlic?"

"Yes!"

"Nik, it's not going to matter, you're not becoming a vampire," angry, Harris snatched my sunglasses off. I squinted from the light. "They haven't changed color. Show me your teeth."

I bared my teeth in a snarl.

"They look pretty dull to me."

"But what about the photo- and phonophobias?"

"Like I said, possible symptoms of migraines."

"Yeah, but my head doesn't ache."

"It doesn't have to for a migraine."

I exhaled, feeling defeated.

"Nik, vampires aren't real, you weren't bitten by one and you're not becoming one. Okay?"

"Fine, but I think you should run some tests."

"Well oddly enough I was just reading in a medical journal that there's now a test to see if you are turning into a vampire," he paused and regarded me sternly then cracked a smile. "Seriously Nik, if you turn into a vampire, then you'd better come back and bite me, but it isn't going to happen."

"Okay, fine," I mumbled, annoyed I had even brought up the subject. "Let's go for coffee."

I awoke late the next afternoon having slept through the day because I was so wired the previous night and I had been unable to sleep. I pulled the curtains back only a crack to test the light and found the weather to be its' usually gloomy grey overcast, but even that brightness did not affect me as it had the previous day.

The rest of the week was spent trying to get my sleep schedule back to normal which proved difficult. I showed no other signs of illness, including symptoms that might show me worsening. I found myself coming home from work early and sleeping for a few hours, then being awake most of the night. Normally I needed a good seven hours sleep but I was surviving on only the three or four after work without feeling the usual sickening exhaustion that normally affected me.

On Friday night, I ventured out to a local club and found myself chatting with a fresh young college student. By midnight I had him drooling over me and ready to come home with me.

When I opened my apartment door, he slowly paraded passed me and immediately sought the bedroom. He seemed more than a little eager to play. I had held back from drinking any alcohol, deciding instead to take a break after my experience the week before. This college student, all of 19, had downed at least five pints while we flirted at the bar and he was now taking extra care to appear sober.

I stood at my bedroom doorway and raked my eyes up and down his slim and athletic body. He eyes scanned my room before falling lazily upon me. Eyes half closed he attempted a seductive smile.

"You're so hot," he slurred before insulting me, "for an old guy." He tried to grab at my shirt but couldn't stand straight enough to allow his fingers to even brush the fabric.

"Fuck you, I'm only 25," I replied. I pulled his crotch up against my stiff cock to steady him, and held his lips closed in a kiss before he could say something else stupid. I was expecting the cocky brat to reply, 'yes, fuck me.'

Slowly I moved my kisses away from his lips, down the soft hairless chin to his exposed neck. He smelled so exotic and his fragrant skin tasted of spice. I pulled his t-shirt over his head and throw it to the floor. He then attempted to help me with mine, but pawed helplessly. Gently I massaged his smooth chest with one hand, feeling his strong firm pecs. I continued to hold him against me, fearing he would tip over. He smiled lazily up at me, a full head shorter, and swept his hand across his crest to push my hand away.

"Ouch," he said looking down at his chest. "I've cut myself again! This stupid ring keeps cutting me." He pulled a ring off his finger and held it to me, the ring was made from three interlocking bands and one had split open, the sharp metal jutting out.

I looked at his chest and saw the small cut that had caused him grief.

"Boy, that's hardly a scratch." Slowly I leaned down and licked away the blood, the cut was indeed only a small scratch. I planted my lips on his again then leaned back and looked at the graceful curve of his neck. A thought suddenly sprang to mind, I was hungry.

I kissed the soft flesh gently then bit down on the neck. Unlike the scratch on his chest, when I bit down the cut was deep and his blood sprayed up into my waiting mouth. I instantly pressed my lips to the skin and began to vigorously suck in his blood. Even in his drunken state he soon started to struggle, but I held him tight against my body with one hand tightly covering his mouth. It seemed to take several minutes before I began to feel full and he had stopped squirming.

Letting the student's body fall to the floor, I went into my bathroom and flicked on the light. The reflection showed my lips wet with his red blood. I opened my mouth wide and examined my teeth, my two canines had grown longer and sharper. I licked the remaining blood from my lips and smiled, playing the tip of my tongue over my new fangs.

After a week of checking myself in the mirror for even the slightest sign of further change, in mere minutes my teeth had sharpened and grown. It hadn't been a dream, I had become a vampire. Reflexively I made my fangs draw back into my gums, but when I ran my tongue over them they were still sharp points.

"I guess he did bite me," I said aloud to myself and thought of last week's one night stand who I couldn't remember. I looked back into the bedroom and the body lying lifelessly on the bed, wondering how I was going to get rid of the corpse now.

From the closet I grabbed my largest duffel bag, one made for previously owned hockey equipment, and stuffed the body inside it. It was easy to carry down to Harris' door. Thankfully I knew he was in with one of his regular internet hookups.

"This is a bad time," he didn't seem pleased to see me and I could hear it on his voice.

I pushed passed him and into his kitchen, dropping the bag on the floor. I smiled, "I promised I would return if anything changed."

When Harris rolled his eyes, I smiled and slid my fangs down. He moved closer, checking my teeth to see if they were real.

"Shit, this isn't possible."

"Well it is, and I kinda drained the guy I picked up tonight," I said, gently kicking the bag.

"Fuck, you brought the body here. What do you want me to do with it?"

"I don't know, you're a doctor, couldn't I dump it in the ally and you find it and pronounce him dead?"

"And then when they do the autopsy and find him drained of blood, the authorities will start an investigation. I can't just find a body, pronounce it dead and it all goes away." Harris looked worried and he was chewing his bottom lip.

The sound of a throat being cleared drew my attention to the front hallway and a young man standing on the first stair leading upstairs. He was lean with small by well defined muscles, and wore only a leather bikini and a collar.

"I think I can help," he spoke softly, then padded barefoot across the hardwood floor to me.

"Who are you?"

"My name is Emre, master," he said addressing me, not the master who had been whipping him. "I can dispose of this body. All I asked is for you to grant me the privilege of turning me into a vampire." He was being polite, speaking submissively and yet excited as a school boy. "I of course would be your servant, and slave." He winked.

New to being a vampire, I was suddenly unsure if it was appropriate to be converting every cute boy I saw. The vampire who had bitten me didn't seem to take much consideration, but then again the world wasn't over run by vampires so not many must be turned. The problem was he was entirely my type and giving me a hard on, and I felt like doing anything to please him, even kill. Normally I would be put off by such pushy demands—I could find my own way to dispose of the body and didn't need him—but he intrigued me.

"Okay, but just so you know, I'm new at this and I can't guarantee this will work."

He smiled and came closer. As he pressed his body against mine, he tilted his head to expose his neck. Carefully I leaned down and thrust my fangs into his neck then removed them with only a lick across the wound. His blood tasted sweat and made my cock pulse. I realized immediately with a slight pang of regret that I didn't know what his plan was or if it would work.

"Thank you, master."

I reached round and spanked him, "that's Nik to you."

He giggled then turned serious. "Okay, we should do this now. I work in a funeral home, I know completely morbid right, but I can get us in and we can cremate the remains," he paused. "I guess you'll be wanting me to keep the job for disposals?"

"No, I'm pretty sure that I don't normally need to kill. We just need to be careful and cover our tracks when we feed."

"Master, how long before I change?"

"I don't honestly know. The vampire who bit me didn't exactly stay around to explain this to me, so I'm sort of going on instinct. I didn't draw blood when I bit you and I think I somehow released something into you that will turn you."

The boy shrugged and smiled, "I trust your instincts." He leaned closer again and laid his head on my chest.

I turned to Harris and smiled, "so you promised I could bite you if I became a vampire, what do you say?"

"I didn't actually expect you to show up with fangs."

"True, but while I'm here, do you want to be turned."

"Um, not particularly."

"What? You who's into all the kinky sex doesn't want to be immortal?"

"Who said you're immortal?"

"Fair point. Still, it's a good offer?"

"No, Nik."

I stood staring at Harris, the boy still leaning against me. I waited a moment for him to give a reason then let the argument pass.

"Okay. But you know, I can't have you revealing what I've become." Before he could respond I throw a punch which connected with his head. He slumped to the floor. "Good thing there's plenty of restraints around here. Help me out here," I said, looking at Emre.

I flung Harris' unconscious body over my shoulder and led Emre upstairs to the playroom. Using the hooks secured in the ceiling, we hung Harris and bound him in a full body leather restraint he had in the closet.

"I hope we won't have to leave him here long, just long enough for you to turn," I smiled wickedly at Emre. He giggled and licked his lips.

Emre pulled on tight leather pants over his leather briefs and covered his upper body with a black hoodie. I had to say, twinks in leather sure looked hot.

Emre and I cremated the body at the funeral home and returned to Harris' before dawn. We slept the day away, though when I woke up around noon I found that I hadn't redeveloped the photophobic side-effect, nor was my skin photosensitive. The light bothered Emre though. When evening came, we went to the now conscious Harris and I decided to try a little experiment.

With a razor I nicked Harris' neck and had Emre lick up the blood. He smiled at me and I watched as his fangs grew in.

"Finish him, Emre."

"Hmm, I wish to share him with my master."

I exposed my own fangs and we fed on Harris. When Emre and I had finished, we kissed.

"Better get him to the funeral home," I said.

"Yes, master."

Immediately I spanked Emre, "I said, call me Nik."

"Yes, Nik," he said, grinning to show off his sharp fangs.

Brotherhood

BY VICTOR HARROW

The tree lined street was one long leafy canopy sheltering the throng of students and parents from the hot midday sun. The shuttle bus had dropped me and the few other parent-less students far from our final destination, unable to maneuver down the street. The road had become a solid wall of people. I stood between the two brick pillars that flanked the entrance to the student residences. Down one side, Greek row spread out with wide empty lawns facing the dense collection of dormitories.

I was being weighed down by a full back pack, while pulling a wheeled suitcase nearly as large as myself and clutching the strap of my book bag and the campus map in the other hand.

According to the map, Tandem Hall, my home for the next year, was not far down the road. With the cars and hundreds of pedestrians clogging the street, moving quickly was not an option. The distance I walked should not have taken more than five minutes but ended up taking half an hour. And the chaos continued out front of Tandem Hall where students were impatiently pushing at the edges of a large crowd.

I had been to a few concerts and I felt like I was at one again, the crowd impossibly trying to advance on the stage, or in this case, the steps leading up to the terraced entrance to Tandem Hall.

From where I stood, the residence was a four story red brick building, the top floor of which were a series of gables poking out from the sloped roof. Two wings extended toward the street on either side of the deeply set back entrance with a large banner hung between them proclaiming "Welcome" and "Registration". Windows were set ever so often along the wings, most of which were open with some students leaning across and shouting to one another. It was unclear to me whether the crowd moved forward much but it didn't seem to grow any larger. After an hour with no advancement, I pushed my suitcase under a large tree providing shade and made a seat with my suitcase and backpack.

I dug out a book, put my iPod on and lost myself until my stomach grumbled and I finally looked up. I consume books rapidly, absorbing myself completely, with the aid of music, in a complete sensory focus. Time buzzes by unnoticed until some external force, the loss of battery on my iPod or the whine of hunger, pulls me forcefully from my daze. I regarded my watch, three hours had passed. I looked up at the crowd and found it had thinned considerably, but not completely.

The wait in line was another hour until finally I reached the finish line and the over worked residence assistant.

"Registration card."

I pulled the laminated card from the side pocket of my book bag and held it out.

"Hold it under the scanner."

He seemed unwilling to take the card and forced me to lean over the table and hold the card under the barcode scanner. The card arrived several weeks after my letter of admission and contained two features, my name and student number in small print under a poorly reproduced university crest, and a large barcode that stretch the entire width of the card. The RA's computer beeped once acknowledging receipt of the code. It also caused the RA to wrinkle his forehead in frustration.

"We appear to have a problem with your room placement," the RA said before tapping a few keys on the laptop.

"What sort of problem?" I asked hopeful.

"Oh, just that your room was reassigned. It happens all the time. What you'll need to do is visit the Campus Residence office and arrange for a replacement when one becomes available."

"I'm sorry, what do you mean when one becomes available?"

The RA sighed in annoyance, "some students don't survive the first semester and drop out, opening up space in the residence, assuming they move out. Go to the Residence office on Monday and sort out a placement. For now you are on the waiting list in the system, but you'll want to double check that on Monday too."

"And just where am I supposed to live until Monday?"

He looked shock for a moment and for the first time, looked my in the eye, "I doubt there will be a space as early as Monday. Next," he bellowed to get me out of the way.

"Wait, you haven't assigned me a room."

"It's out of my hands, I can't help you. Now, please step aside. Next," he yelled louder.

I shuffled away and looked around. I had spent the entire afternoon waiting to be told I didn't have a room and I had nowhere else to stay. I scanned the street which had cleared considerably and my attention was drawn to a large brick house across the street. It was set further back than the other houses, hidden in shadow with darkened windows. The greek lettering was smaller than on the other houses. And I recalled my father's constant storytelling of his days in his own fraternity.

Even before I began applying to colleges, my father had made it clear which ones had chapters of his fraternity. He expected me to pledge. I felt it was a lost cause but my only choice was to seek help in the one place my father would expect me to. I pulled my suitcase across the road and up the long circular driveway to the heavy wooden door baring the letters for Alpha-Delta-Omega. The house remained eerily silent for several minutes after I had pressed the call button. I pressed it again, expecting someone would eventually answer. Another minute passed before the door buzzed then popped inward an inch. I walked into the dark foyer and pushed the door shut. The inner door buzzed at once and I pushed my way further in.

I found myself standing in a dimly lit foyer paneled in dark wood. Archways led left and right with a hallway disappearing into darkness underneath a grand curved staircase. No one seemed to be around.

"Hello," I squeaked. I had no reason to be scared; I already knew what monsters existed and I was safe. But my voice faltered, unsure how I would be perceived by the frat boys.

A figure separated from the darkness at the top of the stairs and slowly descended, apparently sizing me up. I took in the stranger as well. He was tall and wore a tight black t-shirt that defined his firm muscular chest. He worn tight black pants that did little to hide his strong athletic legs. His hair was trimmed short along the sides, but the top was left longer and had been neatly styled to emphasize the honey colored highlights.

He hardly looked 21, but had the well defined face of a model, perfectly portioned with a strong angular jaw line and chin, and flawless skin. Thin manicured eyebrows sloped downward to the natural line of his strong nose. His green eyes were both beautiful and dark. Only his upper lip betrayed the faintness of facial hair. His lips were light pink and full, coming together with a slight upward curve at the ends so that he looked to have a slight smile when showing no emotion at all. I had day dreamed over the image of many a pretty emotionless model but had yet to see one in person so perfect.

When he reached the bottom of the stairs, he smiled and looked me over one final time, "how can I help you?"

I hadn't planned a speech and didn't have a clue where to start. I considered for a moment laying on the overly complicated language my father would use at his fraternity reunions, but couldn't stomach it.

"I'm looking for help."

"Are you lost freshman?"

He picked up my obvious newness.

"I'm sorry, it's just that I've listened to my father talk about his days in ADO for eighteen years and when I found out my residence space had been given away this was right in front of my eyes. Can you help the son of a brother?"

He smiled again, showing his perfect teeth, "are you planning on pledging."

"I'm expected to, yes."

He laughed and extended his hand, "name's Chris."

"Zach," I took his hand and shook it, his skin was soft.

Chris sighed. "I really shouldn't show special treatment for a new pledge, but a brother in need can't be ignored. Let's just see, I think first there's something you need to say."

I rolled my eyes, "do I really?"

"I think you do. Just whisper it in my ear."

I leaned in and recited the special pledge, as I did Chris placed a hand on my butt and pulled me closer to him. His touch was electrifying and I immediately had a hard on. When I finished, he didn't instantly let me go.

"Now that we got that out of the way, I think I can help you out. Luckily you're in the presence of the chapter president, and I can make things happen."

"Am I supposed to be impressed?"

"Cocky little shit," he laughed. "Don't you think you're being rude to the wrong person? Just because you're father was a chapter member, doesn't immediately guarantee your acceptance into our little chapter."

I said sarcastically, "oh that would crush my dreams."

"You can joke, but seriously, if I offer you help, it can't be known by the other pledges."

"I'm good at keeping secrets."

"That's good. You'll need that. We have a lot of secrets around here, even ones your father wouldn't know about. We're the most powerful chapter, the most selective." He sized me up and rolled his lips together.

I decided to keep playing him. "You're being a little dramatic."

"Follow me." Chris turned lifting my suitcase easily with one hand and ascended the stairs; I followed. At the top of the stairs we walked down a long hallway deep into the house then through a door into a large dark bedroom.

"As I said, the other pledges can't know and it may be best if the other brothers didn't know either. I can't just place you in any old room, so you'll need to stay with me as my guest." He gave me a wicked smile.

"Okay."

Chris led me to the walk in closet and put my suitcase down inside, motioning me to do the same.

"I think you need a shower." Chris throw me a towel and pushed me into the attached bathroom, shutting the door behind me.

The windowless bathroom was large and looked like it belonged in a boutique hotel. The entire room was covered in dark glass tiles up to the ceiling. Tiny lights recessed into the ceiling cast small spots of light on the floor. The toilet, designer, the sink, a bowl mounted on a thick slab of glass. The shower was a large walk-in custom shower with several heads.

I stripped and walked into the shower, immersing myself under the heads. Music began playing from several speakers concealed behind larger false tiles that stood out among the sea of tiny glass tiles. Either Chris had the same eclectic music tastes or he had plugged my iPod into the system. I was soon lost in the spray and rhythm.

Finally I finished cleaning myself and toweled off before returning to the bedroom, the towel wrapped around my waist. Chris was laying on his bed, motioning to a neat pile of clothes next to him.

"I think maybe to fit in, you need to dress like a brother."

"I'm a little confused. Am I your guest, or pretending to be a brother?"

"You're a pledge."

"Isn't it a little early for pledge week."

"Partly I'm making an exception for the son of a brother. But in case I didn't make it clear, our fraternity is more exclusive and we carry out the pledge process when we like. Sometimes we find the right pledges during rush week, and sometimes we don't. We've often initiated the real pledges before or after. I think you possess what it takes to be a brother."

I shook my head. "You're being so cryptic."

"I'm sorry. I know I'm moving too fast, but I feel right about you." He stopped and looked down at my towel. My hard on had risen and I was tenting the towel. "I think you feel something too."

I couldn't see my face at that moment but I'm sure I blushed.

"ADO has changed and many of the chapters are entirely special, but we have a lot of secrets and don't want to spread rumors or become branded for excepting only one type of guy." He stood up and came closer to me, removing his t-shirt. "There's also the fact that you're my type, and I'm powerless in your presence." Chris knelt down and removed my towel, leaving me completely naked. He didn't say another word. He engulfed my hard on in his mouth and began sucking. My legs began to shake, there was no way I would be able to stand through this. I pulled Chris' head away and led him to the bed where he continued until my cock exploded.

Chris pulled himself up the bed and brought his face to my, kissing me gently, the taste of my cum still on his lips. He placed his head on my chest and together we fell asleep.

A soft knock at the door stirred me from my sleep. Chris was already moving toward the door and I wasn't sure how exposed I would be. I gathered the pile of clothes and dove into the closet, leaving the door ajar so I could listen.

"Chris, we are gathered in the great room to meet the new pledge."

"Good. We'll be down when we're ready." Chris shut the door and came to the closet. "You should get dressed, you're going to meet your future brothers." He leaned in and kissed me. Smiling down at me he seemed lost in thought, "you are very hard to resist. I'm using all my strength trying not to suck you dry."

Chris walked passed me to gather a clean t-shirt from a shelf behind me then left me to dress. I pulled the underwear on, noticing the monogrammed "ADO" in blood red letters in one corner. The pants were a perfect fit for my small size. I pulled the t-shirt on before attempting to retrieve something from my book bag. When I lifted the lid, the envelope of photos and letters I'd kept close to me fell out. It had been zipped inside an inner pocket but had obviously been pulled out. I opened the envelope and reminded myself of what Chris had seen while snooping. It was clear from the photos of my former boyfriend and myself that I was gay.

I walked out into the room and dropped the envelope on the bed. Chris looked at it then smiled at me.

"Sorry, I had to know. I wouldn't have made a move if I hadn't known."

"You could have asked."

"No, we don't here. I told you we keep secrets, well that's one of them."

"And yet I gathered that was the biggest requirement for getting in?"

"It is, but we find out with discretion. Had you walked in here, as do many guys, obviously gay or publicly out, we would have turned you away. The brothers in this fraternity are very powerful and we maintain our power by keeping our true nature secret."

"I was resistant to pledging because I assumed you were going to be a bunch of homophobic jocks. Instead I find a fraternity full of closet cases."

"No Zach, it goes beyond being in the closet. We only allow gay men to join and receive the gift of brotherhood. If everyone knew the entire fraternity was gay, we'd attract the wrong type of guys and scare away some others. People would also start making connections between our fraternity, its' members and possibly what we truly are."

"And what is that?"

"Not something I can discuss yet. You must first enter into the pledge process. But I need to know something personal."

"More personal than we've already gotten?"

Chris ignored the question and continued, "who is the boy in the photographs?"

"My former boyfriend."

"Former? An ex?"

"No." I hadn't expected to be reminded of my boyfriend and the long future we were supposed to have together. I had somehow managed to keep going, through a darkness that almost took me. "He's dead."

Chris was shocked. He came closer and wrapped his arms around me. "I am truly sorry. I didn't mean to cause you pain. I was being careless with my vetting of your past. Can I ask, how long has it been?"

"Almost a year. It happened last fall. He was special and we had planned our future together just days before he was taken from me."

Without another word, Chris held me tightly in an embrace, expecting to let me grieve. But the grieving had ended, and the future I had expected with my boyfriend was no more.

After several minutes Chris pulled me out of my thoughts, "do you feel ready to begin the initiation?"

I was surprised to be so immediately reminded of Chris' intensions after he had so quickly opened the wounds. But there weren't tears at the moment, just the new future being offered to me.

I smiled at Chris, a naughty thought perked up in my head, "did you know of me before, and plan for me to lose my residence space?"

He shook his head, "no. I guess that was just fate, or if you don't buy fate, just what life handed you."

"It's all just happening so quickly. I feel overwhelmed."

"Don't be. This is right. You'll be happy here and we'll be happy with you as one of us."

"And what about us? You seem head over heels in love with me, you said you couldn't resist me?"

"Oh, slow down Zach. I haven't fallen in love, yet. I hardly know you. I've been talking about lust. Right now it's about the sexual attraction. We need to get to know each other. You might find you're not as in to me. But that won't change the brotherly bonds, if we don't work out, you'll still be with us. Hell, I've been with every brother here, sucked them all. Dated a few, but we don't allow jealousy or pettiness infect our brotherhood."

I felt more at ease, reassured. "I'm ready then."

Chris took my hand and led me out of the room to a panel in the hallway. He tapped and pushed it in a particular way and it swung open, revealing a tiny circular stairwell. We descended below the main floor and passed through an archway into what must have been the great room. Dark red curtains billowed over the walls and created a small intimate room where the brothers were gathered. There was already 14 young men standing silently and dressed as Chris and I were.

The group had been loose until Chris arrived and a tight circle was formed around the two of us. In the center of the circle, a simple round smooth stump of black marble held a knife and a wine glass.

"Brothers, tonight we begin the initiation of a new brother. Zach. He has proven himself an apt pledge and I now ask your permission to accept him into our covenant. What say you?"

All 14 brothers extended their right hands into the circle, palm side up. None made a sound and all eyes were on me. I watched as Chris slid the knife across his left palm and cupped it over the wine glass. The smell of blood hit my nostrils. He held the knife up and slowly one by one the brothers stepped forward to cut their palms and spill blood into the glass.

Finally Chris turned to me and handed me the knife. I slid the knife across my palm and let the blood trickle into the glass. Gently Chris pulled my hand away from the glass and continued to hold my hand.

Chris took a sip from the glass then passed the glass to one of the brothers who took a sip and passed the glass down the line. When the glass was handed to me once again, I didn't hesitate a second, drinking down the coppery liquid. I had drunk my boyfriend's blood before, but this mixture didn't have the same kick. Chris took the empty glass from me and returned it to the marble.

"Welcome Zach, to ADO."

We spent the remainder of the night getting to know each other. I was the only freshman and the remaining brothers were almost evenly split over the remaining three years except with more juniors than seniors or sophomores. It would be a while before I knew everyone's name. Finally around three in the morning, Chris announced the end of the night.

"I'm sure many of you have other things to do become sunrise, so let's adjourn for the night."

Chris pulled me back up the stairs to his bedroom. I was beginning to feel light headed, remembering I hadn't eaten since breakfast. Chris laid down on the bed and I excused myself to use the washroom.

In the bathroom mirror, I examined my pale complexion. The evening had been strange and theatrically. The hunger in my stomach grew stronger before my gums began to ache. It was the blood, I suddenly realized, it was changing me. I fought back the pain as my blunt canines were forced downward by two new sharp fangs. The old teeth clanked into the sink. I smiled at myself in the mirror, licking my extended canines. My stomach grumbled again and I caught the taste of Chris' blood in the air. I willed my fangs up and returned to the bedroom.

I climbed immediately on top of Chris and began making out, kissing his lips, and anywhere I could find exposed skin. Finally, unable to hold back the hunger, I slid my fangs down again and thrust them into the soft flesh of Chris' neck. I pressed my lips against the warm skin and began drinking from the wound, careful not to take too much. Chris struggled only a little under my weight, yet the sudden attack had obviously taken him by surprise. I leaned up onto my hands and met his shocked gaze.

"What the fuck, Zach? You bit me."

"Yeah, sorry. I think drinking the blood earlier finished something started last fall. My former boyfriend was a vampire and he promised to turn me. I tasted his blood for the first time the night before he was killed. He didn't get a chance to finish turning me or apparently explaining I would be able to complete the conversion on my own."

"You're a vampire?"

"Yes Chris, keep up will you. It's funny, all night I was thinking you guys were also vampires, but I could tell you weren't, after all, I had dated a real one. I need to know, what was all your talk about power and feeding me the blood?"

Chris still seemed shocked, unfocused. "The power comes through wealth and well, actual power. We get the best jobs."

"Really, and the blood."

"It's part of the ritual, seals our brotherhood. It's not meant to mock vampires."

"Oh, I didn't think you were mocking vampires. Being a bit theatrically maybe." I kissed Chris and stared into his eyes. "So we have a dilemma now that I've changed and you know about me."

"Shit," Chris finally looked afraid, "you're going to kill me!"

"No Chris, I'm not. You have accepted me into the fraternity and I wish to share myself in return. Or at least I think I have."

"What do you mean?"

"You and the other brothers drank my blood tonight. I'm guessing the entire fraternity will be vampires either in a matter of hours, or when blood next touches their lips. I think the brother's should know."

Chris finally smiled, "you mean you will share your gift?"

"I think I already have. Do you feel any different? Hungry perhaps?"

"No. How should I feel?"

"Well it took a few hours from when I drank the blood, but when I came up here I felt light headed. When I went into the bathroom, my fangs grew in. You drank my blood first so it stands to reason that you will change first.

"But you don't know how long it will take, I mean it took you a year?"

"True," I paused. Thinking about Alexander earlier had brought up my loss, but no tears. Now I couldn't hold back, though I squeezed my eyes tight. I missed him more than ever at that moment, not only would he comfort me but provide me with answers. I tried painfully to recall the night Alexander revealed himself and fed me his blood. Had he said anything, even the slightest off comment?

When I opened my eyes, Chris stared up at me, a smile spread across his face. He began to rub my back to comfort me.

"Alexander fed me to form a bond between us. He had exposed his secret and gave me a choice, be bonded or die. The bonding is the first step to becoming. The brothers are now all bound to me, but I wasn't able to give you the choice."

"So you will kill me if I now refuse?"

"Yes. Are you refusing?"

"No."

There was not a moment to spare. I bit into my wrist and held it to Chris' eager mouth. I soon pulled the wound from his lips and licked away the last drops of blood as the holes sealed.

"There is something else though Chris."

"What?"

"I'm now in charge of this fraternity. The blood works in succession and the sire retains some control over those he has turned."

"I understand," he smiled and pulled me into a long kiss. "Whatever you say, as far as I'm concerned, you're the president now."

"Well, to the brothers that sounds fine, but I think publicly you should remain in charge."

"That does mean we're going to have to share the perks, including this room."

"I can agree with that," I gave him a kiss. "Now how do you feel?"

"The same, I guess. Maybe it'll still take a few..." Chris blinked heavily, "...hours. Or..." he groaned, "...minutes." He winced in pain and held his stomach. I watched as he yawned then as he canines were also pushed out by a pair of sharp fangs. Chris looked up at me and smiled. "Wow, I feel good."

"We need to gather the brothers, immediately."

Chris nodded then reached over to the bedside phone. He pushed only a few buttons then issued a command into the headset. "Emergency gathering in the great home, now."

We made our way back down the spiral staircase to the curtained room and stood at the pillar. I knew from the smiles Chris kept flashing me that his fangs were still drawn and I didn't feel the need to have him retract them. Soon the 14 brothers gathered into the circle, none looking groggy or prematurely pulled from bed.

Looking at the floor Chris spoke, "Brothers, we pride ourselves on accepting the gifts each brother brings to the fraternity. Tonight we welcomed a new member who has an extraordinary gift that we unleashed with our ritual. "He continued to cast his face toward the floor, hiding his teeth as he spoke. "When Zach drank our blood it awoke a gift given to him by his former lover. And tonight, Zach unknowingly passed on that gift to us." Chris raised his head but held his mouth closed, nodding to me to continue.

Standing at the edge of the circle with 14 sets on eyes on me, and before I spoke to my brothers, I opened my mouth wide and slid down my fangs. I watched as each brother recognized what I was, then finally I spoke, "drinking your blood finished my transformation into a vampire. When you first tasted my blood you became bound to me before knowing my secret. Now you know the gift I have shared with you, but your transformations are not complete. Drink from me and receive the gift. You may choose not to accept the gift, however I must protect our kind and refusing will mean your death."

Chris opened his mouth to reveal his fangs. "I made my choice."

I again bit into my wrist and offered it to the brother closest to me. He smiled before leaning in and accepting my blood. One by one each brother broke away from the circle and drank from my arm. Before I had gotten through the 14 brothers, the first one began to transform. As the fangs grew, the boys slid their tongues over the sharp points, or bared them for their other brothers to see. When all the brothers had finished turning, Chris addressed them once more.

"Brothers, we have a new president and master." He leaned in a kissed me on the lips, officially handing the reins to me.

I continued, "tonight you have been given real power, eternal young and immortality. You will need to feed, but you need not kill unless our secret is revealed. The small amount you drank from me should sustain you for several days. While this house is well protected from the sunlight, you need not fear the sun, or stakes, garlic, mirrors, cameras or crosses. I think we may need to have a private party tonight to welcome some of the students back, and for you all to have your first feedings." The brothers smiled at me hungrily. "Feel free to invite one or two guests."

I took Chris' hand and kissed him on the lips. "Good night boys," I said finally, pulling Chris from the circle back to our bedroom.

I woke sometime around noon and looked down at a naked Chris wrapped in my arms. Just 24 hours before I had arrived on campus alone. Now I found myself in charge of the very fraternity I had resisted. I had felt a part of me was missing, and I misunderstood the hole in my life to have been created by the death of my boyfriend, but it had really been remorse for losing the chance to be immortal. I missed Alexander, but he had left me with something as good as our love.

Chris stirred, opening his eyes. He smiled at me and gave me a wink, "was last night all a dream?"

"Feel for yourself."

He reached up and caressed my face.

"I meant, your fangs," I said after descending my own.

His fangs slid down to match mine. We began to kiss, eventually leading to our orgasms. Showered and dressed, we descended to the main floor to discover the brothers preparing the house for the party. The brothers had gathered a lot of alcohol for what would be a small and intimate gathering. When one brother approached me and proudly showed off some date rape drug, I became angry.

"Brothers," I said loudly, causing them to pull together in front of me. "We have no need to drug or intoxicate our guests tonight. Yes, we must guard our secret, but we have other ways. I think I need a human volunteer, anyone got a friend who can be here quickly."

"I do," one of the brothers spoke up. I couldn't recall his name. "My little brother came looking for me earlier, hoping to pledge. I put him to work cleaning the front yard."

"Well then, go get him," I commanded.

The brother slipped out of the room and returned not a minute later to find 15 eager brothers practically drooling over him. I reached into the brothers' minds and utter commands.

"You are not to feed from this boy, I am only to show you what you are capable of doing. Just as I'm speaking to you inside your minds, you can do the same to any mortal. I shall command this one, then you will all take a turn." I looked into the freshman's eyes and relaxed his mind. He smiled, though his face appeared slack and docile. I sent command and he approached as I'm requested. My fangs exposed, I leaned into his neck and took in his scent before looking back to the brothers.

"See brothers, it is easy to cloud a human's mind before we feed from them. When I release him from this trance, he will remember nothing."

I swept my arm around the group, inviting them to command the mortal. One by one the vampires stepped forward and looked into the freshman's eyes. The second vampire commanded him to take up his shirt, the third his pants and shoes. When the forth brother approached, his boxers came off, revealing his stiff cock. His brother finally spoke up.

"Shit guys, that's my kid brother. I don't need to see this," he gave his brother to redress.

The remaining brothers had him perform tasks and simple chores around the room until finally he was returned to me. I gave his mind a quick check. I turned to Chris and gave him a wink. He smiled, knowing what I'd read. The freshman woke from his trance and looked at me, he smiled before approaching me. I gave him a quick kiss on the lips and a gentle hug. Our fraternity had room for at least one more, and he had the just the right qualities.

Immortality found in a laundry mat

BY PERRIN LATIMER

The loud wurring noise died with a click. Sounds of splashing could be heard as water drained from the machine. The lid to the washing machine rose and in the dim florescent light, the young man pulled his wet clothes out and carried them across the broken and grime coated tile floor to a waiting dryer. With the last piece, he slammed the dryer door and feed the machine it's hungrily accepted coins before it belched to life, spinning the wet clothes around inside it's warm womb. The man backed up, reached behind himself, closed the washer lid, places a hand on either side of himself and pulled his body up and back placing his ass onto the washing machine. The dryer show had begun, and it was going to be an exciting episode this evening—guaranteed more interesting then the otherwise empty laundry mat.

There was one other machine working away, a dryer down at the end of the wall lined with dryers that included the one the young man watched. The viewerless dryer had been abandoned it seemed, and there was no one else in sight, not even the older man that normally sat sleeping quietly in the corner by the window protecting the machine or dispensing change if aroused from sleep, which was never. The bright red LED display on the second dryer read 4 minutes, offering the young man the slight hope that someone might return for the clothes shortly.

The man, when standing, stood 6 feet even with light blond wavy and shortly cut hair. His face was framed by a strong cheek bone and firm chin, left smooth from lack of blemish or facial hair. His two blue eyes shone bright with a sparkle that matched his bright perfect teeth smile. His teeth were white, with no hint of stain or filling—a blessing of his dentist for hiding the few fillings well, and his own regimented cleaning that keep the true white without sometimes necessary whiteners. He had been an athlete at the top of his class ages ago when he ruled over his high school as the perfect student / jock. That had been before the move to the city, where he had lost interest in sports, but continued to keep his body at its top form with regular workouts at his gym several times a week. His muscles rippled underneath his tight fitting clothes as he shifted his weighed onto his hands and lean toward the front of the washer.

This laundry mat and a coffee shop below his apartment were the man's two nightly hangouts—one night a week spent with the chore of washing his clothes, the other evenings out spent at the coffee shop that afforded him, like the laundry mat, the opportunity to watch people. The people that passed by or frequented these two places were each unique and held their own story, their histories a secret only in the young man's mind. He had been hugely popular in high school and college, but had made no strong bond with any one person, thus leaving him alone. But through high school and college he had wanted not the popularity or the girls looking for the popularity to rub off on to them, but the companionship of another male. And there had been two fellow school athletes that he had found release with, but neither had wanted to continue their relationships, even in secret. One had been the love of the young man's life through his senior year, but he had ended his own life, taking their secret love with him. It had destroyed the young man, driven him to loneliness that he filled with brief encounters used to satisfy another hunger that lingered inside him.

He made his apartment his home and workplace, preferring to work late nights editing overnight copy for an international newswire agency. There was no workplace relationships to develop and the people that came and went from his apartment building seemed to hang their heads low in the anonymous city. He lived on a schedule without sunshine or the daytime business of the city outside his apartment, never mind the loneliness he felt inside.

But he smiled brightly and felt happy, nonetheless.

Lacking the break in his viewing programme, he slid down from the washer and strode softly to the washroom in the rear. His only comfort when using this bathroom, was the good fortune that just enough light leaked in beneath the door and allowed him to stand and pee while leaving the lights off. It helped to block having to gaze upon the overwhelming grime coating the moist and moldy concrete walls inside the tiny pit.

The young man finished and turned to make his way from the bathroom, back to his seat across from his entertainment. He rounded the corner separating the back hallway to the main room, and stopped short. The missing owner of the clothing that had been spinning in the lone dryer had appeared. He stood with his back to the young man, picking his dry clothes from the machine and depositing them in his bag. From this view, the young man could watch the back of this man who possessed the qualities he was attracted to.

From his years of observation, he had learned to read the back of people and judge how they would look from the front. The man that stood at the dry was 5 foot 6 inches, with jet black hair cut short and spiked along the top. Several silver loop piercings dangled from his ears, and he wore a dark grey hoodie, black cargo pants, and black DC skate shoes. A chain hung down from the center belt loop above his ass dangling around his hip to the belt loop on the front. When he reached in toward the back of the dryer, his hoodie lifted and exposed the band of his boxers and a black leather belt covered completely with steel studs. His whole look suggested a punk look on someone who barely looked twenty—at least from behind, also an area the young man watched closely.

The punk boy turned around, and caught sight of the young man. Not wanting to appear to be staring, he immediately began walking toward his own machine as if he had not been watching for the last minute. The boy smiled at the young man as he passed by. Once at his perch, he turned and leaned back against the washer instead of climbing on top. He dared a sideways glance at the boy who was now packing his bag down to enable it to close. Having placed in on the washer opposite his own dryer, just down from the young man, he made a few glances up at the young man.

The boy looked up again, this time catching the glance from the young man. He smiled in return, which made the young man smile back wider—he felt hungry and horny, the boy would do.

The packing had been completed, and the bag was swung over his shoulder, before the boy slowly strolled passed the young man. He was stopped however by the young man who raised his leg up and planted his foot against the lower dryer, blocking the boy's path. His hand came up to the boy's.

"Hi, I'm Adam," extending his hand for a shake.

The boy returned the handshake, and gently answered with a blush, "Frederick."

The dryer stopped with a click and they both turned to look, glad that the load had finished. Adam looked back at the boy, taking in a good look at the punk boy standing in front of him. Frederick had soft pale skin, no sign of facial hair, luscious full red lips, dark green eyes framed by mascara and eye-liner. Adam suddenly realized the boy was beautiful. Frederick stared back, excited that such an unnatural adonis had stopped him and blatantly flirted with him.

"Well Frederick, I couldn't help notice you when I came out of that bathroom," pointed to the back. "And I'll tell you it was quite a surprise as I've never seen such a beauty as you here before."

Frederick blushed brightly from the overwhelming compliment. "Well I hope you won't mind then taking that fine body of yours and fucking me silly," and Frederick flashed the adonis a smile, showing his own bright near perfect smile.

"Frederick, that's exactly what I intend to do." Adam lowered his leg and moved to pack his not quite dry clothes into his laundry bag, while Frederick came up behind him rested his crotch against Adam's strong leg and wrapped his left arm around to grab at Adam's crotch.

The bag filled, Adam turned and leaned in to kiss Frederick's luscious lips. "You are quite a yummy boy, and I am quite hungry for a young one like you."

"Hmm, I'm rather hungry too, let's go. And don't let these looks foul you, I'm not as young as I appear," he giggled, "and I am not at all inexperienced either."

They wasted no time walking the block and a half to Adam's apartment. They rushed up the two flights of stairs and were in an embrace before the door had closed.

In one move, Adam pulled Frederick's hoodie and t-shirt off his smooth muscular body and began kissing at his nipples, biting them gently to get them hard. In return, Frederick pulled Adam's polo shirt up, forcing Adam's head back to get the shirt off to reveal the hard chiseled muscles of his adonis. Frederick examined Adam's chest, a work of muscular art, budging pecs and a lean ribbed 6-pack, all entirely hairless save the slight dark trail below his belly button dipping into his pants.

Adam grabbed Frederick's hand and led him into the bedroom, allowing Frederick to settle himself upon the bed on his back. Adam straddled Frederick resting up on his knees, hovering above Adam's crotch supporting himself with his muscular arms. He began to bite at Frederick's hardened cock through his pants, before moving up his torso, gently nipping at the boy's smooth body along the path to his lips. The lips were nibbled before he took in the fullness of the boy's lips, not kissing gently but moving their mouths in sync, quickly working their tongues together. At the same time, Adam grabbed hold of Frederick's baggy cargos and pulled the pants down with one motion, using his own feet to squeeze Frederick's shoes off, allowing the pants to come free and be kicked off the end of the bed hitting the wall opposite.

Adam took Frederick's cock in his mouth and began working it with his saliva, sliding it deep into his mouth right to the root where his nose brushed the neatly trimmed pubic hair, before pulling it out again to run his tongue over the head. Frederick clawed at the bed covers and bared down with ecstasy, his cock going back into Adam's mouth for the second time was all it took. He reached his orgasm immediately and his cum exploded into Adam's mouth. Adam eagerly lapped up the white juice as it pumped out of the boy's still hard cock.

'Um, delicious. At yet, I want some more of you," Adam whispered softly smiling down at Frederick.

"Then fuck me, adonis."

Adam grabbed hold of Frederick's legs and pulled them toward Frederick's chest, leaning down to kiss Frederick he placed one finger into Frederick's hole. With his other hand, Adam grabbed a condom from the bedside table drawer. Removing his finger from Frederick's hole, Adam tore the package open with both hands, and rolled it down his hard cock with one hand as two fingers from the second went into Frederick's hole.

Stopping his kissing, Adam whispered, "we can't have my juice in you now can we." He pulled his two fingers out of Frederick's hole and thrust his cock into the hole. Holding on to Frederick's legs, Adam began to thrust his cock deeper inside Frederick, motioning his hips back and forth, all the while nibbling gently at Frederick's lower lip, then along his neck.

Frederick moaned in great pleasure as the cock continued to be thrust back and forth in his hole, digging his clawed hands into the blankets. Adam moved his playful biting back up to Frederick's lips, nibbling at the lower lip, he broke the skin sending blood into his throat. Frederick did not notice the bite over the pleasure from the thrusts. Adam pulled his head back from Frederick's, his eyes shut firmly as he reached his climax. Frederick could fell the rhythm in Adam's movements and was able to tell that Adam was at his orgasm, readying himself for the end.

Frederick had his mouth open, taking great breaths as Adam neared his climax, running his tongue along his top teeth, touching the incisors. At the moment that Adam hit his orgasm, Frederick's fangs slid from their sleeves and he bit down on Adam's throbbing neck. Frederick sucked in Adam's blood as Adam's orgasm came in great waves of pleasure into his condom. Having sucked an ample supply of Adam's blood, Frederick pulled his lips from the wound, licked his lips and drew his fangs back up. Adam hadn't noticed, stilling feeling waves of pleasure pouring over him. He pulled out of Frederick, panting from the workout, and weakened by the loss of blood.

Frederick sensed Adam's confused post-coital state. He reached his hand up to his own chest and used the sharp nail on his pinkie finger to draw a line across his chest in blood, just below his left tit. With his other hand, Frederick grabbed the back of Adam's head and forced Adam's lips to the wound with strength greater then Adam could resist. Without thinking or resisting he sucked at the intoxicating blood feeding the emptiness that Frederick had left from his own sucking. He continued to hungrily drink away at the blood pouring from the little vampire's chest before Frederick stopped pushing Adam's head against his chest and instead gripped Adam's hair and pulled the hungry head back onto the mattress. There Adam passed out from the sexual relief, loss of blood and fill of the powerful vampire blood.

Adam awoke the next morning to find the morning sunshine playing across his face. His eyes blinked to life and he took in the full scene. He found himself naked, with a rock hard erection, the remnants of cum on his cock and a slight pain on his neck. Pulling himself up, Adam placed his feet on the floor and walked over to the full-length mirror covering his bedroom wall. He examined first his perfect muscular body, then leaned in to examine the two fading puncture marks on his neck. He smiled at himself in the mirror, remembering the punk boy he had picked up last night. Adam ran his tongue along his teeth touching his incisors, and watched them slide down. He smiled to himself, the razor sharp fangs glistening in the light, eyes wide and blazing bright orange, pupils small dots.

"This will be fun," Adam said excitingly then looked toward the window. He hoped for nightfall to come soon. He was hungry, not for sex like the night before, but for the sweet taste of blood. Male blood.

Adam awoke for the second time that day, only this time after the sun had set. His hunger and restlessness in the early morning had driven him back to his bed after the excitement of examining his new vampire body in the mirror had worn off. The hard on he had woken with had not however worn off. Adam felt his body charged both with power and sexual energy— more then the usual amount his 24 year old body had normally felt.

When he woke though, he looked over to the empty half of the bed that lay vacant since his sexual companion and sire had left. He realized that he longed to hold the young man that had given him this power gift. The loneliness filled him and he ached for the touch of the boy, and to touch his soft smooth skin. It was not often that Adam longed to hold the another male after the act of sex. Trevor had been his last love, the one who took his own life, and the void until now had been filled with one-night stands.

He smelled the blanket he had slept on naked all day, engulfing himself in the scent of the young vampire, Frederick. He knew he could find him, but first he had to feed.

At first, the lure of his closet and the black leather pants inside, called out to Adam as outfit befitting his new vampire body, but after staring at his reflection in the mirror with the pants held against his legs he decided to go out in his usual jeans and polo. The leather pants had only been worn once before, and Adam had yet to work the courage to wear them out again, regardless of how good he looked wearing them. A polo shirt did not fit the evening, and instead a muscle cut shirt—once a full t-shirt with the sleeves removed to showcase his prominent muscles—would do. He throw on his sneakers, the new and clean ones, ran a small amount of gel through his hair and brushed his teeth, before he was out the door into the cool fall night. Only on the street did Adam realize that he should be wearing a jacket on this night, not to keep warm in any way, for he could no longer feel the cold, but in order to blend in with the humans walking the street with their light fall coats on. He knew however, regardless of his own awkwardness, that he would go unnoticed.

Out on the street, Adam came to a sudden realization regarding his newfound hunger. Regardless of the hunger and his animal instincts that told him to satisfy the hunger with blood, he could not think of a way to secure the blood other then grabbing the nearest body and ripping their throat open. His evening haunt, the coffee shop below his apartment welcomed him with his usual, a coffee and the opportunity to watch people pass while he pondered their lives.

Adam sat down in the old and worn brown leather chair hidden between one front window and the coffee bar, squirreled away in an alcove behind the door. Protected from the café's uninitiated by its irregular placement, it was unused by everyday common patrons, and it became the spot of choice for the few regular customers, most of whom choose not to visit at this later hour. Thus it had unofficially become the chair to be reserved for Adam on late evenings. Sitting in it, he came over with the sudden feeling to mark his territory, but by spilling his blood. He held back though, instead eager to form a plan for his next meal rather then distracting himself with an animal instinct other then to feed and have sex.

This particular night's view from the window offered very little of interest to Adam's hunger. He found that at the same time that he was looking a potential prey up and down, that he was also rating them on their sexual attractiveness. The women that walked by were therefore unnoticed by him. The men however perked his interest, but none that passed seemed suitable. Given the mixed feelings of sex and hunger, Adam was unsure whom to approach, a dilemma that he faced with sexual partners. In the past, he found that he was not attracted to one particular type of person, but instead to the specific person he found relative to the moment. One night he would find himself attracted to a muscular fit athletic body such as the one he had, and on another night to a skinny twinky.

He began to worry that he would find himself in the same perplexing search every time he needed to satisfy his new hunger. But his thoughts were pushed aside when he was interrupted. The younger coffee attendant had squeezed his way into the secreted alcove, a to-go coffee cup in hand. His apron was missing and he held a small satchel over his shoulder indicating that he was most likely finished work for the evening.

Surprisingly Adam could feel two things about the man of about twenty-two years. One, the young man was horny, releasing a sexual scent that intoxicated Adam. Two, this had been the one employee who Adam had been mildly attracted to every time he had seen him, which had not been for a while. The employee was about 5 foot 8 inches and could not have been more then 150 pounds. He held himself tall and leaned gently on his left leg, never standing straight nor could his walk be described as straight either. He had dirty brown hair left messy and long since cut, which hid an almost perfect complexion. His face always seemed to have thin layer of stubble. He almost always had a smile spread across his face, except for the few times Adam had noticed him in a far more bitchy mood, when he generally sported a pout and a overly queer sassy tongue. While he looked lean and not unaccustomed to the gym, he was in no way muscular. And he began to speak.

"Hey, I thought I'd stop and find out what your name is. I mean, I um, I know you're a bit of a regular, but I guess only in the evening since I don't see you during the day, and well I couldn't help think that I should really know your name." And as if he had said it verbally, Adam could hear clearly in the young man's mind, "and I want to fuck your hot body."

Adam reached up and shook the man's hand, "I'm Adam." Making sure to have his hand brush against the man's thigh as he let it fall at the end of the shake.

His cock responded, and the man coughed a pleasurable response, "Dave. My name is Dave."

"Well Dave, I'd think the last place you'd like to do is hangout at work. How 'bout we go up to my apartment and continue this conversation, or...," and he paused looking Dave over, "...anything that might come to your mind."

"Wow, it's like you read my mind. I would like to get out of here." And Dave got up and led Adam out of the alcove. No thought Adam, what I read on your mind is that you want to fuck me.

The trip to Adam's apartment was far shorter on this night than the last. Ten feet out the door of the café, the lobby to his apartment building welcomed them back inside. Dave climbed the two flights of stairs, followed closely by Adam who was finding no need to direct his prey to the proper apartment.

"This is it right," said Dave stopping at the correct apartment door. This worried Adam in some way, given that he had intended not on killing his prey but drinking from him and leaving him as a one-night stand. His prey was already too familiar with Adam, it might not be good if his new secret got out.

"How did you know?" Adam replied, teasing Dave in the same sassy voice he knew he used on those bitchy occasions.

"You're the only A in the building, according to the initials on the mailboxes in the lobby."

"Hmm, smart." And with that, he unlocked the door and led Dave into the apartment. "Welcome,"

Dave dropped his satchel but before it hit the floor, Adam had him against the back of the door passionately kissing him. Adam placed a hand on Dave's hard crotch, and whispered in the boy's ear, "I bet you want to fuck me?"

"How'd you guess?"

Adam moved his hand from Dave's crotch to the deadbolt, "I can read your mind." He giggled making it a playful joke. Kissing Dave, he pulled him into the bedroom and allowed himself to land on the bed first. It was his turn to be seduced, but in the back of Adam's mind a voice rang out, you were the one seduced last night too. He smiled at the thought.

Dave straddled Adam and began to work his lips over Adam's body, first with his lips, neck, then dipping underneath his shirt. As his lips worked their way up Adam's well-developed torso he rolled the muscle shirt up and over Adam's head, stopping to suck deeply at Adam's nipple.

He stopped after a minute, looked up across Adam's chest staring into Adam's eyes and grinned wide, then moved to Adam's cock, biting at it through the jeans. Slowly, Dave began to undo Adam's belt working his way into his pants. Once Dave found Adam naked, he stood up on his knees, pulling own shirt off while Adam worked his own way into Dave's khakis. The khakis were pulled down with the underwear in one tug and Dave's hard 7-inch cock sprang out. Supporting himself on one hand, arm stretched fully out, Dave pushed the pants the remaining way down and onto the floor, while Adam twisted, and grabbed a condom from the bedside table drawer. More condoms would be needed at this rate, he thought. Adam ripped the package open and rolled the condom down Dave's cock. The hunger began to rise within him and he felt the need to rush Dave to get closer to his feeding.

Bending his legs back, knees against his chest, Adam began to assist Dave with inserting his cock in Adam's hole. Dave was taken aback by the eagerness and lack of need for anal foreplay, allowing himself to immediately thrust his cock into Adam's hole, an easy fit. Adam surged with unimaginable pleasure as his hole hungrily welcomed the cock—a task Adam had usually found required great amounts of loosening. But Adam knew that he now had better control over his body and over every muscle that were working to achieve sexual pleasure and then to feed. With the control, he tighten his hole, locking Dave's cock inside the hole, causing Dave a pleasurably tight hole to thrust his cock into and out off, working feverishly to his orgasm.

It had become his singular task to reach his orgasm, forgetting Adam was there. Adam began to feel the pattern of Dave's breathing and knew that the climax was near. He grabbed the back of Dave's neck and pulled him closer to his face, kissing him on the lips then working his lips way down toward the bare throat. Adam allowed his hole to tighten slightly, and Dave moaned in pleasurable excitement. He was close and Adam was ready, his fangs slid down anticipating the blood. Dave hit his orgasm seconds later, curling his toes up and digging his finger into the bed, his load exploding into Adam. When Adam felt the tremble in Dave's muscles the moment it began, he plunged his fangs into Dave's throbbing throat.

For Adam however, he knew that this bite would need to be short, regardless of his own thrusting action that still pumped Dave's cock. Soon Dave would be done his orgasm and would come to feel the sharp pain in his neck. But Adam held his fangs a second too long, and before he could pull out, Dave's orgasm had completed. However he continued to moan and trembled as Adam carried on suck his neck. Adam could feel Dave's excitement, and the pleasure that Dave was getting from the blood letting. This excited Adam, and in a burst of sexual energy he had never obtained before, his hard cock instantly exploded, shooting cum onto his chest.

The hunger satisfied and the sexual energy momentarily spent, Adam pulled his fangs out of Dave's neck, who in turn pulled his cock out of Adam and rolled over, spent from the ordeal. Adam grabbed a clump of Kleenex from the box on the side table and did a quick wipe of his stomach removing the remnants of his cum, which he knew instinctively, would be just as powerful to Dave as his vampire blood, even though there would not be enough to affect a change.

Dave's head rolled back toward Adam, "Wow. That was incredible. I so enjoy finding myself a vampire. You guys really know how to make sex enjoyable, and I get such wicked pleasure out of the blood drinking. I knew that you'd be a good lay after I saw you with Frederick last night."

"Frederick? You know Frederick?"

"Yeah," exhaling a lustful sigh, "that boy is an amazing lay. Really, he's the only other vampire I've been with, but when we get together, it's so fucking amazing."

"You do this regularly?"

"Oh, um, about once a week, if I'm lucky. We seem to just find each other. When I need it, I can find him. Hehe, now I can find you too." Dave leaned in and kissed Adam on the cheek.

"So you know how to find him. Good. I need to see him."

"Yeah," Dave said yawning, "I can always find him some late nights, anytime after 3 AM, going in or out of this old brown stone three blocks up town from the Christopher Street Station. I...," he yawned deeply for a long moment, "...think he might live there, but we always fuck at my place." And then Dave was asleep.

Adam was again excited, having fed and had his sexual release, he also obtained information on where to find Frederick. Pictures of the very building and of the address had risen in Dave's mind as he told his story, giving Adam a great deal to go on. He fell asleep knowing he would soon find the boy he had been thinking of when he woke that day.

The following afternoon came again, and Adam found himself once again in an empty bed lying naked. The day before, he had pulled his bedroom curtains shut, blocking out all the outside light. It was his usual schedule to sleep through the day and work at night, so the room had been set up well before to block out the daylight while he slept.

Unlike the night before, he had felt charged with energy and was unable to sleep, fitting back into his usual schedule. Work was still unavoidable, but Adam had found himself doing his normal 5 to 7 hours of work in 4 short hours while Dave slept. He returned to the bed and found sleep a little after 5AM.

Even though his prey had wondered off without saying good-bye, Adam had obtained the relevant information he needed to find Frederick, and had nearly left around 3AM to find the boy. He knew he could afford to wait.

The thoughts that nested in the back of Adam's mind however, were concerning his new body. He needed to know more about feeding and living as a vampire. After 24 years of working on being a human, he now had to restart the learning process that governed his basic needs. Adam found that he had easily adjusted to the thrill of what he now was, however he was faced with the realization that he had merely adapted rather then take on his new life. Fair, he had already lived several years on the schedule on a night owl, but he had the feeling that his life needed to change to accommodate his immortal powers—if he was even immortal. Should an immortal have to work, or was there a better solution.

One thing he was sure about, he did not feel the same burning hunger he'd felt the night before. His feeding had quenched his thirst, though a dull voice still called for more blood. The amount he took from Dave, while small, appeared to give him a burst of energy and sated his hunger significantly. But how long would it hold of the hunger.

Unable to continue sleeping, Adam pulled his naked body out of his bed toward this closet. He was beginning to enjoy walking around his apartment totally naked, something he only used to do on rare occasions. In the mirror, his skin took on a reddish blush all over his body. His cock was still hard, impressing Adam that he would continue to have this high degree of prowess.

Knowing their were now almost 11 hours until he would be able to search out Frederick, Adam had to find something to fill his waking void. He dressed, again in jeans and a polo.

He ventured into the kitchen and opened the fridge door. It occurred to him that he did not crave the contents, while he knew he could eat anything it contained. Instead he pulled a garbage bag from below the sink and tossed the soon to rot and decay items into the plastic. He stopped himself however at the cupboards. What if he should have company? What would they think of a kitchen with no food? That he was a bachelor basically. Still he left the contents untouched and preceded out of his apartment, the plastic bag in tow.

The garbage bag was tossed down the chute, and Adam ventured out of the building in search of his local bookstore after which he would hit a video store to gather a collection of horror classics and anything that might portray his kind. He figured that it was worth an attempt to find as much information as possible, regardless of its accuracy. The mere information that could exist was important to know if he was to protect his secret and remain hidden from the ignorance around him.

When he had discovered his own sexuality and then been more honest with himself in college, Adam had done the same research for any information that was anti-gay and homophobic and would serve to only spread misinformation. This obsessive response was borne out of an academic behavior he had never been able to shake.

The bookstore held several small wonders, but most of which were fiction including one anthology of gay vampire short stories. How fitting he thought. And only one book that purposed itself to be theory. Adam knew that the truth lay specifically with Frederick, unless another vampire could be found who could shed some light on questions he couldn't answer himself. But Adam wanted Frederick for so much more then for answers. He longed to be with him, to hold him and be close to him. Also he had really enjoyed the sex and wanted to experience it again. Sex with Dave had been different, special in its' own way. Adam realized that if he did need Frederick for the answers, he might otherwise prefer to have Dave by his side.

The video store had an overwhelming number of choices that would take hours to sift through. He ruled out the hammer-horror and disregarded any of the b-movies earlier then 1980. The Lost Boys seemed to be quite well cast, the recent Dracula was unneeded as it had been seen, but another look at Interview with a Vampire was worthwhile. As well its' sequel would be entertaining. Another old release intrigued Adam, The Brotherhood, a B-movie that seemed to contain a number of well-muscled guys. It was all well-meaning research.

After two hours of wandering about gathering his books and videos, and a stop at the drugstore for some more condoms, Adam returned to his apartment and placed himself on the couch opposite the tv.

The Brotherhood came first. There were two movies on the double feature, but only the first one related to the subject of vampires. What Adam saw was an amazingly homoerotic gay version of the famous "tits and ass" b-movie horror genre that amounted to soft-core porn. With the Brotherhood, there was a plot, hot guys, plenty of underwear shots of the guys and a subtext surrounding the relationship between the head vampire and the guy he was trying to recruit.

Next came The Lost Boys, which also got a mention in one of the books Adam had been thumbing through. It appeared to be a cult favorite of the vampire films and an 80s gem for teenage actors. Interview with a Vampire and Queen of the Damned followed and concluded his evening of video research.

After a few hours plowing through his job, the time had come to follow the instructions and visions provided by Dave and begin the search for Frederick. Again Adam left his apartment, this time making his way to the nearest subway station to take him toward the village and the apartment in question. He stopped. A thought rose to his mind, why would Frederick be doing his laundry in a Laundry mat in Chelsea when he supposedly lived near Christopher Street. It made little sense to cross the city to do one's laundry, especially in the hole in the wall he used. He either had to live closer or was there was a reason. Or both. Being at that laundry mat at that time was clearly coincidence and not some scheme of Frederick's. Then again, the thought had to be entertained.

Adam turned around and headed directly for the coffee shop in hopes of finding Dave. The chances were slim that Dave would be working this late, but he could afford the time to chance it and see. Even before he stepped up to the café, the door opened as a late night customer left, and he was sure he could smell Dave. Adam's instincts were proving right. He stepped through the doorway and was greeted by the lone occupant of the café, Dave, who stood behind the counter. He smiled as Adam came in.

"Look at you, hotty. I wandered when I would see you next."

"Well, obviously now. What are you doing here so late?"

"I had to cover a co-worker's shift and pull a double shift. Thank gawd for coffee," he said, throwing back a shot of espresso he'd just pulled from the machine. "What brought you here? Hungry?" and Dave tilted his neck, showing his exposed neck.

Momentarily Adam grew hungry. "No actually, I'm not hungry at all, but I was hoping to see you. I have gotten a little confused about what you said as to where I might find Frederick."

"Oh," and Dave lean on the counter, supporting himself on his elbows, sipping from another cup of coffee.

"You told me to go to the Christopher Street, and I could even tell what place you were even talking about. But I'm bothered you see. I met Frederick across the street at the laundry mat. Now I've never seen him before two days ago, especially at that laundry mat, and can't see why he would have come all the way across town to use that laundry mat. So tell me, what makes you think that he lives on the Lower East side?"

"I don't remember saying that that's where he lives. I did say he might live there, and he might have once."

"Are you saying you know where he lives now?"

"Um," the cover was blown, and an apartment, the inside of an apartment, flashed in Dave's mind. "Well, no I don't really know where he lives but I know how to find him."

"You're terrible at lying. I saw in your mind where he lives."

"Hmm, well yeah maybe where he's staying, but he's not living there for long, I mean he's getting his own place soon. Oh, and by the way, it is totally rude to read someone's mind."

And then it occurred to Adam even without mind reading. "So he's been staying at your apartment then?"

Dave nodded, disappointed that the knowledge had been spilled. "I knew you'd figure it out at some point, but I hoped I could keep you strung along for a little while."

"Why's that?"

"Well I want to keep my vampires separate. I don't want you going off with him, leaving me with neither of you. I mean I know there are a few of you guys around, but I think you're the only one he might think is hot enough for him."

"Why would you think that?"

"Cause I think you're hot, so it stands to reason that he'd go off with you. I mean I pointed out this one hot guy once and Frederick up and killed the guy. I mean talk about jealous."

"I don't know what he like, but you are half right. I want to be with him, so he needs to answer me questions about this gift that he gave me."

"What gift?" jealousy ringing in his voice.

"Making me a vampire of course."

"Wait," impatiently he said standing up, "you're telling me that he made you into a vampire on your first fuck?"

Adam nodded.

"That bitch," his sharp voice ringing out in the café. "He told me there is no way to make a human into a vampire. I mean, I know he keeps me around for the blood and sex, and yeah," he paused to smile, "while I do enjoy both." He paused yet again mulling the idea over, getting himself excited. "It'd be nice if he was honest with me and I don't know, maybe shared the power. Yeah, that's right he's been staying at my place for the last couple of months. I needed the extra cash, and I didn't mind the constant sex and blood sucking, but hell you can have the little fucker." Dave pulled a ring out of pocket and slapped it on the counter. It held two keys. "My apartment is around the corner, the first brownstone on the left. It's the front basement apartment. He should still be there now."

Adam paused, looking down at the keys, not sure how to react.

"Go!" Dave picked up the keys and threw them at Adam as hard as he could. They bounced off Adam's chest and fell into his waiting left hand. Adam rolled the keys in his hand then looked at the distraught young man. He leaned in and kissed Dave.

"Thank you." Adam pulled his own keys from his pocket and placed them in Dave's hand, closing Dave's fist around the keys and held the hand, "I want you to go to my apartment when you get off."

Without waiting for a response, Adam walked away from Dave toward the boy's apartment. Just as Dave had described, he turned left out the café and walked to the end of the block then headed down the street. Finding the first brownstone on the left, Adam took the outside stairs to the basement door and unlocked it.

Dave turned his head to the apartment door, pausing the DVD he had been watching. A creak came from the hallway shortly before the door opened and Adam walked in. Leaving the Lost Boys frozen on the tv, Dave got up and approached Adam.

"Did you find Frederick?"

"No. He wasn't there when I got there and didn't return during the three hours I waited."

Dave went to the bed and laid down, patting the empty side and looking longingly at Adam.

"Dave, you said earlier that Frederick led you to believe that you couldn't be turned, right?"

"That's right. I'm sure I begged enough times, but every time he would say a vampire can only be born a vampire."

Adam laid down next to Dave and kissed him gently on the lips. "So did he tell you much about himself, such as if he was in fact born a vampire?"

"No, he's been pretty quiet about himself. He said he was over two hundred years old. He also said he traveled around a lot and didn't stay in one place too long."

"What makes you think that he was going to get an apartment and settle down here for awhile, if he is such a free spirit?"

"Um, well I guess I just assumed he was looking, but then again, I like having him around. Like I said, he's been helping with the rent and I get plenty of sex from him as well as the feedings."

"You like the feedings don't you?"

"Oh yeah, he has a very gentle and sexual way of feeding," Dave paused and blushed. "I like your feeding style too."

"Thanks, but I've only fed once and that was you. I'm sorry Frederick wasn't willing to turn you. Do you really want to become a vampire?"

"Fuck yeah. I mean I get off on the feedings, but I want the immortality. I want to be doing the feeding."

"Good. Dave, I'm going to turn you. I can understand the need to have someone around to feed off of on a regular basis, but I think you deserve it. And I need another vampire around since Frederick is likely to flee."

Dave laid back against the pillows and allowed Adam to kiss him, first on the lips then down his chest. Adam gathered the fabric clinging to Dave's legs with one hand on each hip and smoothly ripped his pants and underwear off in one pull. Taking Dave's cock in his mouth, Adam brought Dave to the point of orgasm then at the very moment Dave released, Adam slid his fangs down and sank them into the base of Dave's cock. He drank lightly, mixing the blood and cum together.

Dave was still coming down from the orgasm panting heavily when Adam bit his own wrist and offered it to Dave. "Drink." Dave licked his lips and pressed his lips to the cut, sucking in the red liquid. When Adam began to feel light headed, he pulled his wrist from Dave's greedy mouth and gave the wound a lick to seal the skin. Adam watched Dave's eyelids grow heavy until he fell asleep next to him. Just as Adam began to feel his own eyes want to close he heard a soft creak at the foot of the bed. He looked up to find Frederick standing there smiling.

"Hi Adam. I hear you've been looking for me."

"I have," Adam replied and watched Frederick look over Dave's naked form, he smiled wider.

"You've turned him."

"Well you didn't seem to want to do it."

"That's right, I had no intention of doing it myself."

"What do you mean?"

"He likes you; wouldn't stop going on about you. I had to do something. When I first laid eyes on you, I realized immediately how good a vampire you would make. That's when I decided to turn you, knowing Dave would finally find the courage to approach you."

"You could have turned him yourself."

"Aren't you grateful I turned you?"

Adam smiled showing his fangs, "actually, I've very grateful. But you're avoiding the question," he said, standing up and walking up to Frederick.

"As I said," wrapping his arms around Adam's waist when he approached, "I knew you'd make a good vampire. You're independent and smart, and I knew I wouldn't have to take care of you as a newborn. The same couldn't be said for Dave. I just didn't need him clinging to me for the next hundred years."

"You could have left."

Frederick leaned up and kissed Adam on the lips, "no, he deserved to be turned." The expression on Frederick's face seemed to suggest he had something else to say. "He's my son."

"What? Didn't you sleep with him?"

"Oh, he told you that?"

"Yes."

"Okay, he's not my son," Frederick exhaled loudly. He looked up into Adam's eyes and with menace in his voice, and his fangs bared, he hissed quietly, "don't you dare repeat this to Dave, but I turned him to make him happy." Then he smiled wickedly.

Adam pulled Frederick close, "aw, you're a softy."

Frederick giggled into Adam's chest, "I am, but don't let him or anyone else know," he stiffened, "I have a reputation to maintain. Finally, two things before I go..."

"What, you're not going to say goodbye to Dave?"

"No." He pulled two slips of paper from his pocket. "You can tell him I said bye. This," he handed one slip to Adam, "is the number of a Swiss bank account and the number to call to arrange withdrawals. There's a few million to get you by."

Adam took the slip and smiled, "you're kidding?"

"No. And don't tell him about it, or you're dead."

"Second, you must not turn any more vampires without my permission. Here's the best way to contact me, not quickly, but time is irrelevant to immortals." Frederick handed over the second slip.

"How can we be killed?" he asked, since Frederick had made a threat.

"The only way to successfully kill a vampire is by cutting his head off, and then burning the remains."

"I think I'll be able to figure everything else out. I just didn't want to experiment trying to kill myself. Will we see you again?"

"Sure, someday." Frederick kissed Adam again, then said softly, "take care of him for me."

Adam turned to take in Dave who was stirring for the first time, then turned back to find Frederick had vanished. Dave sat up in the bed and opened his mouth to speak, his fangs showing below is upper lip.

"Was someone just here?"

"Yeah, Frederick. He came to say goodbye."

"Why didn't he say it to me?"

Adam got into the bed and kissed Dave, "he didn't want to wake you during your change."

"So he knows. How was he?"

"Indifferent. Oh, except he told me something."

"What?" Dave said suspiciously.

"That you like me."

Dave giggled. "That's not true." He bit his lip and flirted. "I love you."

"I love you too. Now, what say you get dressed and we go pick up someone for dinner."

Dave licked his fangs, "yes, please. I'm really hungry, and horny."

"One thing at a time," Adam teased, then kissed Dave on the lips for several minutes. "There's no rush, we have all the time in the world."

Campus coverup

BY IAN RICHMOND

Josh put the newspaper down and smiled. He had read through the entire feature news story twice and was elated with his hard work. Students were disappearing from campus, their bodies turning up deep in the forest that surrounded the university found ravaged by animals.

After being assigned the story the previous semester, Josh had found the story grow into the biggest story of the year. Normally a freshman wouldn't get such a plum assignment and in this case when the story was assigned it was meant to be a simple test for the rookie reporter. At the time only one student had gone missing and his body had not yet been found so it was assumed he'd simply dropped out of school. When the story grew with further disappearances, and Josh began to take more time to investigate the pattern, he had fought his editor to keep the byline. It may have helped that he had begun dating the same editor.

Keeping the article to himself was easy when no bodies had been found, but once the first mangled corpse was discovered he had to fight harder. Josh had been on the verge of completing the story when the first body was found and a new twist was added to the story. The medical examiner had to investigate, then the report was withheld for weeks until the second and third bodies were discovered. Yet the story had continued to fly below the radar of the local media. Finally the medical report was released and Josh completed the article just in time for this week's edition.

"You should be proud of yourself, I doubt few other students have launched their journalism career with such a strong first piece."

Josh looked up and smiled at his boyfriend. He had been stand staring down at Josh while he'd been lost in thought. Drew leaned down and kissed his boyfriend who was lying on his stomach across Drew's bed.

"Thanks babe, I couldn't have done it without you. And not just because you let me continue to write it, but for all your help along the way."

"Considering all the work I did, I think we should have shared the byline."

"Naw, you're the editor, it's your job to help the writer and not get the credit," I said wickedly.

Drew laughed, "I'd slap you for that comment if you weren't so adorable."

Josh was adorable, but he thought Drew was far more handsome. Well liked through high-school, Josh had been a soccer star but never considered a jock. He kept his dark chocolate brown hair short on the sides and swept in a faux-hawk on top his oval face. His cheeks were slightly freckled above thin but rosy lips that were always smiling. Dimples on each side of his mouth were visible whenever he had a smile across his face, which was most of time. Dark grey eyes shone below thin eyebrows and beautifully distracted from his slightly large nose.

Girls had followed Josh around for years hoping to date him. Instead of ignoring them, Josh made friends and found time for pretty much any girl who approached him. No one had ever suspected Josh was gay, and when he found himself dating one of his teammates and the rest of the team discovered the pair, the rumors didn't spread. The team mates were not suddenly immediate converts to gay rights, but when one junior made an off color comment, Josh was defended. He was their star player, a friendly guy who had gotten each of them out of trouble several times, and he'd also played matchmaker for every one of them, after all he was friends with all the girls.

Away from his high-school boyfriend and across the country from anyone else in his school, Josh reinvented himself at university. Turning down several soccer scholarships, he spent the first month visiting various clubs and organizations on campus until he walked into the newspaper and met Drew.

In many ways Drew looked like the jock Josh wasn't. He was a few inches taller, built of solid bulky muscle with an arrogant, cheeky face. Drew's hair was a lighter shade of brown, so light his eyebrows were almost blond. He was obviously several years older with rugged worn features that looked more mature than Josh's boyish soft skin. Drew spoke with a commanding voice, assure of his good looks which often verged on being full of himself.

"As much as I want to just eat you up right now, we need to get to the office and get working on the next issue. No resting on your laurels just yet, there's going to be a follow up to your article."

"Aww, I have plenty of time."

"Nice try smart ass, I may have let you investigate this story for over three months but now that it's public we need to keep it fresh in people's minds."

The bed shifted as both boys rolled off the mattress and began gathering their coats and school bags. Drew looked less like a senior and more like a graduate student or junior professor, dressed in dark jeans, dress shirt, wool sweater and tweed sport coat complete with elbow patches. He pulled his chocolate brown scarf from the coat peg behind the door and wrapped it casually yet gracefully around his neck. At the opposite end of the spectrum, Josh dressed casually in the all-American collegiate look. Josh's toned soccer star body filled out his tight polo perfectly. His jeans were also tight fitting which Drew particularly liked. Josh throw on his large parka with it's teddy bear fur lining but didn't bother to zip up. He grabbed his canvas bookbag and quickly pecked Drew on the lips before throwing the bag over his shoulder.

Drew's residence was further from the academic buildings than Josh's, but as the room was larger and Drew more demanding, they spent almost all their time there. The big man on campus, Drew would walk around campus with Josh, but never held his hand, including today as they walked to the office.

The dark inky grey sky continuously sprinkled the campus with a light rain that never seemed to stop. Pea soup think fog coated the mountain and gently shrouded the nearly vacant university buildings. The few students brave enough to venture out of their warm residences into the inclement weather scurried quickly from place to place and mostly alone.

The subject of his premiere article on his mind, Josh didn't want to lingered too long on the deserted foot path. The single path from the residences to the main cluster of campus buildings briefly cut through a portion of the woods that crept across the campus like a tentacle extending out from the dense rain forest surrounding the campus. Josh had dashed home after a late class to down a quick dinner while he finished an essay due the day after. He was still hoping to persuade a certain editor to quickly look it over, but it could wait a day. At the moment, he was heading to the newspaper office to meet up with Drew, who was still working away at the late hour.

A cold chill went through Josh as he passed into the short section of forest bordering the academic buildings. The path was lit with lights set only a few feet off the ground bathing only the path and adjacent forest floor in light while the tall trees remained dark above. The dense fog didn't help at this point to make the path visible for more than ten feet ahead.

A distant sound coming from deep within the dark part of the forest made Josh stop suddenly and crane his neck to listen. He could hear the sound approaching, vaguely like the soft beating of wings. The flapping grew louder and more powerful. The closer it approached, the less likely it was a small bird.

In the blink of an eye, Josh suddenly dove into the nearby brush, scrambled around to right himself and face whatever was flying overhead. He crawled through the brush to an enormous old growth tree and kept low as he hid behind it. The beating of wings had stopped getting louder but remained at a slow steady beat as if hovering in one place high above the path. Josh was certain he could feel the air shift with each whip and snap back of the wings, but when he looked up into the trees he couldn't find the shape associated with the sound.

The fog separated like a curtain drawing back and presented a student coming along the path in the direction of campus. When the student had passed Josh's position, the fog shifted further, only from above, as a dark shape descended through the haze. The unfolding scene felt like an eternity but it was within mere seconds that the flying creature landed on the student and forced him to the ground. Josh was horrified as he watched through the mist the head of the winged breast attack the downed student. He strained his eyes to make out the beast. The massive leathery wings, gutting out of the creature's leathery body, had seized beating, and Josh realized the body was physically human apart from the wings. It moved its' legs suddenly revealing boots caked in mud, and a pair of hands starkly white against all the black. In those few seconds the student made only one muffled scream then after a moment of thrashing uselessly under the weight of the beast, he went completely still.

Less quickly than it had descended, the winged man gathered the student limply in his arms with his winged back to Josh. He watched the creature begin to beat his wings and rise up into the fog before disappearing deep into the forest. The sound waning as it flew further into the darkness.

As he crawled out from behind the tree, Josh knew the student was now dead. He walked to the spot where the body had fallen. The smell of blood hung in the air, carried it seemed by the moist breeze. Josh stared up into the dark fog for only a moment before he took off in a run for the main campus.

The newspaper was on the far side of the main cluster of buildings but Josh felt safe once he was under the stronger lights and slightly more populated part of campus. He had just seen the animal that was attacking students on campus, and knew he was wrong. It wasn't an animal.

Running full out, Josh recalled the mental picture of the creature. He wished the images were wrong, that he hadn't seen a man with wings that resembled those of a bat. Moving quickly between the buildings he mentally checked off the list of places bodies had been found; all had been deep in the woods. One autopsy had concluded that the body found had been killed in another location and carried into the forest. Now Josh knew how close to campus the attacks had occurred and just how the bodies were carried away.

Josh came bursting through the entrance of the student center, blowing passed the small mess of spilled newspapers that were the only remnants of a much larger pile. Normally after only one day on the stands, more copies would have remained in the pile next to the busy door. His story had been on the lips of every student that day and now Josh had information for his follow up.

Josh tore through the main office door and immediately came into the newsroom. Kris, the news editor, looked up at Josh with surprise. He'd seen the editor's boyfriend come in late to collect Drew many times but never so out of breath and so seemingly frazzled.

"Are you okay Josh, you seem freaked out?"

Struggling to steady his breathing, Josh took several deep breaths and forced out several words before taking another, "saw the animal."

Kris appeared to know what he had meant. "Are you sure?"

He nodded then added, "wasn't an animal."

"What was it then?"

His breathing was settling but Josh was still at a lost for words. "I don't know. I mean, it looked like a man with wings."

"Hmm, that sounds odd. Are you sure it wasn't an animal and you're just mistaken."

"No, I mean I know it's foggy out but that was not an animal, it had wings, leathery wings and skin of leather. Or not skin, but dressed in leather..." Josh froze and finally looked at Kris then at the jacket hanging off Kris' chair. Kris was wearing black leather pants and the jacket had a long vertical slit in the back. The image that flashed in Josh's mind immediately was of the attack and seeing the creature from behind. Though it had been foggy, Josh had seen enough to know the winged man had only been wearing leather.

"I've never seen you wear so much leather? Some fetish you've kept quiet," Josh said, attempting to make a joke, but he was also backing away while he spoke. "I mean I've seen you wearing that jacket a lot, always did wonder why you have a slit in the back."

The expression on Kris' face was calm and understanding. "Josh, it's not what you think. It's not me."

"Oh right, I know what I saw. You're that monster. You've been killing people!"

"No Josh, listen, I can explain."

"I don't want to hear it. Stay away from me." Josh had completely backed out of the office and quickly turned to sprint into Drew's office.

Slamming the door shut and flipping the deadbolt, Josh rushed over to Drew sitting behind his desk. He instinctively stood and pulled Josh into an embrace, holding him tight. Josh seemed to respond to the security of Drew's arms and began to let the tears fall.

"Everything is okay, babe. You're safe here."

"It was awful."

"What was?"

"The thing killing people in the forest. It's not an animal, it's Kris, he's a monster. He can fly and he attacked a student just now right before my eyes."

"In the office?" Drew asked skeptically.

"No, out in the woods, near the dorms."

"Josh," Drew leaned back and looked into Josh's eyes, "you're being silly, it was an animal, and it certainly wasn't Kris."

"No Drew, I know what I saw, the monster was wearing his leather jacket and had these huge leathery wings, like a bat."

Josh lowered his hands to Drew's butt and stopped, suddenly realizing he was feeling something different. He looked down then looked back into Drew's eyes. He attempted to pull away but Drew's hold on him was firm.

"You're also wearing leather pants?"

"Yep."

"Who's jacket is that out there?"

"That one belongs to Kris, but I had to borrow it. I have one myself, but it's at home and it's a bit chilly out there, especially when flying around."

"Drew," Josh struggled in Drew's arms, "let me go."

"I can't do that babe."

"What are you?"

"You haven't figured that out. Come now, I know you're smart, put the pieces together."

"You can fly?"

"Yes."

"You attacked someone."

"Yes."

Josh swallowed hard upon hearing the quick confession. He thought about the scene again, recalling the attack. Where had his hands been, had Drew strangled the student?

"I didn't see how you attacked him. How do you do it?"

"Oh yes, I imagine if you didn't see this," Drew opened his mouth and allowed his canines to length almost half an inch, "it might be hard to make a conclusion."

"It's not possible. Vampires don't exist."

"And men don't fly, but you saw me do just that."

"Yes, but you had wings... I don't see wings."

"It would be hard for me to walk around with wings gutting out of my back all the time. I can sprout them when I need them. It does hurt a little, but I've gotten used to it. I'd do it now but this room is a tad small."

"And Kris, he's like you too?

"Yes, he and I have been vampires for quite some time."

Josh felt less fearful, but just as suddenly jealous roared inside him. "What is he to you, your boyfriend?" he snapped.

"He's my brother."

Josh seemed taken aback, but satisfied. "Drew?"

"Yes?"

"Please let me go."

"No."

"Are you going to let me go?"

"No I'm afraid you know too much. I told you how good a journalist you are, I can't have you going around spreading the truth."

"So you're going to kill me?"

"Maybe. I did want you to continue writing for the paper, you have a bright future ahead of you. And someone needs to keep writing about the animal attacks."

"But the animal attacks are a lie."

"Yes, but do you think I'm going to let the truth be known? Josh, I've lived for a very long time and I know how to protect my kind."

"What, um, what are you going to do with me then?"

"Ahh," Drew smiled, flashing his fangs. "As I said, I still want you covering the story. I can give you a personal reason to protect our kind, beyond protecting your own boyfriend," he paused and pursed his lips in a pout, "...or maybe you'll be found in the forest somewhere."

Josh shuddered. He looked into Drew's eyes and swallowed, "our kind?"

"Yes Josh. I can offer you immortality and so much more."

"But I'd be a monster too. I'd have to kill people."

"Well you will have to feed, say about once a month, and yes, you will have to kill your donor."

"Can't you just take a little bit and not kill?"

"Sure, if I wanted every donor to turn. I have tried that route. I had to feed sometimes as much as twice a week. That's over a hundred new vampires a year, and I'm 276."

Josh ignored the math and focused on the single terrifying word; vampire. "I don't want to die."

"You don't have to, if you accept my gift."

"I could kill you instead."

"You could try, but you would fail."

"You would say that."

"But it's true. Apart from cutting my head off, nothing can harm me."

"I could do that."

"Sounds simple. Do you think I'm going to let you go so you can find a way to decapitate me before I have a chance to make a move?" Drew shrugged, "No need to answer that. Make your choice now; eternity or death?"

Tears came to Josh's eyes. He looked at Drew's fangs then closed his eyes, remembering the attack in the forest. When he opened them he looked into Drew's eyes and said in a whisper, "I want to live."

"Then you've made your choice."

Drew swung around and unlocked the door. It swung open and he called for Kris. A moment later Kris came to the door. "Hold Josh for me." Kris grabbed Josh gently but held him firmly, while Drew disappear returning with Kris' jacket. He removed his shirt exposing his muscular upper body. Putting the jacket on, Drew took Josh from Kris and smiled at him. "Josh has decided to join us."

"That's great," Kris smiled, his fangs suddenly extended.

"We're going to go for a little flight."

Drew pulled Josh out the back door into the fog filled campus, leading him to a darkened passage behind the student center. He turned and faced Josh then grimaced from the slight pain as his wings tore through his skin and unfolded neatly. The large leathery wings swayed gracefully and Josh could finally see them up close, realizing the wingspan was almost twelve feet.

"Hold on," Drew warned as he pumped his wings and lifted them both through the dense fog until they were floating above it. The rain was now just a mist.

Josh hadn't said a word since making his choice, but when he saw the fog covered city stretching below and felt the powerful beating of Drew's wings he knew he didn't have anything to say. He leaned in instead and kissed Drew. The kiss was long and passionate.

"Since the moment you walked into the paper, I knew I'd make you a vampire. You're going to enjoy this. We're going to have so much fun together," Drew said then leaned into Josh's neck, first kissing the soft skin before thrusting his fangs in. Josh closed his eyes and felt the blood being pulled out of him as the seconds ticked by. Drew withdrew his fangs from Josh's neck and again they kissed. Slowly Josh parted his lips and felt his old blunt human canines pushed out of his mouth, replaced by new sharper fangs.

Drew smiled, "you're now a vampire. You will need to feed—tonight," he paused and let the thought sink in. "It's going to take a while for your wings to be fully grown, until then, you'll fly with me." With a few final pumps of his wings, Drew flew them through the night sky, dipping and swooping as they continued their passionate kisses.

That night, one more student disappeared from campus. He had sat next to Josh in several lectures, but Josh couldn't remember his name.

It didn't bother Josh, he was too hungry to care. He eagerly thrust his fangs into the student's neck and drank the hot red liquid until the body went cold. Standing up from the body, Josh, his mouth covered in blood, smiled at Drew before allowing himself to be carried into the right sky.

Stories appeared in the paper for months, reporting the continuing animal attacks until finally the university was forced to clear the thick forest close to campus. A fence was built to contain the remaining woods, but for almost four years, the disappearances continued.

Rescue

BY LUC RUISLIP

The first thing I realized was that I was sore all over. My muscles felt stiff and asleep. It took effort to open my eyes, and once they were open, it took a moment for my vision to clear. I didn't recognize the bed I was lying on or the room around me.

I caught something move in the distance out of the corner of my eye. A young man approached me smiling.

"Good, you're finally awake," he said. "How do you feel?"

I blinked once slowly, unsure how to describe the pain.

"Oh, I'm sorry, I had forgotten how painful it is to wake up for the first time."

His words confused me, but I felt comfortable having him by my side.

"Your whole body is going to hurt for a little while. It'll help if you drink this."

He handed me a plastic cup with a small amount of red liquid. It smelled familiar and inviting, reminding me of cold medication. I put the cup to my lips and allowed the liquid to pour into my mouth, expecting the cherry syrup taste I could remember. It was a different taste, yet still familiar and incredibly satisfying.

"Do you know your name?" the young man asked. Of course I knew my own name and I could have gotten bitchy but I was beginning to realize just how attractive he was.

"Um," was all I managed. Despite the liquid, my throat was still dry. I swallowed hard, which hurt. "Yeah."

"Well then, what is your name?" he said sweetly, gently pushing to get an answer without seeming to be pushy. He obviously had great patience. I stared at him for a moment, but I felt a fog in my head, I knew my name but I couldn't find the word.

"Oh, don't worry, it will come back to you. My name is Edward. You were attacked and I brought you and your friend to my house."

Attacked. I couldn't remember being attacked, but maybe that's why I hurt all over. And what did he mean friend?

I followed his gaze to the other side of the bed. Another person was lying there still asleep. He was younger than the man who called himself Edward, beautiful and very familiar. His name didn't come to mind but I wanted to touch him, to have skin on skin contact. I forced my hand close to his bare arm and I pressed my fingers to the skin. The feeling was electrifying.

"Do you know his name?"

"Ash," I surprised myself, knowing his name, but still unable to remember my own.

"Is he your boyfriend?"

I stared at Edward, frightened. How could he know that? How did I know that? I looked at Ash sleeping away. He was so beautiful I left lucky; in fact he was hotter than I remembered.

"I didn't mean to shock you. I saw you two making out, before you were attacked."

Edward could have been making it up, I didn't remember. But kissing Ash sounded good. I leaned down and put my lips to his. He seemed unresponsive.

"Look, you're coming out of a long deep sleep, so your mind will take a while to clear out the fog. There's lots to explain but I first want you to be thinking clearly."

"Who are you?" I asked.

"My name is Edward," he had said that before and his calm patient manner was beginning to annoy me.

"I know that," I replied, annoyed and starting to sound bitchy, which seemed familiar. "I mean WHAT are you, a doctor?"

He shook his head, "no, I'm not a doctor. I saw you and your boyfriend kissing, but I turned a way for a minute to watch something else. When I looked back, you were both on the ground and three bigger teens were kicking the shit out of you."

"I don't remember that." I looked down at my body and realized I was only wearing black briefs. I never wore briefs and these weren't even a brand I could afford. Looking passed the underwear I saw no cuts, bruises or marks of any kind. I lifted my legs, and arms to check further and realized I was no longer in pain. "I'm not hurting anymore," I said, but I hadn't wanted to tell him. "If I was attacked, why doesn't it show." I glanced at Ash saw he too was wearing the same black briefs and also appeared completely uninjured.

My reflexes sprung into action and my body uncoiled like a spring. In an instant, the blink of an eye, I was standing in a defensive stance with my back to the wall near the foot of the bed. The move had been instinctive and had surprised only myself. Edward's gaze had casually followed my move and he was still sitting next to the bed smiling. "What have you done to us, are you some sick perv? Is this a fetish for you?"

"Tell me your name?" was all he said.

"Ephraim. Now answer the question."

"Do you remember the attack yet Ephraim?"

"There wasn't an attack. I'm fine. Ash is fine. Look, no marks on either of us. We're fine except you've kidnapped us."

"No Ephraim, I saved you."

"I don't believe you."

"Until you remember the attack, you're going to have trust me. Remembering your name is part of clearing the fog, but the memory of the attack will be buried deep. Your mind may not want to deal with it yet."

"Okay, I'll play along with your fantasy." My voice chimed sarcastically, "Ash and I were attacked."

"Right, gay bashed."

"Sure, gay bashed by Paul, Christopher and Thomas, whatever you say."

"I didn't say their names. The police only released their names this morning. You're starting to remember."

I blinked and an image flashed in my mind behind my closed lids. I closed my eyes again but only briefly and another sequence played, like a movie or like seeing people move about between bursts from a strobe light. The memory was coming back and my eyes were watering heavily. The tears felt good, as did keeping my eyes open. I moved around to the side of the bed, keeping my gaze on Edward, but wanting to be close to Ash, to protect him if Edward made a move.

Edward sat very still. "I don't want to push you, I know it will be hard to relive what happened."

"I remember enough. But it doesn't explain everything, like why we are here, who you are and," I struggled to complete the thought, changing to another topic. "When was the attack?" I finally asked.

"Five days ago."

"What? And we've been asleep the whole time?"

"Yes, in a manner of speaking."

I was ready to object when he shifted slightly in his seat and I thought he was going to attack. I scooped Ash's body into my arms and jumped up. Cradling him in my arms I floated in the far corner of the room staring down at Edward. He only giggled and continued to sit perfectly still.

Looking at the floor below it dawned on me that I was floating about four feet off the floor. I was frightened and only wanted to protect Ash and myself.

"Your instincts are kicking in," Edward finally said. "I'm going to keep explaining what happened and you can continue to float there or you can return to the bed. Now I could make this simple and show you the truth, but I want you to discover it for yourself."

Suddenly Ash made a slight move, his muscles twitched and he began the effort of opening his eyes.

"Maybe you might want to put him on the bed before you have to explain how you're flying," Edward offered.

"No," I snapped.

Ash opened his eyes and looked at me with a smile that appeared to hurt, "baby, what's going on, I'm so sore."

"I know Ash honey, you're going to be alright. Just close your eyes for a moment, the pain will go away and I'll explain everything."

"Mmm kay."

Edward took the cue to continue. "As I said, you were attacked and when I saw it happening I rushed to help..."

"Baby, who's that," Ash said, opening his eyes and craning his neck to see Edward. He didn't seem to notice we were further off the ground then we would normally be. He looked back at me a smiled again, "I like you holding me this way."

"Ash, we were attacked by Paul, Christopher and Thomas. This man, Edward, helped us out. He's just telling us about the attack because I don't remember."

"We were attacked? If you say so. Is that why I hurt so much."

"Yeah, babe."

He looked down, "do you know you're flying?"

"Yeah, now hush up so Edward can talk," I was getting impatient with Ash, who was behaving as if he was drunk—too relaxed and carefree for such an odd situation. I decided to return to the bed and found it easy to command my body to float down. After I laid Ash down, I sat down with my back against the pillowy headboard and pulled Ash up between my legs with his back against my chest and my arms wrapped around him.

"I can move quickly," Edward picked up his speech. "But they had already done a lot of damage. I immediately pulled the three boys off you and disposed of them. You two were in very bad shape, quite close to death."

My head snapped to attention. His words seemed unreal.

"I had two choices, allow you to die or save you. I try not to intervene in human matters, but I found you two so sweet and the attack so revolting."

I wondered what he'd meant by human matters, but he continued before I could interrupt. "I gave you two enough to allow your bodies to heal but because you were so damaged, you lapsed into deep death like comas. The police and eventually the medical examiner declared you both death and you were put in the morgue where I collected you last night before you woke up. I didn't think you'd want to wake up in the morgue, and certainly not together."

I was at a lost for words, unable to comprehend the story he was telling. I just stared, motionless. If we had only been in comas, why were we declared dead and dumped in the morgue? And what had he given us 'enough' of that had healed us? I had all these questions, but I didn't know what to say first to get through his nonsense.

Instead Ash spoke up, "are we vampires?"

It made me immediately laugh, but Edward remained calm.

"Yes Ash, you and Ephraim, like me, are vampires. I fed you my blood and it healed your bodies."

Ash moved slightly, fixing his gaze on Edward. "Did we die?"

Edward shook his head and smiled. "No, it doesn't work like that. You are not an animated corpse. My blood caused your bodies to evolve. Normally the process is done to someone healthy, but I had no other choice. That's why you slipped into a coma for the change, because your body was so near death it had to preserve as much energy as possible."

"This is fucking crap," I finally yelled.

"No Ephraim, you saw for yourself, you were flying a moment ago and you moved with such fast reflexes," Edward paused. "Look." He open his mouth and I watched as his canine teeth grew longer and his eyes went entirely white except for his tiny pupils.

"Cool," I heard Ash say. "When do we get fangs?" he asked excitedly like a little kid.

"Any moment now. But first, Ash, are you still feeling sore?"

"A little."

"Well when Ephraim woke, I gave him some blood and it helped him recover faster. Would you like some?"

"Hmm, yes."

Edward took a second plastic cup and handed it to Ash. I wanted to object, push the red liquid away from Ash and protect him but then I caught the smell and knew he needed it. And that I needed more too. Edward must have read my mind because as I a watched, probably drooling, Ash drink back the blood, I was handed another cup. This time it was full.

I gulped it down and licked my lips, my tongue running over my sharp teeth. Ouch. I had nicked my tongue and could taste my own blood. I immediately felt my gums begin to ache and when I licked my teeth again. My canines had grown. Edward smiled knowingly.

"Ash," I whispered.

Ash turned round and looked at me. "Ahh, cool, you've got your fangs." He leaned up and kissed me, whispering in my ear, "you are sooo hot right now."

"Judging from how quickly Ephraim's grew, yours' should be along soon too," Edward reassured. "In a few minutes I'll give you more blood—it seemed to do the trick for Ephraim."

I looked at Edward and smiled. I twitched my head and he understood that I finally felt safe. He stood slowly then walked over and carefully sat on the edge of the bed.

"You boys are lucky. Had I not been there, you would have died. Instead I have given you immortality. However, because I couldn't prepare you for the change, you will remain the way you are now forever. I gather you are both 17?"

"Yeah." I responded.

"Well you will be 17 with these bodies for eternity. But because your bodies were injured badly, the healing may have made some improves. Sadly you won't be able to build any more muscle or grow any taller."

"Improvement! Shit, no kidding. Look," Ash exclaimed, "I have abs. And muscles. Lean and fit, but yeah damn good improvement."

"Your skin is also clear, honey."

Ash looked at me, "really. You too. Not a pimple or spot."

I looked down at my own body, it too had filled out slightly.

"So what about Paul, Christopher and Thomas?" I paused and licked my fangs at the thought of getting to taste their blood. "When can we get our revenge?"

"No, sorry Ephraim, I killed them immediately before saving you. Snapped each of their necks. But you have been drinking their blood, I didn't waste that. After I fed you, I grabbed their bodies and left the scene. I drained a bit from each boy then tossed them off the cliffs near Tagget

Bay, leaving their clothes on the cliff to make it seem they were diving." Edward continued talking while he took Ash's cup and filled it with more blood and handed it to him. "Their bodies washed ashore soon after and the medical examiner ruled that all three of them had broken their necks diving, it was low tide after all. I left the cliff and doubled back to check the scene of the attack. You were caught earlier on surveillance video being followed by the boys and then your bodies found nearby. Your blood was found on their clothes so it was concluded that they had beaten you two to death before having their accident."

Ash had finished the blood and was teasing his canines with his tongue until they slid down. He smiled at me, prouder than ever. At some point, Edward left the room while we made out. I showed Ash how to fly and we slowly floated around the room making out some more.

I pulled my face away from Ash's and yawned. I hadn't been up for very long, but I was feeling tired. Ash yawned too, but probably as a reflex to my yawn. We looked at the bed then at each other.

"It doesn't feel right?" Ash finally said, amused.

"No, you're right, it doesn't. Let's find Edward."

Together we floated out of the room into a dark hallway that led to a large living room. Edward was seated comfortably on a large L-shaped couch with another young male.

He saw us and waved us to come sit down. "Guys, this is my boyfriend Hunter."

"Hey," we all said in unison.

"I was a bit shocked when Edward told me what he'd done, but he has a habit of rescuing cute guys," Hunter said, teasing Edward then playfully avoiding a kiss. "Welcome to our home. Your home now as well."

"Really," Ash said, the excitement in his voice.

"I didn't say it earlier, but everyone thinks you're dead, so you can't go back to your old life. We'll provide you with a new one. We may want to move, this is a bit of a small place and we don't want you being seen."

"Oh, how about Paris, or better yet, London again," Hunter chimed in, his voice suddenly British, "we have two well-fit lads ready to experience the world. If they can't pass for eighteen, we'll still be able to help them get served in any pub on Old Compton Street."

"I don't see why not, and we do still have the flat near Soho. What do you say boys?"

"Fuck yeah," Ash shouted, bouncing in his seat.

I didn't plan on being away from him and London sounded great. "Wherever, as long as we're together."

"Awww, sweet young love," Hunter teased. I could tell he and Ash were very much alike and would soon be friends.

"Um, Edward?"

"Yes, Ephraim."

"We're feeling a little tired and wanted to go to bed, and the bed in there just doesn't seem right."

Hunter giggled, causing Ash to giggle too.

"Yeah, it's kind of one of those myths that's true. We sleep in coffins."

"Oh no, I don't want to sleep away from Ephraim," Ash whined.

"You won't have to. We have special custom made queen size coffins."

"Edward," I continued my inquiry, "I don't see any windows here and if we sleep in coffins, will sunlight kill us?"

"No, not at all. Hunter and I tend to be very nocturnal. We do wander off to sleep around 5 or 6AM, which is passed dawn in the summer. But we only get about eight hours of sleep and are then wandering about, often out in the sun. It's just that we sleep more comfortably in coffins."

"What will kill or hurt us?" Ash asked.

"Pretty much all other myths are just that. We can eat, including garlic. Religious symbols are benign. Stakes do sting and usually ruin whatever shirt you're wearing, but don't kill us. Being locked in a seriously strong furnace and set on fire might do the trick, but we can control humans, easily making them release us. I'm over six hundred years old and have faced several nutters trying to kill me, all unsuccessfully. Don't worry, we'll teach you how to defend yourself."

"But the best defense," Hunter continued, "is not to let the humans know about us."

I let out another yawn and muttered an apology, but Edward acted regardless, "I'd give you more of a lesson now, but you two should get some sleep."

He and Hunter stood and took our hands and led us back down the hallway, passed the bedroom we had recovered in to the end of the hall. There were two doors.

"That's our room, if you wake and need anything we should be in there." Edward said, pointing to one door. "And this, will be your room."

He swung the door open to reveal a small sitting room with a small couch in front of a fireplace below a massive flat-screen tv. Hunter walked in first and very dramatically flung open a set of double doors I had mistaken for the closet. Behind them was the bedroom, or more like coffin room. The sleek jet black coffin was a huge rectangular box with sharp square edges. It looked modern and nothing like a coffin. Hunter pressed the side of the box and a light pulsed where his finger had touched. Slowly the box split in half and the top rose up on four telescoping corner posts, revealing a sunken queen size bed covered in a tight leather sheet. It looked both uncomfortable and perfect at the same time.

Ash launched himself into the air and floated down onto the mattress. He padded the empty space next to him and waited for me to join him. I smiled at him and laughed. Edward pointed out the two buttons on the interior on each side that would lower and lock the lid. I flew next to Ash as Edward went on about the en suite bathroom, but I was too busy kissing Ash. Out of the corner of my eye I saw Hunter elbow Edward to get him to shut up and leave. I pushed the combined down and lock button and continued to make out with my beautiful vampire boyfriend as the lid sealed above us.

"Wow!"

"What, honey," I said, looking at Ash.

"I can see perfectly in the dark."

"Oh yeah, cool."

"Ephraim," Ash put on his serious face. "Are you happy we're now vampires?"

"Well I don't know if I would have chosen this if I hadn't been attacked, but it does feel really good."

"It does feel good. I've never felt this good. But only one thing would have stopped me from saying yes to becoming a vampire."

"What's that?"

"You would have to have agreed to be one too," he leaned toward me and kissed me. "Ephraim, I love you."

"Ash, I love you too, and I would have said yes in a heart beat if it meant being with you for eternity."

"Well it helps that I'm going to be this hot forever," Ash giggled.

"That doesn't hurt." I planned to make out more but Ash closed his eyes and fell asleep. Wrapping my arms around him, I closed my own and for the first time in my life, was instantly asleep.

Attack

BY ADAM SHEPARD

The full moon bathed the park in dim blue light. Light filtered through the trees sporadically where the thick canopy was sparse and the tree branches skin-and-bones. Only a few lights scattered through the urban park illuminated small pockets of the winding paths below the leafy cover. The lights were few and spaced far apart or not present at all along some paths altogether.

Camden took his usual walk through the park that separated his boyfriend's work and apartment from his own. He had parted company with Aaron outside his work, an all-night coffee shop, only a minute before Aaron's graveyard shift began. Camden had reluctantly let go of Aaron who was attempting not to be late. He watched Aaron go behind the counter and disappear behind the swinging door that led into the back before he finally turned away, the darkness of the park welcoming him from across the street.

The park was relatively safe at night and as long as he struck to the paved paths, Camden wouldn't find trouble, or more than likely, someone looking for a quick fumble, but that would be deep in the bushes off one of the paths.

Pulling the zipper down and opening his hoodie to the warm night air, Camden rounded a bend in the path into a dark and heavily treed portion of the park. Ahead he could make out the outline of two people in a close embrace by the side of the path. The closer he came, the more the pair separated from the shadows, and the more obvious how passionate the embrace appeared. A narrow shaft of moonlight lit the trees behind them, backlighting their scene. One person, who was cloaked in darkness under a long coat, was clutching the second close and leaning into him. Glimmers of reflective clothing gave the suggestion that the second person was a jogger out on a late night run. The couple appeared to be having a romantic moment, normally reserved for the dense treed privacy beyond the path.

Hoping to quietly walk by and not disturb the amorous moment, Camden angled his walk toward the opposite side of the path. He made extra effort to step gently and avoid making too much noise.

When he was about twenty feet from the couple, the cloaked figured turned and locked eyes with Camden. He froze in place. The cloaked man's face was hidden in shadow under his hood, while the runners head had flopped back exposing a neck smeared in the darkness. Camden briefly closed his eyes to take a manual blink, but watched the trees fly by when he opened them again. As he fell to the ground, realizing too late that someone had tackled him, he cried out at the pain. He felt the twin pricks in his neck at the same moment he'd come crashing down on the rocky dirt that edged the path.

The cloaked figure enveloped him with his coat and pressed his face against Camden's neck. Seconds passed slowly as Camden became reoriented and finally recognize he had been forced down and his attacked was sucking at his throat. The pain from the fall coupled with the adrenaline caused from the shock of being suddenly attacked clouded his ability to register the harsher pain coming from his neck.

Just as suddenly, he found himself picked up and held close to the face of the cloaked figure. The man's mouth was smeared with blood and when he smiled his teeth were also dark with blood. Camden stared into the man's eyes feeling the adrenaline coursing through his body. He wanted to turn his gaze, throw a punch or at least run, but he couldn't.

"Feed," the cloaked man whispered. The trees suddenly streaked by and Camden instantly found himself kneeling next to the runner, who was lying lifelessly on the ground. The man whispered again, "drink, there's just enough left. Feed and become immortal."

Camden stared at the runner's neck, blood seeping from two raw punctures in the skin. He felt a surge of energy and he grimaced as his gums began to ache.

Louder now, the cloaked man pushed Camden closer to the wound. "If you want to live, you must drink."

His throat dry, the rumble of hunger reverberating in his stomach and the threat coming from the cloaked man was too much for Camden. He couldn't resist the intoxicating smell coming from the prone body. Camden leaned closer to the neck and slid his tongue slowly across the man's skin then bit down on the throat, creating two more holes. Lips pressed firmly against the skin, he began sucking the blood into his mouth as if gulping back a gallon of water on a hot summer day.

The cloaked man pulled Camden roughly off the runner and stood him up facing the man's back.

"Wrap your arms around me and do not let go."

Camden reflexively followed the order, unsure why until he felt the sudden jerk when his body was pulled through the trees and into the sky. Feeling nauseous and tipsy as if drunk, he closed his eyes tightly and felt the air whip by him, the fabric of the cloak snapping and thrashing about in the air around him.

When his feet again felt the firm earth below him, Camden's arms sprung open and stumbled to the ground. A laugh echoed above his head.

"The first flight is always a surprise," the man said before picking Camden up and effortlessly placing him over his shoulder.

His head bobbed as he watched in reverse while they walked along the stone path, up a set of wooden steps and through a door. His reflexes suddenly quicker, Camden ducked his head close to the man's body the moment the man turned suddenly to shut the door and Camden narrowly missed hitting his head on the wall.

Finally after they had descended a set of creaking wooden stairs into a dark basement, the man put Camden down on a couch. He stared around the room quickly as the man slipped off his cloak and tossed it onto a nearby chair. The windowless room was small with water stained bare concrete walls. The couch, an arm chair and a steel door set into a cinder-block wall were the only features in the dusty basement, apart from the steps leading back up.

The de-cloaked man turned around and settled himself into the arm chair so Camden was finally able to set eyes on him. He was young and beautiful. His suit was black and business-like, and his hair was long and pulled back in a pony tail. He smiled, showing his fangs. Camden saw the sharp teeth and immediately placed his hand on his neck. When he pulled his hand away, he found sticky half dried blood clinging to his fingers. He ran his tongue across his top teeth and felt the distinct protrusions of his own sharp canines.

"What did you do to me?" he finally demanded.

"My boy, I've given you eternal youth," the man spoke with air as if older than his looks implied.

"You're a, um, a..."

"Vampire!" he said lowly with a devilish smile. "Yes, boy. And now, so are you."

"No, no that's not possible. Vampires don't exist."

"We do, and I should say, you can feel the proof of that yourself."

"I don't believe this. I'm having a dream."

"No child, this is real. You may feel a little overwhelmed, but you should consider yourself lucky to be alive. You happened upon me during a feeding and caught me with my guard down."

The memory surfaced on Camden's face, "you were drinking that guy's blood." He froze, tasting his mouth, "you made me drink it too."

"Yes," the vampire exhaled. "I was nearly full when you showed up. What you saw, I simply could not have allowed you to leave remembering. I decided to save you by giving you the gift. It's quite easy, once a vampire bites down and has only taken a small amount of blood from their donor a venom is released into that body. If not immediately sucked back up with more blood, the venom will cause the donor to turn. Fangs grow amazingly quickly in those few seconds, and once the donor tastes human blood the transformation is complete. You will be my servant now, doing as I wish and living here with me."

"No, I need to go home," Camden said, making a move to stand up.

"Do not get up!" the vampire commanded with a firm frightening tone in his voice and Camden felt his legs tighten. He fell back into the couch. "I have the power to command you. You may not leave here until I command otherwise. Your human life is over and you will be considered a missing person. I may, if you show your respect and gratitude, allow you to return to your home tonight to collect a bag of valued possessions."

"But I don't understand. Why did you go this too me?"

"You were unfortunately in the wrong place at the wrong time. Had I been hungrier, you would not have survived. But ultimately you made the choice. You accepted the blood from that donor, and the gift of immortality it sealed. Do you not feel the power coursing through your body?"

"All I feel is adrenaline and fear, and..." he stopped and smiled looking at his arms as he opened and closed his fists. "No, actually I feel like I've just had a good work out followed by the most amazing sex."

"And?"

"And I feel good, better than I've ever felt. Oh," Camden moaned, "this is incredible." He breathed deeply.

"Let me take you to our resting chamber and show you how you now look," the vampire rose gracefully and went to the steel door. Effortlessly he pulled the thick door open and led Camden into another room. Sitting raised above the floor were two sleek black coffins, one of which was open. Each had drawers in the platforms they rested on.

The vampire pulled Camden's hoodie off then lifted his t-shirt over his head. He gestured toward a full length mirror leaning against the far wall.

Camden stood in front of the mirror and examined with delight his increased muscle size, the sudden lack of any body fat and the overall firmness in his physique. He leaned in and playing his tongue against his very real fangs.

"So we have reflections?" Camden said, not look away from the mirror.

"Oh yes, almost everything is a myth. Stakes, garlic, mirrors, crosses, sleeping in native soil. Almost all the myths are just that, except," he paused and allowed his face to grow dark and serious, "not the sun, its' rays will harm you."

"Anything else?"

The vampire eyed him with suspicion and held back his answer, choosing to continue his other thought. "It actually takes several hours of full noonday sunlight to burn us completely. I've escaped many fires but one could prove deadly when tramped."

Camden pondered the warning and rolled around one thought he kept to himself. "So if I'm carefully, I can live for a long time?"

"Eternity, my boy, you are now immortal," the vampire whispered seductively. "I have not survived over three hundred years without being vigilant."

"Wow. You're so beautiful for an old man."

The vampire seemed amused by the acknowledgement of his beauty, casually glancing at his own image reflected in the mirror. He turned and placed a hand on the closed coffin.

"This will be yours. We shall obtain new clothes for you, which you can put underneath. For now, I shall show you the rest of the house after which we shall collect your things."

Camden followed the vampire to the main floor and through the various rooms, most of which were empty. The living room held a few modern pieces of furniture, the dining room only a table and chairs, and in the library with its' shelves bare, a desk with a tidy pile of papers. In the kitchen, Camden was shown the wine fridge with individually cooled sections for the reds and whites.

"The blood sustains us. Most food holds little taste, but wine, good wine at least, can still be enjoyed," the vampire said with a pleasant smile.

The second floor was completely empty, except for the bathroom which appeared to be used often. They returned to the basement and the vampire gathered his cloak. Camden pulled his hoodie back on, and zipped it only slightly to leave his bare chest exposed.

"Let us retrieve a few of your things, and I will show you how to fly."

"Um, what do I call you?" Camden finally asked.

A smiled spread across the vampire's face, "while addressing me Master would be proper, I shall allow you to address me as Lawrence."

"I'm Camden." Lawrence nodded, though he didn't seem to need the name. "Come, my boy."

Out in the yard, he slowly began to float up into the dark sky leaving Camden standing on the ground with no instructions. He closed his eyes and imagined himself lifting off from the ground. When he opened his eyes he had indeed begun to float higher and higher above the lawn. Lawrence was flying around house in large circle, waiting for him.

They flew quickly to the cluster of apartment towers in Camden's neighborhood. Lawrence flew close to Camden and had him point out the exact apartment from blocks away. They were able to race toward it unnoticed and land silently on his balcony, twenty stories up. Camden slid the glass door open and reentered his human life.

"Don't take much that might be missed by family," Lawrence whispered.

Silently Camden swept around the one-bedroom apartment and gathered a suitcase full of treasures and some clothes.

Packed, he glanced around one last time at his apartment before launching himself into the night sky following Lawrence. As he flew, Camden watched the city roll by and memorized how the journey would look on the ground. Back in the basement, Lawrence allowed him time to organize his possessions under his coffin while they sipped away on a bottle of red wine. Indeed Lawrence had been right, the wine exploded in his mouth in an eruption of delicate flavors unlike anything he had ever tasted before. Lawrence kept to himself and mostly ignored Camden.

Just before dawn, Lawrence climbed into his coffin without a word and shut the lid with a firm thud. Camden opened the lid to his own tomb and climbed in, feeling the interior lining and stretching about to get used to the space. It was roomier than he had imagined, and comfortable despite having to lay on his back.

He felt the moment when the sun rose, and his strength was drained out of him. Although he felt tired, when Camden closed the lid and tried to sleep, it did not come. He rolled onto his front trying to match his normal sleeping position, but sleep still did not take him.

Feeling sexually aroused and missing the touch of another person, Camden climbed out of his coffin and went to Lawrence's, got in and began to undo the vampire's pants. He pushed the pants and underwear down then swallowed Lawrence's member full and proceed to pump the cock with his mouth.

Lawrence woke and regarded Camden with disgust before lifting the young vampire's head. "What are you doing?"

"Giving you pleasure, master," he said, playing up the submissive role he found himself in.

"Servant, are you perchance a homosexual?"

Camden looked at Lawrence in the dark coffin and mused over the clinical old world term. "I'm gay, yes."

"And what gave you the impression that I am also?"

Camden shrugged, "I thought vampires were overly sexual and well, you're so hot. I was certain you were at least bi."

"You were wrong. I sleep in this coffin alone and when I do take a lover it is a female. Return to your own coffin."

Lifting the lid and holding it while he stepped out, Camden avoided the vampire's eyes. "Sorry."

"You are not the first to make the mistake, but I would prefer this be the only time you make such a lapse of judgement. Good night."

Lawrence went to pull the lid close but Camden held it open. "But if I can't be with you, master," he said shyly in a respectful tone, "may I turn my boyfriend?"

"No you may not! I do not make it a habit out of turning humans often. Maybe you do not fully appreciate how fortunate you are to have received the gift instead of death. Good Night," he finished while closing the lid.

Camden returned to his own coffin but lay awake sulking with the lid raised. If there was one trait most annoying about Camden it was his stubbornness and with it, his obsessive need to fight back. He wanted his boyfriend beside him, to share with him the gift. Camden decided to rid himself of his homophobic master, but he couldn't risk the sunlight himself and didn't have a way to hold Lawrence out in it long enough.

Silently he lowered himself to the floor and found a treasure in one of the drawers. He held the long length of flat steel cable, a memento from an engineering job the previous summer. Camden tried to steady his breathing as he placed himself at the head of Lawrence's coffin.

Once ready he flipped open the lid, pulled Lawrence's shoulders until his body slid up, then expertly he wrapped the cable around the vampire's neck, giving both ends a sudden and forceful tug in opposing directions just as Lawrence opened his eyes and attempted to reach back at Camden.

As Camden had planned, the cable sliced through the vampire's neck although it appeared to have stopped at the spine. Lawrence struggled more, flailing his arms trying to make purchase, the blood gushing from his neck, but Camden was far enough beyond the vampire's reach. He wiggled the cable, sliding it up against the bone and pulled tight again. Finally the head flew off and landed with a thump on the floor. Camden looked at it with surprise. His plan had actually worked.

Camden allowed his breathing to steady, and his adrenaline to calm, before searching for the next task.

Wearing Lawrence's cloak to cover his entire body, he brought the vampire's remains out to the backyard and with a single match from a fancy hotel bar matchbox found in the kitchen, set the corpse ablaze.

Safely back at his coffin, Camden found his cellphone and dialed Aaron's number.

"Hey sweety," the groggy voice said on the other end.

"Hey babe, how was work?"

"Long and boring. Aren't you at work?"

"No, something came up. Have you gone to bed yet?"

"Not yet."

"Can you come see me, I'm not at home but it's really important you come by?"

"What is it?"

"Something major went down last night and I, well I need to show you. Please?"

"Can't it wait until tonight, or can't you come here?"

Camden took a deep breath and turned on his sultry seductive voice, the one that worked on Aaron. "I can't imagine waiting until sunset to be with you."

"Okay, give me the address."

Camden finished the call by giving the directions to the house, then made another call to a florist for a rush delivery bouquet. He felt relieved when the flowers arrived before Aaron, and ushered the delivery boy into the dark house to pay him.

Minutes later Aaron arrived with two coffees in hand. He followed his boyfriend's instructions and went directly to the basement to find Camden lounging on the couch.

"Hey babe, I'm so happy to see you," looking up from the couch.

"Sweetie how can you, it's so dark down here?"

"Oh I forgot, my eyes have adjusted to the dark," he said, lighting some candles he'd found in the sleeping chamber. "Here, come sit with me."

"What's with all the mysterious behavior?"

"You'll see," Camden said slyly. He lifted the bouquet from behind the couch and presented them to Aaron.

"Oww, my favorite," he said, putting them down on the empty chair and settled on the couch to kiss Camden.

"I missed you so much, and well I kind of had a very strange night."

"Oh, how strange?"

Camden took a deep breath and began, "it started when I was walking home through the park. I found some guy attacking a runner and before I knew it, he attacked me and dragged me back here. I eventually fought him off, but see he was different."

"Different how? He didn't rape you or something?"

"No, he was straight and didn't touch me sexually."

"But he touched you another way? Did he hurt you? You don't look hurt, actually you look good." Aaron pushed Camden's hoodie open and ran his hand over the firm chest.

"Yeah here's the thing," he paused and looked into Aaron's eyes. Before he could comment further "I love you, you know that right?"

"I know it, and I love you too."

"Well the guy was a vampire and was feeding from the runner in the park. I surprised him so he bit me too, but instead of killing me, he turned me into a vampire."

"Cam, seriously, don't joke around!"

"I'm not joking," he said then slowly opened his mouth to show his fangs grow longer.

"Shit, oh shit," Aaron looked shocked for a moment, then smiled, "you are playing a joke on me."

"No Aaron, this is real."

He became nervous.

"When he wouldn't let me bring you here, I killed him. I didn't plan on being eternally young without you."

"What are you saying?"

"I want you to become a vampire. Be with me forever."

"No, you're scaring me, I can't do this," Aaron began to get up but Camden held him on the couch.

"Babe, I want to give you the choice he didn't give me. You have to trust me, I was freaked out at first but then I realized how good it feels. And look," he pushed his hoodie open all the way to reveal is muscular chest and sculpted six-pack, "see how good I look."

Aaron smiled and ran his hand along Camden's smooth chest, but shook his head, "I can't."

"Do you love me?"

"Yes, but..."

"No buts, as long as you love me then it's all good."

Camden leaned forward and kissed his boyfriend.

"I love you, Aaron."

Before Aaron could see Camden move, he'd bit into his neck and sucked up a small amount of blood. He pulled his sharp teeth out when he felt the serum inject into Aaron's blood stream. Sweeping Aaron up into his arms, Camden carried him to the sleeping chamber and stood him in front of Lawrence's coffin. He lifted the lid to reveal the delivery boy tied up inside. His neck had two punctures and blood was beginning to dry around the wounds.

Camden pushed Aaron's face toward the blood and whispered, "drink."

"No!" Aaron tried to yell, but the smell of the blood was hitting his nose and his gums began to ache. "I won't be a monster!" he hissed through his fangs.

"It's too late, feed or you will die." Camden pushed Aaron's mouth closer but he resisted.

"No, please no."

"Aaron, accept the gift, you're already a vampire, finish it. Feed!" He said with anger and worry. He began to sob, "I won't live an eternity without you."

"NO!" Aaron yelled again.

Camden pressed his hand to the dripping wound then slid his fingers across Aaron's lips. He did it a second time, only this time Aaron's tongue darted out and licked up the blood.

"You can feel me coursing through your veins. The desire for immortality, and to be with me. Take it."

Aaron was already lost to the bloodlust. His face slammed into the exposed neck and his fangs cut deep. He sucked the delivery boy's blood until it ran dry.

"Come, lie with me." Camden placed Aaron in his coffin and climbed in on top of him where they instantly fell asleep wrapped in each other's arms.

Both boys felt the moment the sun disappeared below the horizon. They kissed and silently explored each other's improved bodies. Camden pushed the lid open and took Aaron's hardened cock in his mouth, sucking deep.

He released the cock from his mouth then ran his tongue down the whole length, finally reaching the balls. Camden sucked on each ball before taking the whole length into his mouth again. Aaron moaned.

His eyes focused on his lover, he moaned, "fuck me."

Camden broke the kiss. Lifting Aaron's legs, he impaled his hard cock inside his boyfriend. He leaned close to Aaron's neck, kissing it gently before his pointed teeth broke the skin and released a dribble of blood. His hard thrusting in and out of Aaron increased as both guys discovered the extent of their increased senses. Camden placed his wrist at Aaron's mouth, who quickly bit his fangs into flesh and lapped at the blood seeping from the twin holes.

Aaron was experiencing levels of ecstasy he'd never thought possible. Camden's thrusts were sending waves of pleasure through his entire body and he felt close. For several minutes he felt ready to release, but found he was able to hold the pleasure at the very moment when an orgasm would ripple through his body. Their bodies shook in sync as if they were cumming over and over again. Aaron drank from the wrist and continued to hold Camden's face to his neck while he constricted the muscles in his ass tightly around the thrusting cock causing Camden to moan loudly. Aaron's own cock oozed pre-cum as it bounced off his drum tight belly. Camden's body stiffened as he pushed one last time into his boyfriend's hole and his cock exploded. Aaron's body shuddered when he felt the hot cum inside him. Releasing the bloodied wrist he let out a deep whimper as his cock shot a stream of white cream across his belly and chest.

Camden continued licked at the rivulets of blood dripping from Aaron's neck while their heavy breathing slowed to normal. Both were glistening, their bodies wet from the activity more vigorous then ever before.

Finally Camden slid his tongue one last time across Aaron's neck then raised himself up and stared into his lover's eyes. "So babe, how do you feel?"

"Incredible. Shit, this is amazing, I feel like I'm high, and not just from the sex. I feel so alive and then the sex, that was incredible."

"Told you."

"Fuck, I'm so sorry I resisted. Cam, I love you."

"I love you too."

They continued to lay in the open coffin wrapped in each other's arms, sweaty from the sex and enjoying the moment.

"Cam," Aaron finally said, revealing his fangs, "I'm hungry."

"Me too," he replied, seductively showing his own elongated canines.

A happy accident

BY OLIVER SLOANE

He was going to dump me. I stared into his eyes, hoping he'd at least not freak out when I told him what I'd done. Getting him to forgive me, that was something else.

Daniel and I had an agreement, when either of us was out of town, we were allowed to play around. As long as we keep the affairs out of town, we wouldn't argue. Of course since Daniel is a flight attendant, he's almost always out of town. Convenient for him really. I'm also not the most horny of guys. Not every guy wants sex several times a day. Or week. Or month for that matter.

When Daniel is in town long enough for us to spend time together on a normal schedule, we do have sex, but really we're lucky if we average once a week. At the opposite end of the scale, Daniel is sex mad. Our little agreement would have to include home base if he wasn't out of town so much; he needs to regularly get off.

I think any other couple would have given up once it was obvious they were incompatible. But we've stayed together because we honestly love each other. This is why I tell Daniel everything. He knows everything about me, including my fetishes and fantasies.

He took a sip of his wine and leaned into the couch, sitting sideways to face me. A wicked smile crept across his face.

"So I can tell you have something to say."

"Yeah. I want to tell you what I did for Halloween."

Again he smiled, settling himself in further, preparing to hear my story. That's how he is, willing and content to listen.

"Well I finally got a chance to go to that private after hours club near the village, Underground Vault. I spent the evening with the boys from work at the pub, but they went off to the big party. The weather was still nice so I decided to walk home and happened to take a route passed U.V."

Daniel chuckled. He knew where Underground Vault was, and it wasn't 'on the way home.'

"Okay, you're right, I went out of my way. I was curious. I'd heard the rumors and it was Halloween so I had to indulge my fantasy."

"And how were you dressed?"

"Just one of my plain old t-shirts and jeans." With my lean toned physique, I tend to wear just tight t-shirts and jeans. I'm not very muscular, but I've managed to keep myself pretty thin.

"So I wandered down the alley passed U.V. and found myself standing outside. I didn't figure I'd get in, from what'd I've heard you have to be pretty damn hot to get through the door. But the doorman saw me staring and told me to 'either stop hanging around and come in or get the hell out of there'. It seemed like the perfect chance to see the place so I went in. Oh Daniel, it was fantastic; exactly what I'd hoped for."

"Really," the wicked grin was back and his dimples were showing.

"There weren't a lot of guys in there; it was still early, before midnight at least. But the few guys in there were hot. The staff were all shirtless with tight black leather pants and these leather harnesses with hoods. And for effect they were all wearing fangs and had red contacts in. Very hot, let me tell you. I started talking to the bartender while ordering my drink. He was friendly but didn't seem too chatty, at least not with me. But I had to engage him, he was so perfect."

"I went up to him and when he asked 'what'll you have?' I replied 'A bite from you'. He just smiled, baring his fangs but said 'you're not my blood-type princess'.

"Oh, I'm sorry," Daniel said to comfort me. "So, the rumors about the place?"

"Not true. Maybe they'd heard the rumors and I thought they must have taken the chance to get dressed up for Halloween in the spirit. When the bartender bared his fangs, I noticed they were fake. I mean, they're like the theatrical ones I buy and if you mold them correctly, it's very hard to tell they're fake, but I could see the molding plastic overlapping his teeth. Still he made a beautiful vampire; they all did. My perfect fantasy."

"Exactly. Your deepest fantasy," Daniel reached his hand out and gave my shoulder a squeeze. Over the years he'd indulged me, putting on a pair of fangs I'd bought for him and fucking me, playfully biting the whole while.

"They seemed to be the only people in the club who'd gotten dressed for the occasion. I thought I might as well have a seat near the end of the bar and enjoy the view. Most of the room has these built in couches set up in alcoves for groups to gather in. I sat through two drinks, watching the staff mostly. The place started to fill up but didn't get too packed. Mostly the customers were muscle marys, a few I knew played on several of the gay sports teams. Eventually a few guys came in dressed up, a three-some who came as two vampires all dressed from the eighteenth century, and their victim, shirtless with blood pouring from his shoulder and looking seriously pale. I remember a few sailors, two shirtless guys wearing a matching angel wings, shorts and knee high boots, except one was all in black and the other in white."

"Standard stuff for a gay bar, at least for Halloween."

"Yeah I know. This wasn't the creative costume crowd. Like I said, most people weren't dressed up. Anyway, so I just had my third drink delivered by the waiter, who was a little more friendly than the bartender when I chatted him up."

"What'd you say to him?"

"Ah, when he brought me the drink I had been racking my brain for another good vampire line, but this one was hotter than the bartender. Very twinky with pale skin and light blond hair, so his face stood out really well under the hood. His red eyes seemed to shine, and he'd done a much better job with his fangs; they fit perfectly. Actually they were the more expensive dental caps. He had at least put in some effort. So I was nervous and I blurted out 'you're a very hot vampire and if you want, I would let you bite every inch of me'. He smiled showing off his fangs without baring them in a hiss like the bartender. Then he slipped me a card and said he'd do just that, but it would be an extra charge."

"He didn't?"

"He did, yeah. Pretty much advertised he was for hire," I shrugged my shoulders and looked into Daniel's eyes. "But again, he wasn't real."

Daniel nodded in understanding. I smiled back at him and closed my eyes, remembering how the rest of the night had unfolded.

"When he'd left I noticed that someone had taken a seat not far from me. Cute guy; pretty plain like me. It didn't seem like he tried hard to present his best features, hiding behind messy hair and glasses. He was wearing a baggy sweater so I couldn't tell what he looked like underneath but he didn't really carry himself as someone with something to brag about. But he looked over at me and started up a conversation. 'He's pretty cute?' he said to me. 'Hell ya, just my type, but probably out of my price range.' I showed him the card.

'No kidding. He offered his services right here.'

'Pretty much. But that outfit is extra.'

'Really? That's nothing special.'

'Sorry, what do you mean.' I asked him.

'Oh, that's what they wear every night. Fangs and all. I guess you haven't been here before.'

'No. I didn't think I'd ever get in.'

'Naw, they aren't that strict really. That's just a rumor. I mean look at me, they let me in all the time. Name's Chris.' He told me, extending his hand. He had a strong grip, but a gentle touch and soft skin.

'Mike,' I replied

'What did you say to him to get his card?'

'Oh I told him he could bite every inch of me if he wanted.'

'No kidding. I guess he gets that all the time. They must get various lines like with the outfits they wear.'

'I told the bartender he could take a bite too, but he said I wasn't his blood-type. I figured it was special for Halloween, playing up the rumor that this place is full of vampires.'

'Well that's not actually a rumor since they do it every night. I'm just not sure why, this isn't a goth or fetish club. They're not dressed properly for either of those, more like a mix of both. And comments like that bartender made are a little cheesy. I mean vampires are not that particular about blood types. Blood is blood.'

'I'll let him know.'

'So are you here alone?'

'I was out with friends earlier but they went to the party at Boys' Den.

'Yeah, I was thinking of checking that party out. What were you looking to do?'

'I just dropped in here on my way home. It being Halloween and from what I had heard of this club I figured I might find something interesting.'

'Or someone?'

'Or maybe someone, sure.'

'And as you said, it being Halloween, it's a good night for something different.'

'True.'

'I don't have plastic fangs but I'm sure I can still bite you all over no matter your blood type.'

I looked him over and figured I didn't have a chance with any of the bar staff and their fake fangs. 'Okay, your place or my?'

'I live two blocks away. You any closer?'

'No. Your place it is.'

We left and walked the short distance to his place. I don't think we said a single word along the way. He lived in a converted loft, but I don't remember seeing much more than the couch where we sat down when we came in. We started making out pretty much right away, until he broke away from our kissing.

Chris whispered in my ear, 'I'm so sorry Mike. I just can't wait, I'm too hungry'.

And that's when it happened. He bit me. I had no warning, just the sudden shock that someone had bitten into my neck. And it's an odd feeling when it happens for real. It wasn't like the times you've playfully nipped at my neck. When Chris pushed his fangs into my neck it was like this great pressure against the skin and muscles. And I could tell they were fangs by the odd twin pressure. It wasn't at all like having a needle inserted into your skin. The fangs might be sharp, but they're much bigger than a needle.

When his teeth broke the skin, he pressed his lips against my neck and sucked, but it was pretty quiet. I was too surprised to push him away at first, but when I did try to push him, I found he had me pinned.

"The event impacted me most when he pulled away and kissed my lips. I tasted my blood on his lips, but then he pulled back and looked at me. His face showed a look of satisfaction and sympathy. I hardly noticed his fangs, dripping with my blood. They could have been fake like the club's staff, covered in blood to hide the imperfections. The fakeness. It was the sadness on his face that I was focused on. His eyes were watering.

'I'm really sorry,' he said. 'I lost control. I know that's no excuse, but that's it. I haven't fed in a few days and the smell of your blood was all I could think off. I should have asked you, let you choose before I violated you.'

He laid his face against my chest and began to cry. I didn't know what to think. My first real vampire and he was not only sorry for attacking me, he was crying. I felt like he'd had a pre-mature ejaculation and he was making excuses.

I tried to comfort him. 'I was asking for it. You did what I have always wanted. It was very sudden and I think I'd built it up as this great sexual experience, when really that was... shit I don't know, I'm shocked really. And excited now that I think about it. I think if you had warned me I'd have been in fear of the anticipation.'

He sobbed into my chest and continued, 'It's a bit like donating blood. You're going to be weak for a while, but you'll be fine. There won't be any side effects. You won't change into a vampire just because I bit you.'

'I won't? How would that happen?'

He raised his head and made eye contact. 'I know you want that. It's pretty simple, I need to feed you now. A vampire doesn't need to feed from someone first, the blood will turn them on its' own. But you've been weakened and that helps. My blood if like a virus. The cells will attack every cell in your body and convert them. You won't die, you will change. It's not painful, just tiring. Are you sure you want this?'

'Immortality?'

'Yes.'

'Will I have to give up daylight?'

'No, that's one of those silly myths. But Mike, I need you to know, I already have a boyfriend so don't think this means we're together.'

'Well that's for the better, I'm also seeing someone.'

I stopped replaying the story and looked into Daniel's eyes, letting him know he was that someone.

"So, what happened next? I'm loving your little tale."

"Tale? Daniel do you think I'm making this up?"

"Well yeah, I know how you like your vampire fantasy and all."

"Daniel, does this look like a fantasy?" I said before I seductively smiled at him and allowed my fangs to grow.

He dropped his wine glass in surprise, "shit. You're a vampire," he shouted as the wine glass crashed to the floor.

Before either of us could deal with the broken glass or the small amount of spilled wine, I launched myself on top of him, pressed my body against his and planted my lips against his. I could feel his tongue dart into my mouth and explore my fangs. "The change happened pretty quick. I came home and woke of the next night completely transformed. I couldn't wait to tell you," I finally said when I pulled my lips away from his. I stared into his eyes. "Daniel, I love you."

"I love you too," he smiled up at me and struggled with what to say next. "What do you want, or I mean, er, Mike this is scaring me a bit."

"Oh baby, I don't want to scare you, but I have to give you a choice. Will you join me for eternity?" I paused and looked deep into his eyes. "We can be together forever, never growing old, and our out of town arrangement doesn't have to change."

"Really, you don't mind me continuing to hook up with other people?"

"No, it's something you have to do."

"And if I say no?"

"It's best if I tell you after you say yes," I replied with a pout.

"Because?"

"Daniel, I need you to trust me. I could say 'you would do it if you loved me', but this is a choice you need to live with forever."

"You're not telling me something, are you?"

"No Daniel, I'm trying to protect you," I couldn't stop the tears from coming to my eyes. "Once I've fed from you, you'll need to decide." Before he could say anything I sunk my fangs into his neck and began drinking his blood.

After several minutes a pulled away and gave him a kiss, his blood now coating both our lips.

Daniel focused his eyes on mine. "Yes," was all he said.

I smiled then kissed him again. I bit into my wrist and offered the wound to him so he could drink from me just as I had fed off of Chris. When it was done, I carried Daniel into the bedroom and we both fell into a long sleep.

The next night, when Daniel woke he rolled over to face me and smiled. His fangs had grown in.

"Hungry," I asked him.

"Unbelievably!"

"Me too. Maybe we should go pick someone up. When was the last time we had a threesome?"

"Ages. Is this how's it going to work, we're going to feed together?"

"Well not when you're out of town. We can feed alone then."

"Hmm, sounds like you'll be breaking our rule?"

"I could always go somewhere else when you've flown off somewhere, well and just because I'll be feeding off some guy doesn't mean I'll also be sleeping with him."

"I know, it's okay, I know you'll always be here when I get back. And if you hadn't bent our rule you wouldn't have met Chris and finally fulfilled your fantasy."

"And neither of us would be vampires."

"That would have sucked. I can't believe how good I feel right now."

"Yeah, isn't it great. Just wait until you feed."

Daniel smiled and briefly closed his eyes before asking again, "so what couldn't you tell me last night about saying no to this."

"Chris explained to me, when a human discovers us they can't be allowed to remember us. If you had said no, just as if I hadn't wanted Chris to turn me, I would have had to drain you. The other option is to brainwash the human before biting them so they don't know it's happening; it's sort of hard to do that after."

"Then I'm glad I said yes," and again Daniel smiled and flashed his fangs. I smiled to reveal my fangs in return before we kissed.

Secrets

BY MATT CAMDEN

I realized today that I've been with Kyle for six months now and it's beginning to get serious. Also I can't stop staring at him as he re-stacks one of the shelves, especially when he squats down to fill a low shelf and his tight jeans pull over his beautiful ass. Or when he reaches for the higher shelves and his shirt lifts and I see the small of his back and the gentle curve downward to the slightly exposed crevasse.

When his work schedule overlaps mine, I'm completely unfocused. It's my own fault though. The day he entered my used book shop clutching his resume I was ready to hire him. And as it is my shop, I'm here a lot, although I shouldn't be, after all I have enough employees to run the place. The shop makes good money, even when I'm not involved. It probably does better when I'm not around. Nearly all my employees are competent enough, though I favor Kyle the most.

So this morning, I arrived at work and found him carrying a bouquet of flowers. I looked at them and became immediately jealous, ready to hunt down the bastard who was making moves on my boyfriend. But then he handed them to me with a kiss and wished me a happy six month anniversary.

Whoops.

It wasn't that I had forgotten. I'm a little older, well a lot older, and six months didn't seem like a milestone. Now I have to get him something. I can't decide the right gift though, and I suspect it's because I care enough to get the perfect present. I'll take him for a fine meal and make love to him tonight, and yet these are commonplace events for us. No, I need to show how I genuinely feel. Even if I couldn't bring myself to give him the one gift I most truly wanted to give.

Kyle has turned around and said something to me, it was registered, but I was still deep in thought. "Top floor, back wall, third shelf to the left of the exit," I said, answering his query. He smiled, and turned to retrieve the book meant to fill the new prominent display of queer writers. "Wait," I stopped him before he left. "I need to run an errand. I'll be out for a few hours."

"Okay," he smiled again, inching toward the till I stood behind. "Do you need me to watch the floor?"

"No, what you're doing is more important." It was, and it was also his idea. He'd come to me, wait, no it was a postcoital discussion, and suggested gathering all the works be queer writers in on section for pride. I easily acquiesced to his suggestion. "Send Malcolm down from the second floor. He'll cover the till."

He nodded and turned to leave, "wait! I did not dismiss you, come here." He came to the desk and leaned over, knowing all to well my intensions. I looked deep into his eyes and gave him a kiss. "Okay, my angel, I'll see you later."

He turned again and climbed the stairs heading for the third floor and his conquest. Even if I thought I was dispensable, that my employees could run the store easily without me, I knew where every single book was kept. I can be away from the shop for months, or years and upon returning, I just need to walk through the stacks over the four floors and scan the spines to memorize the location of any tome.

Legs appear on the stairs, then a torso and finally Malcolm descends at the speed of a glacier. He tries my patience, and I'm a very patient man.

Finally he steps behind the counter and sits on the spare stool. I bite most of my words and depart with a terse statement.

Out on the pavement, I begin the search for that perfect gift. Over six months I have become more than a tad fond of my little angel. He has become my world, and I want to share my world, my life, with him for as long as I manage to walk the earth. But there is too much to explain before he will know me fully, and I him. I know he has a troubled past, which we do not discuss. I have shared few of my own secrets, and he is keeping a few himself.

Now on with the gift. Kyle loves three things, food & cooking, books and sex. I only allow him to work four days a week in the store so that he has time to spend perfecting his artistry in the kitchen. I over pay him severely so that he can work less and afford ingredients. Soon after I began working for me, I found him the most adorable flat with a professional kitchen in a building not far from my own home. The landlord was charging a surprisingly low amount because I own the building and gave instruction for it to be rented to him cheap. Of course without him knowing.

He thanked me for finding him the home by cooking me an incredible meal. My oversensitive taste buds exploded over the flavors in his concoctions. We unfortunately missed dessert when I became a bit over excited and had a night of wild sex with him. That marked the night we began dating, apparently according to him.

Since the kitchen is well fitted out, there's no need for an unromantic stove or mixer. He has most of the tools he needs, but I worry sex tonight will be a little restrained or won't happen at all if I give him a spatula or rolling pin. Not unless we take it to the bedroom.

I want to give him a ring or another piece of jewelry, but it feels too soon. Yet I can imagine someday giving him one ring to bind our love, but I'm a patient man and I can wait. I do find it amazing how young he makes me feel, not that I'm physically that old, and at the same time his energy and youthful impatience at times makes me want to rush our future.

A leather shop has opened on this high street, the thick aroma of the skins pours out into the street. I have a few pieces I've worn over the years, and I can just imagine how beautiful Kyle would look in leather, especially with his tight ass and firm physique. It's hard to tell, given how my body responds to him all the time, but just the thought of Kyle sheathed in leather has made me even harder. Ah, but as I now find myself standing in the store, I wonder if he'd appreciate such a gift and really, I'd need to bring him here for a proper fitting.

The shop keep has looked up from a magazine he's been flipping through on the counter. He's young, maybe a little older than Kyle's 23 years, muscular with a shaved head, and tattoos covering his upper body, which is bare. Tight leather pants cling to his legs.

He smiles, and I am hungry.

"Hello, I'm looking for something for my boyfriend," I say, demanding his service immediately.

"Of course," his smile has fallen a bit. "Anything in particular?"

"No, nothing comes to mind. It's our anniversary and while it's still too early for some things, I thought some leather might appeal to him. I guess pants and a shirt or harness would get him started."

"Well we have plenty of styles to choose from," he came out from behind his counter and ushered me over to several racks of pants. As I came to stand next to him, his scent hit my nostrils. Intoxicating.

I caught his eyes and locked onto them. The store was otherwise empty and my scan of the place had found only a security camera at the front door. I pulled his body against mine then quickly bit into his throbbing neck, sucking back a small amount of his blood. It was sweet, pure and laced with caffeine. I pulled my fangs from his neck and dragged my tongue across his tattooed skin, watching the wounds quickly begin to heal.

He had become catatonic as all my prey become, until I will them out of their trance. After planting the suggestion he looked at me and blinked several times, disoriented as was normal, and smiled weakly.

"Sorry, what was it I was saying?" he asked, genuinely confused.

"Oh, you were just pointing out that it would be best for me to bring my boyfriend here for a fitting."

"Yes, right."

"Thank you for your time," I smiled and left the shop. Normally I wouldn't risk returning after feeding, but I really did want to see Kyle in leather someday. Such a gift was possible, yet I planned to have something else in case he balked at coming into the shop later.

I had not been throwing my money around too much and Kyle probably assumed I was comfortable, rather than extremely comfortable. Over the years my investments have netted me a considerable portfolio, mostly through wise real estate purchases, and not just the building Kyle lived in. I wanted very much to buy Kyle the world, or at the very least a new car, which he had no need for. But I had resolved not to shower him, least his love be tainted by wealth.

Finally I came to stand in front of a jeweler. It seemed fitting, the gift I wanted to give the most was the one with no material value. But it was still too early to share my immortal secret and I certainly had no intention of turning him without his express wishes. He would become my partner for eternity by his own choice. For now though, a ring would have to express my love.

I entered the store and sought out the rings. It would need to be simple. Possibly with an inscription if I could be appropriately poetic quickly enough. The gentleman behind the counter was attractive and carried a wonderful scent, but my hunger had been sated.

"I am in need of a ring for a young man."

"What type of occasion would this be to celebrate?" he asked, even though I hadn't hinted at a celebration.

"Six month anniversary. I do not wish something too flashy or suggestive."

"Of course sir," he slid toward one case and pulled out a tray of bands. "These would be most appropriate. Silvers and stainless steels, oh and a few made of titanium."

I raked my eyes across the tray and immediately spotted a wide thick band made of silver and unadorned by jewels or motifs.

"That one," I pointed.

"Wonderful choice, sir."

"And I would like an inscription. Unfortunately I am short on time."

"Not a problem at all, sir. I can do that immediately."

"Right, please inscribe, 'I wish to measure our love in years'."

"How nice," he smiled. "I shall just ring up your purchase and if you'd prefer, it will take a few minutes, you can wait here or return in an hour."

"Fine, I think I won't rush you by hovering around here."

I paid in cash and returned to the jeweler over an hour later to retrieve the ring.

I find myself hanging around the shop far too late these days. It's Kyle's fault, I am required to wait for him to finish his shift. Or is it my fault for not booking him for a shorter work day. I really must do a better job at setting his hours based on my needs. Surprisingly he doesn't take advantage of his position with the boss, begging off work early or coming in late on mornings when I know his head must be hurting.

"Are you ready to go?" I finally ask him the second the clock ticks over to five. I'm comforting the flowers against my chest, the ring tucked inside my jacket.

"Yes, but stop hurrying me, dinner can wait," he teased back, moving slowly to retrieve his bag from behind the counter.

"Well I wish to stop on the way to the restaurant and pick up something."

"Oh baby, I wanted to surprise you with a nice meal at home."

"You're certainly full of surprises today. But it's a special day, would you not prefer to enjoy a meal cooked for you for once?"

He put on his pout, the sexy one I couldn't resist, "well that's the thing, it is special and I have a special meal planned just for you."

"Alright, I just want to spend the night with you."

His smile was wide. He'd won, but I hadn't fought him.

"Just one stop, if you are game?" I asked suggestively.

"What do you have in mind?"

"I passed by a new shop today and it made me think what a wonderful treat it would be to buy you a new outfit. However, I don't know how you'd feel about leather?"

"Really! You want to try leather?"

"Well angel," I placed my hand on his ass and pulled him to me. "I already have, it's you I want to see."

"I'd love something, I've just never been able to afford it. That's so sweet of you, such a wonderful gift."

"Pretty angel, that's my gift to me, yours will come later."

He blushed, "okay, quickly then."

I took Kyle's hand and strolled slowly down the pavement, fighting a raging tide of workers rushing to make their trains or the Tube home. The same young man was in the leather shop when we entered. Again it was empty, and he seemed pleased to see me.

"You have returned, with the boyfriend."

"Yes, now lets find him the right outfit. Trousers, harness, shirt, boots, and underwear, and the same for me."

A huge smile broke across the clerk's face. I knew he was happy to make the sale that would make his day. Within minutes, Kyle was trying on several trousers to find the right fit. The clerk cupped Kyle's ass and balls several times, probably his usual seductive sales routine, except I was standing watching and not appreciating the groping. I would have to pay him another visit and show him who is truly master.

Kyle chose a tight pair of leather jeans with riding seat that helped lift his already perky butt. He paired it with a tight v-neck short-sleeve leather shirt. I couldn't have gotten any harder, then he began modeling the harnesses and low-cut leather briefs. As he mulled over which two items to get, I had the clerk do a fitting for my own trousers. I whispered in his ear before he slipped into the back to hem our trousers, "whichever harness and underwear he decides on, stick the other in the bag, but don't let him see."

He gave me a wick before disappearing with the two pairs for tailoring.

"I just can't decide, I'm sorry, I'll hurry if you're hungry," he said talking to my reflection in the modeling mirror, once I'd walked over and stood behind him.

"I had a good lunch, I can wait as long as it takes. The clerk is adjusting our pants, so it will be a few minutes regardless."

"So which do you prefer, these or the last pair I tried?"

"Both."

"Thanks, that's not helpful."

"Actually Kyle, it is customary to try on the underwear over your own. It may be a health violation, so I'll probably have to purchase both pairs."

"What, seriously?"

"Yes, I am afraid so. You weren't to know, so don't scold yourself, but I may have to purchase a paddle and reprimand you later."

He rolled his eyes and giggled, "I don't like you spoiling me."

"I understand. However, if you feel so strongly that I don't treat you as I know you deserve, then you can purchase them yourself. Unfortunately I will have to ask you to submit a bill for all the meals you've cooked for me. I won't except a single meal for less than 50 pounds and you've cooked me," I paused pretending to calculate the meals we'd shared, "...76. Therefore I want a bill for 3,800 quid."

Kyle huffed. He did that every time I stood my ground and went on a rant to win an argument. "Fine. But I won't enjoy them," he teased.

I gave his ass a slap, "yes you will."

He pulled closer to me and I felt his hardening cock press against my body. He whispered, "we'd better not get them soiled just yet."

The clerk cleared his throat. He stood behind us, the pants folded on the counter behind him.

"Ring those up, which Kyle will wear home, along with these," I commanded, and handed the remaining garments to the clerk. I looked at Kyle and flapped my hand, "go on, put your clothes on."

"I want to wear the trousers home," he said after a short pause that I assumed was a challenge.

I didn't give an answer. Instead a turned to clerk and received both pairs as I had reached into his mind and commanded him to do.

Kyle pulled his pair on over the leather bikini briefs, and zipped his hoodie over the harness, while I removed my denim and replaced them with my new pair. We laced up our boots and I paid the clerk while Kyle continued to check himself out in the mirror. Our walk home, hand in hand, did get a number of stares, even for London.

When we walked into Kyle's flat, he unzipped his hoodie and looked at me. The stare was suggestive, hungry. I pulled my shirt off and pulled our bodies together, the leather creaking as we moved about. Without any further words, dinner was postponed as I pulled him into his bedroom, my hand grasping the straps of his new harness. I resisted undressing him. I wanted to enjoy our time together, but he soon fumbled to open my trousers.

Within seconds his mouth found its' way to my still hard cock. He engulfed it quickly, hungry. I had learned over the years to control my body and enjoy sex at length. Kyle proved to test my will power. I often took him to be hoping to make the most of the night, but even before his own stamina gave out, I craved release. Tonight would be enjoyed.

I stopped Kyle's oral fixation and pulled his face to my, kissing his gently. The leather clung tightly to his legs but I easily pulled them off. His erection was barely contained inside his tight briefs. Pre-cum oozed from the tip which was poking above the brief's top band. I dove on his stiff member, pushing the leather away and burying my face into his crotch. The scent of his sweat mixed with the new leather. My fangs wanted to ache, but my earlier feeding would control my need.

Kyle gave me his look, the one where he bit his lower lip and twitched his entire body. He wanted me to fuck him. I reached into his bedside table and pulled out of a rubber and the bottle of lube. When I had turned back the underwear was on the floor. I pulled my own trousers and pants off and rolled the condom onto my leaking dick. Kyle had pulled back his legs, presenting his hole to me.

"Do it now, fuck me hard," he yelled dirty.

Without hesitation I thrust my lubed cock his ass and plunged in and out slowly at first, then quickening the pace when I Kyle tight his anus. I pushed deeper, going faster and thrusting rougher than before. He moaned and grunted with every plunge of my dick. Several times he wrapped his fist around his own dripping cock, but I slapped his hand away. He needed to save his seed.

I knew I had the will power and the resolve to thrust into Kyle for hours, until he was raw, but I wanted release and I knew he needed it desperately too. When he opened his eyes, his face and body moist with sweat, still hoofing loudly with a moan on each of my thrust, he smiled at me. It was enough. I released a torrent of cum into his gut, as well as a loud guttural yell.

Kyle was even more desperate for his own explosion, nearly pushing me off his before I had completely finished gushing. He slide a rubber on his own cock as I repositioned myself. His cock plunged into me easily, even without the lube he had forgotten to apply. Kyle's thrusts were short and delicate, his breath held as he tried to control his building orgasm. With far better control over the muscles in my hole, I tightened around his cock, providing him the push over the edge he desired. His thrusts stopped and he let out a soft sigh as his seed burst into the condom. It took him minutes to regain himself and pull out, before lying down beside me.

"Happy anniversary, baby," Kyle whispered, his body still glistening with sweat.

"That reminds me, angel," I hoped out of the bed and retrieved the little jeweler's box. "Your gift." I knelt on the bed and extended the light blue box for his waiting hand.

He snatched it up and pried it open. He squealed with joy when he beheld the ring. I pulled the box away from him and properly placed the ring on his finger.

"It's beautiful, thank you," tears were in his eyes and he pulled me down to him. "Aidan, I love you."

"I love you too, more than this ring can say."

Kyle giggled then flayed out his fingers to take in the sight of the ring. I would have wanted him to discover the inscription himself but I was impatient.

"There's something inside the ring."

His face was confused for a moment before he pulled it off and struggled in the low light to read the lettering.

"Oh baby," more tears fell from his sentimental eyes, "that's so beautiful. And here I've skipped your gift."

"No, the flowers and the thought of dinner was enough. It's a special night, one you should have off, even if you enjoy cooking so much."

He pouted, "but I had something special planned."

"It is quite alright, I will survive."

He smiled, closing his eyes and sighed. After sex he was talkative, but the words came in bursts, intermixed with periods of deep reflection. I knew every detail of his personality, every curve and feature of his body, but his past was still a mystery to me. I desired to dip into his mind but the promise to myself was more important. I also knew that questions posed to him might result in the same to me and my lengthy history.

Before his eyes opened I ventured a question. Just above his hip along his side abdomen was a faint scar. "Kyle," I traced the raised skin with my finger, how did you gain this?"

His eyes opened slowly, filled with sadness. "That was from an ex back in Manchester." He looked away, into the distance. "I don't want to talk about it right now." He stifled a tear, holding it back long enough to depart for the toilet. When he returned over ten minutes later, he scooped up his briefs and pulled them on. While his eyes were red and puffy, he smiled weakly and yawned, mostly for show. I pulled my own new briefs on and climbed into the bed beside him. He inched his body back into me. I draped my arm over him and pulled him close.

When I opened my eyes, Kyle was lying next to me still sound asleep. We both have the day off and I wanted to spend it with him, but no, he has a cooking class.

Shit.

No, it's an extended course in Norfolk studying under some fancy celebrity chef. Only four students, all paying through the nose. He would be gone five days.

It's nine, and his train is in an hour. Screw it, I'll drive him.

"Kyle honey, time to get up," I said, giving him a gentle shake.

"Mmm, what time is it?"

"Nine."

"Fuck, I'm going to miss my train!" he jumped, throwing the sheets back and hopping out of bed, still wearing the leather briefs. Actually, as I look down, I'm wearing my too.

"Angel, don't fret, I'll drive you out there. Finish getting ready and I'll go collect my car."

"No baby, I can't make you do that," he said while checking himself out in his bedroom mirror. "Damn, I look good in these."

"Yes you do," I crawled out of the bed and came up behind him, wrapping my arms around him and pulling him against my body. "I'm going to go spend a few days at my country house, so driving you is not a problem. I insist. And you are late, so you have no right to argue."

"Fine."

I slapped his ass then reached down for my trousers.

"Are you going to wear those today?" he asked, checking me out as I pulled the leather on.

"Probably."

"Good," he sighed, and began to whine, "oh, I don't want to go now, I'm going to miss you so much."

I gave him a long kiss. "It'll be worth it. And if you ever need me, I'll be close by."

"Yeah but I'll be too busy in class and working the restaurant."

A blink passed my eyes. I'd actually forgotten, each day the students had to cook a meal from scratch. The course ran once a month and for four nights the school become an exclusive restaurant. Bookings were full for the next three years. Kyle would be working 16 hour days, as least.

"I'll get the car, get packing," I gave him one more kiss and left while pulling on a shirt.

I returned less than an hour later, and Kyle was in a frenzy, still throwing clothes into a bag and running about the flat in a panic. The drive out to the farm in Norfolk was quick once we cleared the M25. Kyle fidgeted with a map, but the satnav led the way. We arrived after Kyle's missed train, but he still had plenty of time before needing to officially arrive.

We made full use of the time making out in the car. Finally he pulled away and looked at me with mist in his eyes.

"I'm going to miss you."

"As will I. But don't worry, my pretty angel, the time will fly very quickly."

"I know."

I had made a promise to keep out of his mind, but I gently gave his nerves a nudge. He needed to focus on his course and not pine for me, and I set his mind on that very track. Kyle smiled and without another word, got out of the car and took his bag into the large farm house.

While I had said I was going to stay at my place in the county, I knew Kyle wouldn't call until he was back in London. I decided I would surprise him on his last night and enjoy a meal in the restaurant. Getting a table booked hadn't been a problem for me. I pulled the car out on the road and guided it back to the nearest A-road bound for my flat in Manchester. I wanted time away from Kyle to think, but I certainly didn't plan to do it in the country. And I had someone to hunt down in Manchester.

Kyle looked completely exhausted. The restaurant had slowly emptied, the kitchen had been cleaned and Kyle dragged himself through the kitchen door finally out of his uniform. He could barely smile when his eyes cast upon me.

"Would you mind if we drive back to London tonight, I'm done here and I don't want to stay the night?"

"Absolutely. You can sleep the whole drive back, it looks like you need it," I wrapped an arm around him, mostly to support him from falling.

I settled Kyle into the passenger seat and retrieved his suitcase. When I passed two of the other students, they appeared in even worse shape. The hour was late, which allowed me to drive along traffic free motorways directly into London. Kyle slept the whole way, and remained sound asleep when I carried him into my house and my waiting bed.

Strangely enough, he had allowed me to schedule him to work the next day. It was clear he'd need sleep and I had no intention of letting him go to work. I woke cuddled next to him early in the morning and called my assistant manager letting him know neither of us would be in to work. Kyle finally woke around two in the afternoon, his movement rousing me from my own sleep.

He yawned and tried to look into my eyes though the sleep was still evident around his eye lids.

"Wasn't I supposed to work today?"

"You were, but you are in no condition to work, even caffeinated. For your own health and safety, I wouldn't allow it, after all I'm not a slave driver," I joked to him.

"Well, not at work, but I like being your slave when you drive me," he tried firing back.

"So, how was the experience?"

"Fantastic. I am completely drained and I almost feel like never cooking again, but I know this is what I want to do."

"I know someday you'll have the top restaurant in London."

"Thanks, but you're just saying that because you're sleeping with me."

"True, but I also have every intention of investing in the restaurant of your dreams."

"I can't let you do that," he smiled weakly.

"I am afraid you have no choice. But that will be when you are ready."

He smiled, knowing I wouldn't rush him.

We spent the remainder of the day causally laying about my house enjoying each other's company. While Kyle had managed a good night sleep, he still seemed mentally drained. He also had not much of an appetite, which was understandable. The day wore into the evening while we cuddled and kissed.

"Baby, I need a few things from my apartment and I want to go for a bit of a walk," Kyle finally said some time after ten.

"As long as you come back to me," I said, looking up from the couch.

Kyle smiled, bouncing with energy. Having slept most of the day, he was probably wide awake despite the late hour. He came close and gave me a kiss.

"I won't be long, maybe an hour."

"I wait with bated breath for your return."

He rolled his eyes and walked out the door. Nearly an hour later, he sent a text announcing he was on his way home and would be quick. The walk normally took less than ten minutes, so after 10 I became concerned.

My link to Kyle is weak. I've never tasted his blood and unless he is physically close to me, I can't reach into his mind. However I began to sense something was not quite right. I slipped out of my house and sped down the pavement, heading for his place. Not a block from my door, I picked up his scent. It was strong, and I was smelling his blood in the air.

I turned and ran down a pathway that created a short cut to Kyle's flat though it passed through a darkened park normally gated at this late hour. In the darkness, my sight could clearly discern his body lying on the grass.

The smell of his blood grew stronger as I approached. My mouth began to water, the hunger rising in me. I reached him in the blink of an eye. He was still, lying prone. When I turned him over, my hand brushed against his blood soaked shirt. A deep cut in his belly was seeping blood at an alarming rate. I know from instinct that he was close to death.

My fangs grew in an instant and I tore viciously at my wrist. I immediately pressed the wound to Kyle's mouth to allow the blood to drip onto his lips. He only needed the tiniest amounts to save his life.

Without me drinking his blood first, he would not turn just yet. No, the blood would revive him and heal him in good speed. Soon I'd be able to fly him back to my house, and let him sleep off the attack.

A strong light suddenly spread across the park. I both froze and slipped my wrist away from his lips. The light landed on us and it was far too late for me to move. I turned my head and could, despite the bright torch directed into my eyes, make out a police officer moving quickly toward us.

"Help, he's been stabbed!" I yelled.

The officer came next to me and barked an order into his radio.

I could already feel Kyle's heart beat increase, he would survive, but I allowed tears to form in my eyes. I looked at the officer and sobbed, "please, help my boyfriend. I shouldn't have let walk home alone. I knew something was wrong when he didn't get back."

"Sir, don't worry an ambulance is on the way," he snapped into action. "Take his sweater and press it against the wound."

The wail of an ambulance was growing in the distance, just reaching the edge of my powerful hearing. I pulled Kyle's sweater and applied pressure against the wound. I knew it would be able to heal quickly, though a drop or two of my blood on the cut would have been able to speed the process, if only the officer hadn't arrived. The cuts on my wrist had already healed.

In the distance, the siren grew louder; the officer could now hear it.

"Sir, it won't be long now, paramedics are coming," as he said this, the flashing lights appeared in the distance, reflecting off the rows of houses outside the park.

Kyle was whisked away in the ambulance, leaving me to answer questions as more police arrived and the park was taped off to create the crime scene. Lights were set up and soon a junior officer discovered a knife lying in a shrub on the edge of the park. Kyle's wallet was also retrieve nearby, empty. I saw the police handle the evidence carefully and was able to sniff the air for the criminal's scent.

Shortly after taking down my initial statement, an officer drove me to the hospital where I found Kyle still in causality. He was heavily sedated, and already bandaged up. They were awaiting a bed in the ward before moving him, but a young doctor informed me that Kyle was lucky, the wound hadn't been as deep as feared and the blood had begun clotting when he was stitched up. My blood was doing the work, probably too quickly for medical science.

Kyle was finally moved into the ward in the morning, and remained sedated throughout the day. I slipped out after sunset and returned to the park to pick up the attacker's scent. The trail was strong and I was able to find him in an estate in South London within an hour. My fangs tore into his throat and I drained him in a fury. His choice of mugging victims had been a poor one.

After two days in the hospital, Kyle was released. I brought him home and would have put him immediately to bed but he was too full of energy. We curled up together on the couch and enjoyed just being with the other. The silence between us was comfortable, but I could see Kyle struggle with his thoughts.

"What is it my angel?"

"Oh, I just been doing a lot of thinking."

I didn't want to push too hard, instead I coaxed gently, "hmmm."

"I came very close to dying. I'm certain of it. The doctors were amazed that the cut wasn't life threatening, but I still heard their whispers. I mean," he paused, "I know this will sound odd, but I swear my senses have been on overload and I've been hearing hushed conversations clearly in other rooms."

It was a side-effect of my blood. I had to reassure him, "that's understandable with a traumatic event."

He shook his head, "the doctors swore I should have been dead from the amount of blood I lost and the size of the cut which should have resulted in a deeper cut."

Again, the healing properties from my blood worked too quickly, ahead of the doctors' actions.

"They must have been wrong. You recovered quickly, so it must not have been too bad." I didn't want to stifle his questions and I wanted desperately to tell him the truth. But if the truth sent him away, I couldn't stand to lose him.

Tears came to his eyes. He sniffled and continued. "I thought about other move important things. Namely us and my past. I need to tell you about my life in Manchester."

"You don't if it hurts too much."

"No, I've kept this a secret far too long. I need closure. I need to share my secret and release it. Then maybe we can be together. I tried to tell you on our anniversary, but seeing my life flash before me made me realize I had to get it out in the open before I could move on."

"I understand." And I did. I knew he was in a great deal of pain.

"When I first moved away from home for school, I met Chad. I fell in love and allowed him to run my life. I barely made it through sixth-form, but I stuck with him." The tears were streaming from his eyes, he continued to sniffle, but I don't think he noticed.

"He abused me. Again, I was young, dumb and madly in love. I let him emotionally abuse me, physically abuse me and basically rape me when I wasn't in the mood and he was."

I pulled Kyle tightly into my arms, I knew as much, but he needed to let it out before taking the next step.

"Then after three years together, he found someone else. He brought the boy home and treated him like a prince, but forced me to watch him make love to him. I feared for the guy, but I took my chance and fled. If they're still together, I'm sure he's abusing the guy, and I didn't do anything to stop it. I'm sure of it."

"You're right."

"Sorry," he paused and looked finally into my eyes, they had stared into the distance while he had shared his pain. His eyes were red and puffy. "What do you mean?"

I knew the truth and he wasn't to blame, though my sudden outburst made it seem he was at fault. "Your ex is a predator, he'll keep repeating his pattern. We can still stop him. You can stop him from abusing anymore guys."

"No, I can't!"

"Angel, I know how much pain he has caused you. I am sorry, I've been burdened with my own secrets. While you were on your course, I went to Manchester. I knew from the way you talked how much pain this guy caused, and I had to find him."

"You did."

"Yes, it wasn't hard. He may not be with the same boyfriend, but he's still abusing. We can stop him. I can give you the power to stop him. To take your revenge."

"I don't want revenge," Kyle responded in a the smallest of voices, "I just don't want him hurting other people."

"Well you can do that instead, the result will be the same."

"So you want me to call the police, send them after him?"

"Sure, in this day in age that should work, but there are other ways."

"Like what?"

I swallowed hard. This wasn't the way to do it and I realized I had travelled down the wrong road.

"I have kept another secret from you, one that has caused me to lie in other ways. I love you terribly much. I will not lie to you, I have loved other men over the years who have come and gone. Each has been special, and I've only shared my true self with a few. Some have excepted me, others have not."

"You're scaring me."

"I'm sorry. You were right earlier. You were about to die when I found you in the part. I healed you. I fed you a few drops of my blood and would have given you more if that police officer had not arrived."

"Aidan, you talking crazy."

"No, hear me out. Angel, my angel, I am what you call a vampire. Would you like me to show you?"

"Fuck you," he pushed me back and tried to rise from the couch but I held him firm. He still lashed out verbally, "I can't believe you, you're sick you know that, sick. I pour my heart out and you mock me."

Before he could react I leaned in and kissed him on the lips. His desire for me won out and he didn't fight his need. His tongue soon began to explore my waiting mouth. I felt his tongue slid across my descended fangs and knew he felt them too.

I pulled away and smiled, my sharp teeth showing in my grin.

Kyle swallowed hard, "shit."

"I have wanted to tell you since the moment I first laid eyes on you. As I said, there have been others before you, one who I loved from his thirties until the day he died an old man at 74, and two who I've shared this gift with."

"What happened to them?"

"One killed himself and the other fell out of love with me. I know love's a fickle thing, people change, grow apart. I love you Kyle, and I want to spend either the rest of your natural life with you, or if you'll accept, an eternity."

"You want me to become a vampire?"

"Yes."

"And when I give up my soul and have no conscious, you want me to take revenge on my ex."

"You will retain your soul, and the burden of all your actions as an immortal. I don't kill often or lightly, only for a reason. And you don't have to seek revenge in the form of killing if you don't want to. But you can save the other guy being abused now."

"When did you last kill?"

"The night after you were stabbed."

"Was it my attacker?"

"Yes."

Tears returned to his eyes, but he smiled.

"I had been so well behaved. It had been over a three decades since I lasted killed. But he hurt the one I love."

"Should I say thanks? I want to," he paused, then continued slowly, "I feel bad to think that he deserved it."

"Kyle, you were good as dead."

He closed his eyes and sighed.

"I don't expect you to decide immediately. You need time to think this out, as much as you need."

"And if I say no, what will you do to me?"

"That depends if you still want to be with me. I said before, I want to be with you, it doesn't matter if you decline the gift. I will still love you."

"But what if I don't want to see you again?"

We were both now crying.

"I will respect your wish."

"This is too much," he stood and I let him. Kyle pulled on his coat and walked to the door. I let him. His hand rested on the nob. He was frozen on the spot and trembling. "I need to think."

"Of course, I said take all the time you need, years even."

"But I don't want to leave. I'm afraid of being alone."

"Well you can stay too." I moved closer until he turned and rushed at me, throwing his arms around me. He buried his face on my shoulder and wept.

"I'm tired, please let's just go to bed."

I wrapped an arm around him and led Kyle to my bedroom. We lay on the bed, nestled together for hours, each pretending to sleep until finally I felt his breathing become shallow.

Kyle woke midway through the morning, and he repositioned his body to face me. His movements woke me. He locked onto my eyes and smiled.

"I'm still not ready to decide. But I have questions."

"As you wish."

"I've seen you in the daylight, and seen your reflection and photos of you," it wasn't a question, but the statement was left to comment.

"All myths."

He seemed put off. Kyle had apparently come to some conclusions and didn't need me confirming them. "More importantly, I have cooked dozens of meal, one's you claimed to enjoy. Were you lying to me?"

I shook my head, "no, I never once lied to you about your art. Eating what you create is one of my most treasured moments. I have superior senses, the increase to your own hearing caused by my blood is only a fraction of how I feel. When I eat your food, the flavors explode on my palette, and I can pick out every single ingredient you used and often how you cooked them. Over the years I become used to the overwhelming tastes, yet I still avoid bad food. The first time I ate after becoming I had an organism the flavors were so intense."

"My passion is cooking, I couldn't give that up."

"You won't have to."

"And I couldn't be without you."

"I do not wish that either."

"How old are you?"

"Over a hundred."

"That's not an answer."

"I was born in 1873 and became a vampire at the age of 25. My immortal age is 110 years old."

"Shit, you look good."

"Of course my angel, vampires stop aging when they change."

Thoughts began to percolate in Kyle's mind, a pensive look spread across his face. "Should I wait until I'm 25, I like how I look now."

"You are beautiful, and I am positive you will be just as beautiful in two years and in 20."

"Oh, I'm not letting myself get that old."

I did not wish to apply pressure and appear too eager, though Kyle was close to a decision, ultimately he would have to come to his own conclusion.

"How often do you, well what do you even call it, drink blood?" he asked skeptically.

"I feed," emphasizing the term I preferred, "taking a small amount, not even half a pint, once or twice a week. While I can enjoy the taste of human food, it has no nutritional value for me, only blood is necessary for survival."

"What is it like?"

"Feeding?"

Kyle simply nodded.

"It is quite enjoyable. Over time you learn to taste the variations, similar to recognizing the subtle differences between wines. There is a physical high you experience when you feed, a burst of energy and an arousal."

"Have you ever bitten me?"

"No, never."

"Why not, were you afraid I'd notice?"

"I have the power to cloud a human's mind. Few ever know they've been fed on and the bite heals quickly. You would not have noticed, but I did not want to cloud your mind, you deserved to always be free from my control."

"Your control?"

"Yes, once I've fed, I have a stronger link to that human. Take for example our visit to the leather shop. I happened upon the place on my errands and drank from the clerk. When we returned that evening I was able give him mental instructions. Otherwise I need to look deep into their eyes to cloud their minds and bend them to my will, or merely to give them suggestions."

"Aidan, I want you bite me now and drink from me?"

"Are you sure?"

"Yes," he paused hoping I would immediately jump him, "I need to know what it feels like."

Slowly I opened my mouth and allowed my fangs to lengthen. I placed my lips on Kyle's then zeroed in on his neck. He tilted his head to further expose the soft flesh that curved gracefully from his ear down to his shoulder. I pressed my lips to the skin in a kiss before dragging my tongue across the smooth derma, the saliva would help to numb the bite and close the wound after. Kyle was tensing him, fearing the worst. I reached my hand up under his shirt and gave his nipple a pinch. He moaned and I sunk my sharp teeth into his flesh. I sipped a small amount and sampled the taste before taking a full drink.

Laced with the medicines from his stay at the hospital, Kyle's blood was sweet and fresh. It was a delicate flavor not to overwhelmed with testosterone or the adrenaline caused by fear, and free of caffeine, nicotine and alcohol. I drank in more of his blood, enjoying his unique bouquet to the fullest. It had been freely given, making the drink all the more sensual. I pulled my fangs from the wounds and released a deep moan.

"How am I?"

"Amazing."

He pulled my face to his, and kissed my lips, tasting his blood on them before his tongue forced its' way into my mouth to explore. Soon though Kyle's eyelids became heavy and he yawned. He fell asleep without another word.

I cuddled next to him and synchronized my heart beat and breathing to his until I was roused from a deep sleep by his movements several hours later. I cleared the sleep my eyes and checked the clock. The sun had set. Kyle stirred some more, finally opening his eyes and searching for me in the darkness. I flicked on a light for his benefit.

He smiled up at me and stretched his limbs.

"Am I a vampire yet?"

"Not yet. Does this mean you accept my offer?"

"I do."

I smiled and gave him a kiss. "I love you and I want to spend eternity with you, but do not fear you must always love me in return. We will be connected, but even as I will be your sire, we will be equals."

"What needs to happen? Do I need to die?"

"No my angel, you will never die. We have already performed the first stage. I have drunk your blood and allowed time enough to pass for it to be absorbed into my system. And you have rested, which has helped you to regain much needed strength. All that is left is for you to drink my seed."

"Shit, really, I give you a blow job and swallow to become a vampire?"

I nodded, giving him a smirk. "Another reason I had not fed from you before."

Kyle slid down the bed and pulled my underwear off, freeing my cock. He swallowed the entire length in one go and immediately created suction. Pumping his lips along the shaft, his tongue swirled over the head. He massaged my balls and pumped faster, eager to taste the nectar. Though I wanted to savor and relish the moment, I felt more impatient and wanted to turn Kyle immediately. I tensed and forced my body to release without reservation. The hot liquid spurted inside his waiting mouth. Kyle swallowed and sucked greedily, keeping my cock in his mouth until nothing more would release. He let go and sat up, looking over my body lazily.

"Can I do that again" he asked without shame.

"Yes, but it won't speed the results."

He pouted.

"Come on, let's shower and go for a walk, we need the fresh air and it'll be better than waiting here."

Like an obedient puppy he followed me into the hot shower. We washed each other and kissed until the water threatened to run cold. In the bedroom we throw on our leather pants, black t-shirts and pulled on a pair of black knitted jumpers with oversized hoods I had in the wardrobe.

We must have walked everywhere, making our way into Soho, with a stop at Comptons, then up through Islington and down through Shoreditch to the river. We followed the path that edged the Thames as far as Embankment before walking back through a still lively Soho, into Regent Park and over the dark canals to Primrose Hill. Together we settled into the worn grass at the edge of the hill and watched the sun rise over East London.

In the early morning hour, we walked back down to Kensington through Hyde Park, as the city slow came to life for another day. We reached my house as the first commuters began to crowd the streets pushing to reach their jobs.

Kyle plopped down on the couch and looked over to me, a smile on his face. Apart from our light conversation outside the bar, barely any words had crossed our lips during the entire walk. We had simply enjoyed the night together.

"I'm not at all feeling tired or sore from that walk, and it was long."

"Well no, you wouldn't now. Your body received a powerful dose of vampire semen and aside from changing you, will probably keep you up for a few days."

"Really? Thanks for telling me."

"Would it have made the slightest difference?"

"No," he nestled in beside me as I sat down, the leather on our legs creaking as we cuddled together. "How much longer?"

"For what exactly? The change began when you drank my sperm, but do you mean when will it be complete?"

"When will I have fangs," he said with a slight hiss.

"You should have them by now. Open your mouth."

Kyle stretched his upper lip back as he bared his teeth to me.

"They have grown in, you just need to learn how to release them. It takes practice. You need to learn to flex a new muscle in your gums. Just imagine your pushing them down, and if you need to, think of blood. Here," I leaned my head to one side, exposing my neck, "see the veins along my neck."

I heard Kyle grunt and looked back to his face. He had succeeded, his fangs had descended. He ran his tongue over the sharp points, then in a show of bravado, hissed at me. The attempt at a menacing display quickly turned to giggles.

"How long before I need to feed?"

"Best to do it either tonight or tomorrow."

"Good. Fancy a drive to Manchester?"

"Now?"

"Yes," he said slowly with an ounce of venom. His face changed to shock, his eyes wide with fear. He looked at me, "I suddenly wanted to tear his throat open and drain him. But I don't want to do that."

I gently squeezed his shoulder to reassure him.

"I want to taste his blood though, but I just need to make him stop and to protect whoever he's abusing now."

"Well good. I will show you how to feed without killing, and to control him. You can implant in his mind the desire to stop, or to turn himself into the police."

"You're right, I want him to stop and to pay for his crimes."

I stood and pulled Kyle up, heading for my car. I turned to Kyle and whispered in his ear, "angel, you should probably retract your fangs before we leave, after all I do care what the neighbors think."

He giggled and covered his mouth while he learned to slide them away. He kissed me on the lips, his fangs hidden. "Let's go." I gave his leather sheathed ass a slap and guided him back out to my car, bound for Manchester.

The Ex-boyfriend

BY ISSAC HOLLAND

The phone rang. But the sleeping body remained still, dreaming of another place and time where a loud ringing sound confused him. The phone rang again. This time Daniel snapped awake and wondered if the ringing was not in his dream. He paused and waited for another ring to confirm this, while he scanned his dark bedroom and examined the alarm clock—2:00PM. Finally the phone rang again. Daniel pulled himself from his bed and slowly walked out into the living room, not sure if he wanted to answer the phone, cursing himself for leaving the ringer on. It rang once more as he journeyed to answer it and was about to make it's fifth attempt when Daniel finally lifted the receiver.

"Yeah," his voice scratchy from sleep.

"Daniel, hi, I know I probably woke you, but I need to see you," said the voice on the phone, with a shakiness in the voice.

"You did wake me, but that's ok. Is everything all right?"

"No it's not. It has to do with my ex. He's back and I'm scared. That's all I can say. Can you come over so I can tell you everything?"

"Sure, just let me get dressed and I'll be over shortly."

"Ok, I'll see you soon. Watch that you're not followed."

"Do you want me to bring you anything, I need to grab a coffee?"

"Yeah, a non-fat latte."

"Alright. See you soon."

Daniel was now quite awake. He walked from the phone to the bathroom and examined himself in the mirror. He looked awake and even composed. Lately he'd had great luck with his hair—he would wake up and it would be perfect without an ounce of grooming.

Back in the dark bedroom, Daniel pulled a pair of jeans from the row of several dozen pairs neatly hanging in the closet. They were arranged loose to tightest, and today he felt like a medium tightness. Spencer might be scared, but Daniel still had to arrive looking good. Grabbing a muscle shirt from the drawer and slipping on socks, Daniel was ready. On the way to his front door—while he threw on his thin leather jacket and shoes—he smiled at himself in the mirror a wicked cunning smile, and stuffed his cell phone and wallet into his pocket.

At the nearest street corner, Daniel entered the local coffee shop. He co-owned the cafe along with his brother, and because Daniel had a smaller share of the business, he always ended up working the graveyard shift—his brother didn't trust the late night staffs' honesty. Spencer's call had woken him in the middle of his normal 8 hours of sleep.

Daniel gave a wink to the barista, who nodded and marked up two large paper cups with his order. Daniel grabbed the completed drinks and turned to leave, finally realizing who was sitting near the back. Gracefully, Daniel walked through the maze of chairs and patrons, who were all suddenly moving into his way, to the friend in the back.

"I'm surprised to see you in here at this hour," the young handsome man said.

"Yes, and I would say the same. I'm off to see Spencer, actually,"

"Really, how is he doing?"

"He's good. Things are going perfectly. He's a little frightened right now about an old boyfriend, but I'm sure everything will be fine once I go over there. I'd say he'll be even better by the end of the night," Daniel said with a wink.

"Good. Well don't let me stop you now. I'll see you soon." And the man winked at Daniel.

Daniel returned the wink and left without a word. The bright afternoon sun had emerged from behind the early springtime clouds causing Daniel to stack the drinks while he pulled a pair of designer sunglasses from his jacket pocket. Of the many pairs he owned, this pair was a recent gift, normally too expensive even for him. To Daniel, it was more about the style and hiding his eyes then about blocking the bright sunlight, which these were designed specifically to do.

Daniel firmly believed that he had the most alluring eyes in the country, a bright blue color that radiated and sparkled in any light. Daniel knew he was vain, and had become even more so in the last year when he had become, in many people's eyes, even more beautiful. Daniel was now twenty-one, with perfect clear complexion, a strong jaw line that helped to accentuate his high cheekbones. With a lean muscular body standing six foot one, he looked good in his muscle shirts, or even no shirt at all.

Daniel's inner reflection lasted the full five-minute walk down to Spencer's apartment building. He let himself into the lobby and walked directly into a waiting elevator to take him to Spencer's top floor apartment. Spencer's door was locked, but the chain was not drawn, allowing Daniel to let himself in with his set of keys.

Spencer was sitting nervously on his couch, rocking back and forth with his legs press against his chest, distantly gazing out the large living room window. When he looked at Daniel, he immediately appeared relieved. Spencer was the older man, twenty-four, though often mistaken for being younger then Daniel. He did not have Daniel's model-worthy features, but instead had his own beautiful cuteness about him based solely on his charming smile, accentuated by his adorable dimples and slight green eyes. He spent hours keeping his skin soft and clear, his eyebrows perfectly manicured and his hair, which took the most amount of time, was made tousled and messy just right.

He got up and crossed the distance in two strides, pressing his boxer-brief clad body to Daniel's, one hand on Daniel's lower back, the other gently rubbing his boyfriend's chest. Standing five feet seven, Spencer had to look up slightly to face Daniel. They smiled at each other then kissed passionately for a full minute. Spencer pulled away from the kiss and placed both arms around Daniel, and pressed the side of his head against Daniel's shoulder.

"I'm glad you're here, I've been freaking out," Spencer finally whispered after a long drawn out embrace.

"You sounded so frightened. Now what's this about your ex-boyfriend?"

"I thought I saw him last night, and again this morning I am sure he was watching me from the street."

"It's okay, I'm here now to keep you safe."

Spencer relaxed even more, squeezed Daniel then released to take the latte. "That's why I love you."

"So you think you saw him last night?"

"Yeah, when I was coming home from the bar, I kept feeling like I was being followed, and only once did I see someone in the shadows, and I couldn't see the face, but the shape of the person reminded me of James. I forced it out of my mind until this morning when I looked out the window and there he was down on the street looking up at this building smoking away. I think he'd been there for awhile, I mean I checked through the binoculars and there were cigarette butts all over the sidewalk."

"It's okay, you don't need to worry, he's not going to harm you."

"Harm me," Spencer broke into tears. "Of course he's going to harm me, he's a monster and he has wanted to get me since we dated. Look I don't expect you to believe me, even with my evidence, but he's a monster."

Daniel looked at him concerned, "You have evidence," Daniel sputtered out, his face expressing shock before he quickly found composure and continued, "um, of what? What do you have that makes him a monster?"

Spencer grabbed Daniel by the hand and led him into the bedroom to his iMac, which Spencer used for video editing when not at work as a video editor at a porn company. Spencer sat Daniel down and manipulated the mouse to pull open a video file which began playing.

"Back when I was dating James, he showed me what he truly was. I couldn't believe it, because it was something unreal." The video played.

Spencer was lying on his bed with James next to him, James' face was clearly observed by the camera. Daniel watched as James transformed on screen. The video wasn't perfect, but there on screen James grew a set of fangs and his eyes changed color to a bright fiery blood red.

Spencer hit the keyboard and paused the video, the still frame showing James' new face.

"It's real. He's a vampire. He wanted me to join him, to become a monster like him. I told him no." Tears began pouring from Spencer's eyes. Daniel wrapped an arm around Spencer and held him.

"I know it's hard for me to believe, but I do. That was over a year ago, what happened before I came along?"

"I met you shortly after I broke up with James. I told him I didn't want to be a monster and to get out of my life. He told me that he could force me, but wouldn't do it. He said that I would eventually become a vampire, and couldn't stop it."

"But he went away?"

"Yeah, he did. But when he left, he told me he'd be back in a year and that if I didn't choose right, he would change me anyway."

"So did he tell you what it would be like? Would you be immortal, staying young forever, and have great power?"

"All that, yeah. But I'd be a monster. I'd have to kill people and drink their blood."

"He told you that?"

"No," Spencer blurted out, frustration building on his face. He took a breath and continued, "he tried to tell me that all it took was a small amount of blood once every week or so. But I didn't believe him, I could tell he was lying." Spencer fell to the bed and through tears looked at Daniel. "I found out that he'd been feeding off me. While I slept, he'd bite me and taken my blood."

"But he didn't kill you," Daniel paused and looked at his distressed boyfriend. "Sorry, I know you felt violated, but if he fed off you a little bit at a time, doesn't that prove he didn't have to kill?"

"I guess. And maybe I feel like he should have trusted his secret before feeding from me."

"So what are you afraid of, becoming a vampire or how he treated you?"

"He scares me. He was never the nicest person in the world, but I ignored his bad behavior, until I realized I'd be forced to spend an eternity with a monster."

Daniel moved to the bed and held Spencer tightly to his body, rubbing his hand along Spencer's back. "It's okay. He's not going to harm you. You don't have to worry. I am glad that you can trust me with this."

"Of course I can, Daniel, I love you. I was never in love with James, it was just about the sex. Immediately after he left, I went into the woods to work on a porno and stayed at the resort for a few weeks after to let things blow over. When I got back to town, I met you, the only time I went into your cafe. I was still scared and couldn't sleep, and well your place is the only one still open at 4AM." he paused at took in Daniel's face, "I am so thankful that I met you."

"I'm glad that I met you too. You're very brave, standing up to him and getting away from him, especially turning down the chance to stay young and beautiful forever. You know, I couldn't resist his offer."

"But to live as a monster. Would you give up your soul and humanity?"

"A monster. What makes you so sure vampires are monsters? We're gay and were once considered deviants and monsters to the norms of society. He too is different and has to live a closeted life as an outcast. And pardon me, but did he tell you that you would lose your soul or your humanity?"

"Well no, we didn't get into a discussion of the details. You have such an open mind, believing that he could be good."

"You've only seen evil vampires on television and in movies, you're expecting him to be something he's not."

"Yeah, but that still doesn't mean I want to be with him for an eternity. Look, Daniel, let's stop talking about it for now. I'd rather you fuck me," Spencer said, sliding his hand up Daniel's inner thigh before placing it on top of his cock.

Without a word, Daniel began kissing Spencer passionately starting on the mouth, then working across to the left ear and down his neck. Daniel paused for a minute, sucking on Spencer's nipple, while pushing him down onto his back. Spencer grabbed at Daniel's shirt and pulled it up and off. Next he was undoing Daniel's jeans, and pulling them down too. They both continued to make out in their underwear losing themselves for almost an hour, moving the mouths slowly across each other's bodies.

Finally Spencer pulled Daniel's boxers off and placed his mouth over Daniel's erect cock, playing his tongue across the tip. Daniel lifted Spencer's body and spun him 180 degrees so he faced his boyfriend's crotch. He reached up and pulled off Spencer's boxers and went to take Spencer's large erect member in his mouth when Spencer stopped him and wagged his finger. Spencer got on his back and pulled his legs to his chest, inviting Daniel into his hole. Daniel moved into position and slowly ran his tongue around Spencer's hole, finally pushing it in.

Spencer fumbled inside the night stand drawer for a condom and the lube, tossing the items to Daniel. In one expert movement, Daniel rolled the condom down his cock. He squirted the sheathed cock with lube and ran two fingers through the liquid collecting enough to help in further loosening Spencer. After one finger went in and out again, two fingers went in and came out. Spencer moaned with excitement, clasping the sheets in his fists.

Daniel finally inserted his cock and began to work his member in Spencer's ass. Within a minute of the rhythmic thrusts, Spencer's moaning grew louder and intense as his breathing turned to heavy panting. He looked into Daniel's eyes, getting the knowing nod, Spencer released, erupting a burst of cum between them. Daniel immediately followed, tensing and slowing his thrusts as his own load shot into the condom still in Spencer's ass. He pulled out, removed the condom, tied it off and tossed it into the garbage. Spencer was still regaining his breath so he allowed Daniel to wipe the cum off his torso with a Kleenex.

Daniel lay down next to Spencer who gave him a quick kiss. "Daniel, you got me thinking. I prejudged James as a monster. I don't care about him and I don't want to be with him. It would be different if you were to change me, because I love you."

"Do you mean that?"

"Yeah, well you're more convincing. I want to tell you a secret," he paused for Daniel's reassuring word.

"Go ahead."

"Well when I came back from the woods after the porn shoot, I started to think long and hard. I knew I didn't love James, but I'll tell you it was tempting to be eternally young and beautiful. I couldn't get the image of James as a vampire out of my mind—but it was not an image I feared, no I was turned on. I struggled with the thought of being a soulless killer for eternity and was close to saying yes to James. Then you came into my life and I soon realized I couldn't leave you for James just to be a vampire."

Daniel smiled and looked deeply into Spencer's eyes, "I love you and I want to spend eternity with you," and Daniel kissed Spencer, who had closed his eyes to enjoy the kiss.

When Spencer reopened his eyes, Daniel had transformed, his beautiful blue eyes were now blood red, and his fangs had slid down. Spencer's breath was briefly caught in his throat unable to speak, Daniel continued.

"Spencer, I am a vampire, and I want you to be one too. You will retain your soul and you won't have to kill if you don't want to. I won't lie, you will need to feed, though not much. James was right about that."

Spencer regarded the vampire for a moment, realizing his good fortune. There was no fear in his eyes, only love. "I want you to turn me."

"I have to come clean first. You must know that shortly after we started dating, James came to me. He turned me, promising me eternal young, and shit you know how vain I am, I couldn't turn him down. After I had turned, James revealed that he had given me the gift so that I would turn you. He wants you for himself and I don't know what he'll do—I love you too much and won't be willing to give you up. I'm just sorry I kept this a secret from you."

"Did you ever feed from me?"

"Never."

"And when he told you his plan for me, were up going to just hand me over?" Spencer asked with a pout.

"Spencer, since I was fifteen I've wanted nothing more than to be a vampire. I couldn't pass up James' offer. We weren't very serious at the time, but I've grown to love you. And I know deep down that if you love me more than James, you will choose me. I fear that even if you do choose me now, James won't be happy without you."

"Well if he can't accept what he created, then we'll run away or kill him if we have no other choice."

"You're right," and Daniel kissed Spencer on the lips again. "This will hurt at first, but then it will soon be over."

Daniel kissed Spencer once more before running his tongue down to Spencer's neck. He kissed the soft skin then gently pushed his fangs into the flesh. Spencer tensed and drew in a sharp breath, it hurt but he was determined to hide it. Daniel sucked the blood pouring from the wound for a little over a minute then pulled back, licking the blood from his lips.

Looking down at his love, Daniel spoke, "you now need to drink some of my blood to become a vampire, otherwise you will recover in a day or two from the blood loss with no side-effects. Do you still want it?"

Spencer barely had the strength and awareness to answer, but still uttered a whispered, "yes."

Daniel raised his index finger to his chest and with his nail drew a line across his left pec just above his nipple. Blood began to well up in the cut. With the same hand, Daniel reached behind Spencer's head and lifted it to his chest, guiding the lips to press against the cut. The blood trickled into Spencer's mouth and after a moment, his energy returned enough for him to wrap his arms around Daniel. Spencer increasingly licked at the blood pouring from the cut, drawing as much blood as he could, an act that continued for several minutes until Daniel gently pulled Spencer's determined mouth from the wound and laid his head back onto the pillow.

Spencer immediately passed out, but was revived ten minutes later with a glass of water placed at his lips. He drank a small amount, swallowed, stared at the ceiling for a moment then doubled over from a sharp pain in his gut. All he could do was curl up in a ball and shake as the pain shot through him. He could feel every muscle in his body stretch beyond its' limit then contract, and he felt a series of shocks go through his body. Tears streamed from the tightly closed eyes while Daniel held him close.

Slowly after several minutes of the most intense pain, Spencer began to notice the pain subside. An hour later the pain had died away completely until Spencer realized he had been focusing on the distant sounds down on the street, a conversation echoed in his ears so clearly it could have been in the same room, many more sounds grew louder until he felt that he was in a crowded room deafened by the noise level. Suddenly there was silence and he could only hear the sound of Daniel's heart beating softly next to him. Spencer turned over and looked to Daniel and smiled. Daniel leaned close and kissed him deeply. These new kisses sent waves of ecstasy through Spencer's body and instantly he was hard.

"It's done. You are now a vampire. It will take some time to get used to your new senses and to practice releasing your fangs with control."

"I feel so alive. So strong and powerful. And so incredibly horny."

"That is all normal. I am so glad that you chose this. I love you."

"I love you so much, Daniel. For being here and for giving me this gift."

"Well I can see I came at the right time," spoke a third voice from across the room. Both Spencer and Daniel turned quickly to find the man Daniel had spoken to earlier that day in the cafe. "Daniel, you've done an excellent job, which I obviously hadn't been able to do myself. Spencer, glad to see you've finally embraced the change. How do you feel?"

"Wonderful, James"

"See, and you wanted to resist, silly boy. Thank you Daniel, that will be all," James finished, not turning his gaze which was locked on Spencer. Once it became obvious that Daniel wasn't moving, James turned and faced him, "Is there a problem?"

"I'm not going anywhere. I created him, and he's my."

"And I created you, now leave."

"No! You created me to turn Spencer, but you can't control our love."

"Yeah, you monster, you'll have to kill us both, I'll never be yours'," Spencer finally said, barely his fangs for the first time with a hiss.

James bared his own fangs, "kill you, don't be stupid, I can't kill either of you any more then you can kill me. No, I am afraid I am stuck with you two. Spencer, I can give you the choice once more. I am an old and powerful vampire with more money then we could ever possibly spend even as immortals. Come with me and live eternity like a king or choose to remain with this servant."

"I've made my decision. I don't love you, I love Spencer."

"Fine. What a waste of time you two have been."

Spencer stared at James, a look of shock and suspicion across his face. "That's it, you're giving up without a fight?"

"I thought you made your decision. I'm offering you the world, Daniel has nothing to offer you."

"But you tried so hard, turned Daniel and spent more than a year trying to turn me. I can't believe you're just going to walk away."

"You two are so young. A year is meaningless to a vampire my age. I've spent far longer prepping humans for the change. But you don't understand, I still won, you're a vampire."

"What, is this a game to you?"

James smiled wickedly, "yes that's exactly what this is, a bet." He shook his head, "did you really think I loved you that much, that I wanted to spend eternity with you?" He didn't wait for an answer. "No Spencer, you were a bet, and I won. You agreed to be turned, and I didn't force you."

"You sick monster! I can't believe I had even reconsidered and was going to say yes to you. I was right to think you're evil. Are you even capable of love?"

James rolled his eyes. "Stupid little queer. Love," he laughed. "You're not going to survive eternity on love."

"Just watch us." Daniel tightened his hold on Spencer then leaned in and kissed him.

"I bet you can't stay together for a hundred years."

"Screw you!" Spencer screamed. "We're not a game to you. We're not going base our relationship on proving you wrong. I think you should leave."

James scowled and turned away. The sound of a piece of furniture being against a wall came from the living room followed by the slamming of the front door.

Spencer turned to Daniel.

"Hungry?" Daniel asked, showing his fangs.

"Yes, how do we do this?"

"We need to find a donor. What do you think about a threesome?"

"Anyone in mind?"

Daniel nodded and pulled out his phone. He tapped a few buttons and handed the phone to Spencer to show him the picture of a younger male.

"He's my regular donor. We don't have sex, I just feed off him, and I'm sure he'd be okay with two vampires."

"This guy knows?"

"I pay him and well I promised to turn him when he feels old enough. He's a barista in my cafe and he should be getting off shortly."

"Oh, I know which one he is," Spencer licked his lips. "Call him, now!"

Spencer handed the phone back to Daniel; it was already dialing the boys' number.

"Hey Kenny, do you feel up to coming for dinner now?" A smile crept across Daniel's face as he listened to Kenny's response. "Okay, check with my brother." Daniel covered the phone and looked at Spencer.

"He's just getting my brother."

Spencer rolled his eyes, annoyed.

"Yeah Pete, let Kenny go early, I need him to bring me and Spencer coffee." He paused. "Yes, the usual, but send him to Spencer's." Daniel smiled. "Okay, later." He ended the call.

"Is he coming?"

"In five minutes."

Spencer pushed Daniel against the mattress and smothered him in kisses. A knock at the door several minutes later broke their foreplay.

"Come in," Daniel yelled.

A moment later Kenny came wandering through the door holding two coffee cups. Kenny smelled of coffee but had changed into fresh clothes— tight black jeans with a hoodie pulled up over his head, with his messy black hair falling across his face. The 18 year old wore a lot of black and usually sported an emo look. He smiled at the two naked vampires.

"Hey Spencer, glad to see Daniel turned you."

Spencer looked taken a back, "you knew?"

"Yeah, Daniel tells me everything." Kenny put the coffees aside and stripped. He climbed onto the bed and gave Spencer a kiss. "Daniel, I'm charging you double, I don't care if it's his first time."

"Hmm, trying to negotiate while flaunting the goods, maybe I won't turn you after all," Daniel teased.

Kenny giggled, "nice try, I'm black mailing you too well."

"So that's how you're getting him to turn you?" Spencer asked.

"Um, Kenny," Daniel gave the boy a wink, "it's not a secret anymore, Spencer knows."

"Oh, right," the young man looked rejected.

"Don't worry, I promised."

Kenny looked at Spencer and smiled seductively, "so, are you going to bite me or not?"

Without an answer he pulled Kenny close and bit into his throat. Spencer immediately sucked at the blood that sprayed out from the wound. Daniel leaned into Kenny's crotch and bit into his thigh just below his cock, who moaned as the two vampires fed from him.

When the boys were done feeding, Kenny lay back and fell asleep.

Daniel grabbed Spencer's hand and dragged him away, "I need a shower."

"You know what I need?"

"What?"

"To fuck your brains out."

"Charming," Daniel said pushing Spencer into the shower one hand around his boyfriend's hard cock.

In the bedroom, Kenny slept soundlessly as James slipped back into the apartment. He examined the wounds on the boy and smiled. With the flick of his finger he cut his wrist open and held it above Kenny's mouth. Slowly drops of blood fell on the boy's mouth. His tongue slid slowly across his lips then he accepted the wrist which he sucked at eagerly. Once Kenny had been fed, James left the apartment, leaving the boy to turn.

Skater boys

BY VIAN WATFORD

The old bus pulled away from the isolated bus stop, as Nat reached its'
tail. He had started sprinting flat out across the deserted parking lot
the moment he'd seen the bus lumber down the street toward the small
gathering at the stop. He examined his watch as he panted heavily in an
attempt to regain his breath.

Under his breath, he cursed the salesman at the warehouse he'd just
run from. With an hour between buses, Nat had consulted his watch
often during his purchase to make sure he didn't have to stay an extra
hour. But the salesman continued to vent about the proper way to install
the wireless security camera system Nat was buying. Paying him no
attention, Nat thought out his own plan for installing and catching the
thief who'd been hitting the store he managed.

The thefts didn't bother Nat at all. It wasn't his concern. And he
hated the job, which gave him long hours and all the responsibilities but
thanked him with a nice small paycheck. Quitting wasn't the answer, he
was comfortable after all. Nat already stole from the store and there was

a good amount of room for him to write off all thefts from the store. He was just bored and needed to focus all his energies on catching the thief.

Having sufficiently caught his breath, Nat looked down the empty street line with warehouses. He had seen a strip mall very close by when he'd ridden in, and it stuck him as a way to kill the time. The parcel secured in his backpack, Nat began to follow the path of the bus.

Misjudging the distance entirely, Nat found himself at the strip mall 15 minutes later. There was room for ten stores, four of which were vacant. Two were take away pizza places that sandwiched a florist, a Chinese restaurant and a porn shop. The last opinion was a liquor store at the far end separated by the empty stores.

Unable to decide which to enter, Nat instead turned his attention to a group of four young guys skateboarding around a skate park across the road. They all had the same skater look familiar among the customers in Nat's store, baggy pants, a tight graphic tee and messing hair.

One boy stood apart from the other three. He had been standing holding his board, watching over the others. As Nat studied him, he turned and looked toward Nat. A moment passed then the boy waved for Nat to come over.

Seizing an opportunity to break the boredom standing in the parking lot, Nat ventured toward the skaters. The other three continued to skate around the concrete curves while the other continued to stare at Nat. It unnerved him, but he felt compelled to approach him.

Nat got to the road and paused. He was impressed by what he saw. They were much better skaters than Nat, and hot as hell. Crossing the street, Nat was entirely focused on the one who'd summoned him, not even turning his head to check the traffic. Likely there was none.

Reaching the mound the boy stood on, Nat just stared into the bright blue eyes of the blonde cherub smiling back at him, dimples and a big white smile and all. He was young, and though Nat called him a cherub, he was at least 19 or 20.

He wore items Nat sold in his store, the pants, shoes and even the blue graphic tee that read "okay, bite me" in large gothic blackletter type. The blonde's hair was a mess, and it looked to have taken an hour to style right, or that's how long it took Nat. Unlike most of the pimply young guys that came into his store, this one had flawless skin and barely any facial hair showing. And his lips were large and pouty.

"Hey dude, the name's Vian," and he reached his hand out to Nat and woke him from his thoughts.

Nat swallowed hard, "Um, Nat."

"Well Nat, see I'm wondering if you might be able to do us a favor," he said as the others skated around ignoring Nat's presence, "well you look old enough to buy beer, and we're not. We don't even have IDs."

"Do you need money," Nat stammered, unsure why he asked, questioning why he suddenly felt willing to pay.

"No, we have cash. Plenty of that, but not IDs and we don't even look old enough. So here's what I'm thinking, if you're willing. I'll give you enough money for a case of beer for us and you get something for yourself. You're even welcome to join us," Vian stopped, a perfect seductive smile spread across his angelic face.

"Sure. Anything in particular?"

"Surprise me," and Vian pulled two twenties from his pocket.

Taking the money, Nat turned and returned to the strip mall. He walked directly to the place he'd been before, out of direct sight from the liquor store, then strolled along the shop fronts to the last one. Nat had played out his paranoid scenario. Rather than make a beeline for the store after talking to the boys, he meandered so not to be too obvious.

The store was empty except for the clerk and the dust covering the product. Grabbing a bottle of rum and the first 24 case of beer he saw, a brand that meant nothing to him, he walked up to the clerk. Without so much as a look at Nat or mention of ID, the clerk rang in the order and took the outstretched green.

Slipping the rum into is backpack before setting out, Nat noticed the boys had begun skating down the street to the far end of the strip mall. He set out and tried to decide what to do next. He reached them before he made his decision.

"Dude, thanks. You rock," Vian said, his eyes now almost covered by is mess blond hair. Then one of the guys with black hair approached and took the case. His hands suddenly free, Nat received a hug from Vian without warning..

"You're going to join us, right?" Vian said, having leaned away, but still holding Nat by the shoulders.

Nat nodded yes. He wasn't about to miss hanging out with them, even as he now found he wasn't able to speak.

The pair turned and followed the three still skating down the empty road, without a word. Nat noted where they were going, keeping track of the deserted buildings and over grown weeds. Not far down the road they turned and walked to the end of a shorter road, its worn pavement showing neglect and disuse. Where this road ended, another was around the corner, but this short street led them to turn again onto a street marked with a sign proclaiming "No through road". Nat followed as they hooped over a short chained gate, its' metal frame and lock so rusted the gate must have been locked decades before. He'd also lost his bearings after turning left and right so many times.

Nat looked into the complex beyond the gate and saw a grouping of old brick and stone buildings some with pipes connected to others buildings high above the road. More pipes and other debris cluttered the road. Each building bore markings carved into stone and cemented into each corner, stating the building number. The one they filed passed was marked "Distillery". They turned at the building's corner and followed a narrow alley lined with bricks choked with weeds. The pathway turned around the back of the building and began to slope downward. Nat watched as they approached a large metal door. Vian grabbed and pulled down a lever on the building wall causing half the door creaked open a foot.

Through this opening they filed into the darkness. Nat's eyes adjusted, but when the door creaked shut, he was plunged into complete darkness. He then felt someone hold his hand.

"I forget, we're so used to the way, we get in just fine," Vian said, quite softly just for Nat's benefit. "I'll lead you."

Nat put his trust in Vian's hand, and allowed himself to be brought through the darkness around a number of curves and up one staircase. Then in the distance another door creaked and moments later, dim light broke the darkness.

Vian continued to hold Nat's hand all the way into a large room that looked like a nightclub. The walls were painted black, there were two long bars and a grouping of leather couches. As Nat examined, it turned out to be one long winding semi-circle of seating in black leather with the exposed plywood base showing along the bottom.

Taking a seat, Nat scanned the rest of the room. It was a large room with two lofts running its' length on either side. The only source of light coming from dim vertical light boxes recessed into the two rows of thick wood posts that ran up to the roof. The rows of pillars created the large cathedral-like central space with a loft on each side hugging the wall. Nat then noticed that the three without names had removed their t-shirts and were walking around sporting smooth muscled upper bodies. Their chests and arms were toned but not too bulky.

Turning to see Vian, Nat watched as Vian also pulled his graphic tee off and hung it off his belt as if he were at a rave.

"Welcome to our home," Vian waved his hand around the vast space.

"You live here?"

"Yeah, we're not ones for normal society. We'd rather kick back here. This used to be an underground nightclub, but we took it over. The whole place was a distillery until a long time ago when they banned alcohol. It's been empty ever since. We're not actually squatting since this place used to be run by my family and I still hold the deed."

"That's crazy."

"Yeah I know, but no one knows we're here and we like that."

The black haired boy came out of the darkness and handed Vian a bottle of beer. In one move, Vian twisted the cap off and pitched it into the far corner where it hit with a soft metal clank.

"This here is Aaron, the first to join me," Vian said of the black haired boy. He came forward and shook Nat's hand, smiling warmly. His eyes were a pale blue that shone green when he turned slightly. He had a hoop piercing on his left nipple, and an otherwise unblemished upper body. As he turned, Nat saw the top of a tattoo showing on his groin.

When Aaron had departed to sit behind Vian, Nat noticed a similar tattoo showing on Vian. The remaining two quickly blocked this view. "Marc on your left and Pax on your right," Vian said from behind them. They both smiled and then shook Nat's hand before sitting down next to Aaron with the beers.

"So Nat," Vian paused and look him over before looking back at the other boys, "what's 'Nat' short for?"

Nat looked puzzled for a moment as he wondered about the strange request. "Actually it's Ignatius."

Vian was grinning, "Really? That's great and such a great name," Vian continued to smile as the others had stopped and were looking directly at Nat, also smiling.

"You're kind of weirding me out here."

"We'll weird you out even more. Yeah, sorry we're just excited. Ignatius," Vian paused placing emphasis on the name, "do you know what your name means?"

"Yeah, fire or something like it."

"Fiery one. Very fitting."

"I'm so glad," he said slightly sarcastically. "You."

"Oh, Vian is English for 'full of life'. Marc is short for Marcel, which is 'young warrior' and Pax means 'peace'."

"You're really up on the meaning of names," Nat added as a comment.

"Yeah, it's something that interests me."

"Well you should try my middle name."

"Shoot."

"Isaac."

"Two names beginning with 'I'?"

Nat nodded.

"Isaac means he will laugh. Maybe we'll make you laugh."

"Here's hoping." Nat reached into his bag and pulled out an open bottle of coke with a quarter already gone, and his rum, which he opened and used to top up his coke.

Aaron, Marc and Pax each finished their beers in several gulps and walked away, likely looking for more. Vian sat down next to Nat and looked over at him.

"I'm probably going to call you Ignatius rather than Nat."

"That's fine with me."

"So dude, I think you're hot, if you're straight, sorry to come on strong."

"You're not offending. Thank you. And I'm not straight," Nat paused, "and I think you're very hot. Certainly hotter than me."

"Well, beauty is in the eye of the beholder."

"Listen, Vian, I want to ask you, just how old are you guys?"

"How long do we look?"

"Um, 19 or 20."

"Well that's it."

"You're 19?"

"Well no, I look 19. I'm a little older."

"How much older?"

"Well I should explain. We often bring guys back here for a little bit of fun. In the last few years we've met a lot of guys, and you're the second with a name beginning with 'I'. See I have this silly tradition that I will bring guys into the group in a certain order. It's really the stupidest tradition ever, but I'm having good luck so far. Okay, starting from me, Vian, then there's Aaron, Marc and then Pax. You would be Ignatius and the next two would have names starting with R then E." Vian stopped and allowed Nat a moment to think.

"Right, so you're adding friends to spell the word vampire?"

"Um, it's more than that Ignatius. I'm giving you a choice. You could choose to join us or not. Joining us would give you immortality and actually you would grow younger to the age of 19; your looks and body would be at their peak. If you are worried about not being attractive, don't worry, you'll be as hot as I am now. You're other choice will be your death."

Nat looked at Vian and laughed. "Dude you had me going until that death part."

"See I knew I'd make you laugh. Hopefully I won't scare you when I show you."

Nat watched Vian as he broadened his smile and slid his canine teeth down extending them half an inch to two sharp fangs. At the same time, his irises went from bright blue to blood red.

"Shit. You weren't lying."

"Nope," Vian said through his fangs.

"I mean I didn't think you were. I was laughing because I find vampires a turn on."

"You've met one before?"

"No, never a real one, just in books and movies."

"So does that make your choice easy?"

"Yeah, too easy. What gives?"

"Okay, I'll come clean. I spotted you a few months ago, at Dark Vault Books. Most of the people that hang out there are goth wanna-bes, but I could tell you were different. I followed you to your store. I've been watching you a lot since then. Oh, and we're the ones pinching clothes from the store. Did you suspect it was us?"

"No," Nat whispered. The clues were there, he'd just ignored them. He had forgotten the busy afternoon they had come in and cased the place, trying on the clothes they now wore, or at least half wore.

"It was a trap really. I wanted you to follow the clues right to us. I was glad to see you today, happy you'd found us."

Nat nodded, "I guess I did, but not because of the clues. I was picking up a few small security cameras down the street."

"Right, and what made you come all this way to pick up something you could have bought near your store?"

"There was a flier on my desk for the warehouse and the prices were cheap."

"And the other flier?"

"There was only one flier."

"Shit, really. Oh well I'm sure had you seen it, you'd have been here sooner."

"What was it?"

"I left one for a rave. Not a real rave, but one that should have gotten you here. It said 'Vampire Nightclub: the hot spot for gay boys to party'. A little obvious?"

Nat nodded, "It would have worked. When is it?"

"Every Friday night at midnight. So we've been here the last two Friday nights."

"And tonight?"

"Well you came early without even knowing."

"True. Has anyone else shown up?"

"Not yet. If someone other than you had shown, we'd have had a nice dinner."

"The morning I came to work and found the flier, an employee had opened the store. His name is Ryan. And he's a little party boy twink."

"Ryan. Hmm, it's a little early to be thinking out the next boy to turn."

"Oh, yeah that's right, I hadn't thought of him that way. No I was thinking if he took the flier he might show up here."

"Well I mentioned what we'll do about that."

"I want to be the one to do it."

"Absolutely. That must mean you're going to join us?"

"Of course."

"Well let me explain. Oh, keeping my fangs down isn't bothering you is it?"

"No, but I want to kiss you."

Vian smiled flashing his fangs. He leaned in and pressed his lips to Nat who returned the kiss. After a few seconds, Nat slipped his tongue along Vian's sharp canines.

"Vian, you are so hot. And I am so glad you chose me," Nat said, pulling away from Vian's lips, his eyes focused on the teeth then slowly moved up to the red eyes.

Vian pulled a little further away, "I should explain myself first."

Nat smiled and allowed Vian to continue.

"I was born here in 1897. My father had already established this distillery and once he married my mother they were ready to have a family. I was their only child. When I was ten my mother died, causing my father to become deeply depressed. Slowly I began taking over the business, as my father increasingly stayed away. In all that time, he never drank. The day after I turned eighteen, he had a heart attack. I found him in his study after it was too late. I buried myself into the business and we produced a large stockpile of liquor, which I had the foresight to hide. Four years later, prohibition hit and I had to shut down the business. I managed to unload some the hidden liquor soon after to the local gangsters for a good profit. They came for the rest at a lower price. I wasn't ready to sell the rest, but one late night when I was 26, they came looking for me.

"It was that night that I changed. Two large men held me as a third beat me with a baseball bat. That is when I tasted my blood and almost immediately felt the surge of strength. I tossed the two off with such force that they crashed into brick walls and were killed instantly. I lunged for the leader, sinking my new teeth into his neck. The bodies were later found at their speakeasy, stuffed in whiskey barrels. I tied up my affairs, put the business and assets into a trust, took a huge chunk of cash and fled to Europe. As I waited in New York for the boat trip, I began to change further, becoming younger and more beautiful with each day. By the time I sailed across the Atlantic, I had settled on the body I still have now. On that boat, I met a young man who I fell madly in love with. Men had always aroused me, but I hadn't acted on it. Adam was more forward and I spent the remained of the voyage in my cabin with him. Not once during that time did I drink from him. I wasn't hungry and I didn't feed again for two years.

"I lived out the 20s and the depression with him in England. But in the late 30s Adam began to notice I wasn't aging as he was. I knew he wanted to ask me, but he put it off. Soon after war broke, he was on his way home when he was killed by a German bomb. That night I planned on confessing my true nature to him, and offer him immortality. At the time, I wasn't certain how to turn someone else, but I knew it could be done. I was angry at losing Adam, so I joined up and was sent into Europe soon after training. When the other troops were slaughtered in one of the worst losses to the British, I had managed to work my way past the front line into Europe. I found refuge in an abandoned barn, where I found Aaron hiding for his life. He had fled from the German's insane slaughter and found a hidden cellar, beneath that barn, the night before I arrived.

"He was frighten for his life, but let me into his cellar. In that dark stone cell he shared his secret. His family had all been killed but he'd escaped and survived. I told him that I would protect him and bring him to safety. I showed him what I was and offered him the same. Very frighten by the German's hunting him above, but also the monster hiding with him, he accepted. Instinct kicked in and I turned him without thinking how to do it. Two German soldiers soon found us, but Aaron had enough time for the initial change. Before they had their guns up, he had pounced the furthest. The other spun round and fired a shot. As it hit Aaron, I leapt up and bit down on that soldier. Aaron survived the shot easily. We took their uniforms, dumped their bodies in the cellar then ran. We found our way to a small village in France where we took up new lives. I already spoke perfect French, and soon taught Aaron. With our advanced abilities, it takes no time at all. I foolishly thought we were somehow safe in France, but once we were found, we were captured. Since we hadn't been around during the invasion, the Germans decided we were spies or working for the resistance, either way we were dragged us in front of a firing line. We were shot."

Nat looked at Vian, sitting across from him over sixty years later, and still breathing. Looking closely at Vian's chest, he watched it rise and fall with each breath.

"How did you survive?"

"We held our breath. For two days actually," Vian paused and smiled again as he held his breath for a moment. "I discovered swimming one day that I could hold my breath, however, after a few hours, I would blackout. That's what we did. We held our breaths and were buried alive, thankfully together in the same grave. The sound of digging woke us and we found our new friend, Jean-Louis, the first vampire I've met. He pulled us out and the three of us went into hiding in his chateau. Occupied by German's above, we lived away in the catacombs and hidden passages below. We survived the war and Jean-Louis taught us everything he knew. It turned out he was my great-great-great grandfather on my mother's side and explained that the blood that ran through our family had evolved us into vampires, triggered by the violet beating and drinking our own blood. After fathering a son, Jean-Louis had been captured during the French revolution. He turned while he was tortured and eventually managed to escape.

"After the war, Aaron and I parted ways with Jean-Louis and returned to England before setting out for America. As the acceptance of gays slowly rose in the US we found places to be and eventually found Marc in the 60s. Marc had wandered over to America to study while Paris burned during the riots. Once I had turned Marc, I noticed I was starting a trend so I figured I would watch and see what happened and who came along. Then in the 80s we met Pax, and it wasn't a question because of his name, but rather he just fit. That's the same feeling I get from you."

"Thanks."

"It's not a problem. And now you know most of my story. You will become beautiful and 19 forever. We can't be killed and as far as other vampire stereotypes, we're not dead, we can walk around in daylight, eat and drink normally including garlic and if you want, holy water. Stakes usually ruin the shirt you're wearing and tickle a bit. You will be able to heal almost immediately if hurt. I do expect you to give up the life you know. Since you'll look very different in a few days, we won't move immediately, but we're likely to relocate when we get bored. After you've changed, we can go back to your place and gather up a few items you want to keep, then you will disappear."

"Sounds good."

"Okay, let's go up to my loft and we'll do this," Vian picked Nat up carrying him in his arms, then kicked off from the floor, flying up to the loft. Nat was placed on a large square leather bench with Vian straddling his legs.

"This is quite simple. We need to cycle our blood. I will offer you a cut on my neck, and as you start drinking my blood, I will bite you on the neck, we will then continue for about ten minutes."

Vian stood and pulled his pants off revealing tight black boxer briefs. He then reached down and pulled Nat's pants off then his t-shirt. Resting himself again on his knees and straddling Nat, Vian pulled a ring from his wrist band and placed it on his middle finger. The ring had two fang shaped spikes protruding from the base.

"They're like brass-knuckles, only molded after my own fangs. I had it made a few years ago, and haven't used it to turn someone yet."

With that Vian lined up the metal fangs to his neck then pushed them deep. Vian pulled the prongs out then brought the exposed neck to Nat's lips. He licked the blood beading on the skin then pressed his lips against the two bleeding holes. The sweet red liquid hit Nat's tongue and as he pressed harder, Vian thrust his own sharp canines into Nat's waiting neck.

Nat couldn't get enough. He was in utter ecstasy as Vian's blood flowed through his mouth while Vian was pulling out his own blood. Eyes tightly shut and enjoying the moment beyond an organism, Nat barely noticed that the ten minutes flew by so quickly it felt like two.

Vian pulled his fangs from Nat's neck, gently licked the wound then straightened up.

"You're done," Vian stopped and licked his lips. He looked down at the blood smeared over Nat's mouth. "When you feed, it will be even more intense than that."

Catching his breath, "if it's that good, what stops you from feeding everyday?"

"Feeding is so intense that you really don't want to do it too often. And besides I forgot to mention it, as a vampire, your orgasms are even more spectacular than feeding."

Vian smiled and leaned in to kiss Nat.

"Thank you Vian. Thank you so much."

"You are very welcome. One last thing," he paused a took a breath, "the change is going to hurt at first and then you will feel amazing. Kind of a hint as to what an organism will feel like."

"Okay. When does that..." But Nat answered his own question and collapsed to the bench, his fists clenched and eyes screwed tight as sudden pain surged through his body. Every cell was changing, every muscle stretching, all impurities expelled and his teeth were pushed out by a new set.

The final waves of pain diminished slowly after ten minutes. When his new set of teeth had finished growing in, Nat was beginning to ride the wave into pleasure. As the pleasure grew, two of his new teeth slid down and his muscles became more defined, chiseled hard and larger then before. His skin cleared and Nat was able to lie back, taking in the mounting enjoyment coursing through his body. Slowly as the energy subsided, Nat opened his eyes to reveal his blood red eyes.

He looked at Vian and smiled.

"I think I'm hungry."

"You should be. Well first, you need to wash up. You reek from your body cleansing itself."

"I don't think I'll want to wear these clothes either."

"Oh don't worry, remember, I removed clothes from your store, including a set for you. I'll go grab them and you head down to the washroom," Vian pointed to the end of the loft where a door lead away.

Nat rose from the bench, which was slick with his sweat and body fluids. He stood and realized the strength he felt in his changed body. Stepping forward, Nat floated off the floor and rocketed through the waiting door.

Inside the bathroom, Nat found a large room that stretched to the other loft built like a large public washroom found in a chic club. Through the doors, Nat saw that the stalls were individual rooms with a toilet and sink. Tiny spotlights in the ceiling, cast shadows off the dark tile and designer fixtures, lit the whole space. At the end of the row sat two larger rooms, each with a large walk in shower enclosed by glass.

Nat removed his soaked underwear and stepped into the shower. He washed away the remainder of his former self. When he stepped out of the shower, he felt reborn. He studied his new naked body in the small room's full-length mirror, the large muscles and fangs especially. Nat continued staring at himself until Vian came to the door, holding a box. Vian looked at Nat then opened the box to reveal a pair of black boxer briefs laid flat. Nat lifted and put on the new garment.

"What are these made off?"

"Nylon and lycra. Custom made for us."

"You're kidding."

"Nope. You'll have noticed we tend to walk around in only our boxers, and I wanted to make sure we had the best. And Pax is a fashion designer, so he designed them."

"Cool."

"If you're ready, the boys brought home dinner."

Nat followed Vian out through the bathroom door then down a wide curved staircase that arced under the loft to the floor below. Skating with Aaron, Marc and Pax were two other guys also around 19. More lights had been turned out and now Nat realized that a half-pipe ramp had been under the other loft the whole time. The curved plywood structure bent below the floor, leaving only the two decks at floor level. Plenty of padding was attached to the walls around it, but the skaters seemed able to avoid the walls. Marc especially pumped hard when passing the flat bottom before shooting up one quarter and spinning three times before landing perfectly. He, Aaron and Pax were without shirts again.

Nat looked down and realized he was only wearing the boxers. Vian looked at him and shrugged. He too was wearing only boxers. One of the new guys slid his board along the deck edge then jumped up to land on the regular floor. He skated around Nat and Vian once before hoping off the board and kicking it up.

Standing in front of Nat the guy had long messy dirty blond hair that almost hid his brown eyes. With a slightly round face he was adorable yet lean as evident from his muscular arms. He wore a tight tee and baggy dark green pants with a few patches of duct tape near the knees. The skater smiled and walked closer to Nat and Vian.

"I'm Todd," shaking Nat's then Vian hand. He smiled again then pulled off his tee, wiping his face of sweat to give its removal a purpose. The muscular arms lead to a nicely toned and lean chest with a dusting of dark hairs.

Vian walked away but turned back to make Nat and Todd follow. He led them to another lounge couch, but further from the main one and hidden by a wall blocking the view from the half-pipe. They needed the privacy.

The three sat, Vian and Nat on either side of Todd who started by leaning over and kissing Nat. Surprised, Nat found he was instantly turned on and kissing back with passion. Todd broke away and smiled, resting his hand gently on Nat's cheek. He turned and began kissing Vian, who darted his eyes and made contact with Nat.

Nat grimaced as a wave of hunger passed through him. He was hungry not horny. Nat opened his mouth and let his fangs extend down. Fangs drawn, he leaned into Todd's neck. Pausing briefly, Nat pressed his fangs on the skin then thrust them in. Blood sprayed up, but Nat quickly clamped his lips against the throat.

Todd moaned then started to notice the pain. Vian had his mouth occupied and his was face turned away from the new vampire sucking at this throat. But he began to struggle, pushing away from Vian's lips and squeezing out a short yell before Vian's hand was on it. The scream carried over to Todd's friend, who lost his balance on a spin off the deck and came sliding down the quarter to rest on the pipe bottom.

Aaron, Marc and Pax immediately pounced on the fallen skater. Marc found the soft neck, slid his fangs down and thrust them into the flesh. Aaron pulled the boy's arm up while his own fangs slid into place before he bit down. Pax, his fangs already out, pulled down the boy's baggy pants and bit into the soft flesh of his inner thigh. With the three boys' mouths pressed against the skater and holding him down, he barely had a chance to struggle up.

Briefly satisfied, Nat pulled his fangs out of Todd's neck and licked his lips. Vian looked at him, his own fangs drawn before biting into the other side of Todd's neck. Nat resumed now biting into Todd's arm. After another minute, Vian pulled away and gave Nat a nudge. Nat looked up, pulling his canines from the arm then pressed his lips against Vian's. The body was pushed to the floor when Vian came to lie on Nat.

The others had finished, pulled their dinner out of the half-pipe then wandered over to Nat and Vian.

"Did you like that?" Vian asked, standing up.

"Ohhh, yeah. That was incredible. I have a hard on from that and I feel so powerful."

"Good. All normal signs. You've handled yourself well, Ignatius. I'm proud of you. Pax there didn't do such a good job his first time."

"Well it was easy. I didn't think about it. There was this voice in my head and well I just did what it told me."

"Dude that's great. There's a lot left to teach you, but it'll come in time."

"Right. So let's start with that fantastic orgasm," Nat finished then pressed his lips to Vian's. His arms wrapped tightly around Nat, Vian lifted him up to the loft and his waiting bed. The others pulled off their pants then returned to half-pike, skating and flying about beyond human skill, the whole while their fangs slid down and eyes burning blood red.

The new boy

BY SEBASTIEN TERREAN

I stared at the blackboard. The white chalk letters swam meaninglessly. Romeo and Juliet were boring, the language too old and foreign. I always dreaded the token Shakespeare play we had to study each year, especially the story of two lovers I couldn't relate to. But I was able to fill the time daydreaming, imagining myself with Romeo who had cast Juliet aside for me.

Mr. Vital cleared his throat. I jumped in my seat, panicked. Had he called me while my mind wandered? I searched his face but he was looking at a piece of paper.

"Class, we have a new student. Reid Wilton," Mr. Vital said reading from the sheet.

I turned and looked toward the doorway and my heart skipped a beat. Shit, I thought. The new boy is absolutely gorgeous and I couldn't take my eyes off him. The moment began to feel surreal, unfolding like an after school special. I tuned out whatever the teacher was saying and watched Reid be directed to the empty seat in front of me.

Mr. Vital was known to be an easy going and boisterous teacher. Unlike with other teachers, students were not assigned desks and filled out the room starting from the back. This left all the empty seats up front. There were many to choose from and Reid had his pick, even one dead center but slightly further back, but instead he sat in front of me. It was probably a good spot. Mr. Vital had a habit of sitting on a desk facing the students and those of us on the edge would have to turn inward to see him.

When Mr. Vital took his seat perched on that very desk and began rambling about the star crossed lover, Reid turned in his seat. I couldn't help but stare at him since he was there. He didn't have a copy of the play, so I slid mine forward.

I was so nervous I didn't trust myself to speak, least my voice break, so I whispered to him. "Do you want to share with me?"

He turned and locked his honey colored eyes with mine. Slowly he smiled warmly and I thought he said, "I know it by heart, but sure." It was hard to hear what he was saying over my fast beating heart. He sounded British. I took an inventory of his beautiful features. His light brown hair highlighted with strands of blond, cut short on the sides but longer on the top sweeping messily forward and to the left coming to a point above his eye. The eyebrows, revealed the true chestnut brown, were full and arched only slightly. His skin had a dark color but not so much that it seemed he over tanned himself. His complexion was clear, lips full and pouty, a slight dimple on his chin. The looks were boyish and sad, but his eyes held a warmth and kindness the pouty expression tried to mask.

The thin cotton shirt material didn't seem to be able to hold in his well-defined muscles, while my own body was flat with milky pink skin. Unlike his hair, I didn't have any highlights, and though it was shorter, it was styled similarly to his. Where my face was round with little definition, his was square with a jaw that angled sharply then rounded at the chin. At least my lips were just as full, but a much lighter pink. My brows were more sunken, which were often hidden with shadows underneath. I always thought I looked angry or pissed off. Reid's face seemed expressionless until the edges of his mouth would curl slightly in a smile, then his whole face would light up.

I held the book open on the desk, turned so we could both read it, but my hands were shaking. This prompted Reid to reach out and put his hand on my hand to steady the shaking book. At that moment I almost died. His touch was gentle and instantly I had a hard on.

He leaned in and said, "I'm the one who's supposed to be nervous."

"I can't help it."

I don't know how I got through the rest of the class, but it went very quickly. I'm sure the clock sped up while I sat there with his hand touching my, moving away only when we needed to turn the page. Had it been a regular day I'm sure the clock would have dragged slowly, torturing me with as much Shakespeare as was legally allowed.

The final bell rang and most of the students had instantly picked up there books and were heading out the door. Mr. Vital was already behind his desk stuffing his briefcase.

I dared to look once more at Reid. He smiled again. I wanted so badly to be his friend. I was the lone gay student and if I wasn't ignored, I was bullied. Until Reid knew and made real friends, I might have a chance.

He locked his honey eyes on me again and spoke, "look this is forward, but I'm rather new and I could use a little help being shown around."

I was dreaming again. I blinked my eyes. "Sorry, what?"

"I said, would you be able to show me around."

"Um, but it's the end of the day." I stopped, actually it was Friday. "The end of the week," I added uselessly. I stopped, I'm screwing this up, stating the obvious.

"Yes, and the headmaster already gave me a tour. I was hoping for..." he stopped.

Mr. Vital cleared his throat again, tipping his head to the door. He probably wanted to get home.

"Let's continue this outside," Reid finally said and walked away. I grabbed my bag and followed, holding the bag in front of my crotch.

He was wearing the wrong clothes for a teenager in this city. Probably even this country. But it wasn't like he showed up like all British school boys, with a shirt and tie. I pictured watching Skins and remembered students our age didn't have to wear uniforms. Maybe they didn't in other grades either. His jeans were dark blue and tight, I mean painted on tight. I couldn't help it, I just started at his ass as I followed him. No student would wear such tight jeans, or Diesel sneakers. I followed him outside, not sure when he'd continue the conversation.

He stopped and I ran into him. Shit, I was being a complete space case.

"Sorry," he said.

"No, I wasn't watching where I was going."

He was leaning against a black Mini Cooper.

"Wow, is this your car?"

"Yeah, I made my parents bring it from Manchester."

"Where?"

"The north of England."

"Oh, it's so cute. Er, I mean, sweet wheels."

Reid giggled. "Would you like a ride?"

"Yeah!" I said, with too much excitement.

Reid walked to the driver's door, opened it, and ushered me to get in.

"I don't think you want me driving your car. I'm still shaking a little," I lied, I was shaking a lot.

"As if. No one drives Cooper but me."

I looked into the car and suddenly realized it was from the UK and had the steering wheel on the wrong side. I got in and he carefully closed the door for me. The interior was all black with leather seats. It was tiny and boxy, but really comfortable.

I watched Reid go round the car, and slide into the driver's seat. "So like I said, maybe you could show me around the neighborhood."

"Sure. What do you like to do?"

"Mostly hang with friends. If anyone's older brother or boyfriend was around, we'd go for a few pints, but I'm not old enough here."

"Yeah, that must suck."

"At least my parents let me drink at home."

"They do? What cool parents."

"Yes, they're British..."

"Really," I interrupted. I couldn't believe I had blurted that out. I was being so stupid.

He giggled, "well my dad is. Robin is Canadian. But they let me drink because they know I miss Manchester."

"Who's Robin?" I asked as Reid pulled the car out of the parking lot into traffic.

"My dad's partner."

I held me breath. No one used that kind of language, could it be that he had two dads. I wanted to ask, but I was sure my voice would give me away.

"I hope that doesn't make you uncomfortable."

"What?" I answered and sure enough my voice cracked.

He turned and smiled at me. "That I have two dads."

"Um," I didn't know what to say. I couldn't believe I was right. But what about Reid?

Shit, I had to answer to give. Reid looked at me, waiting for the response, probably getting worried I was a homophobe. Finally I shrugged noncommittally. He smiled.

"Look, I hope you don't mind, but I need to stop at home. I don't have a mobile yet and I need to check in with my parents."

"Sure, whatever."

The drive didn't take more than five minutes since we hit all green lights and Reid lived pretty close to the school. Actually, it probably took him longer to drive because he had to weave around the bendy suburban roads instead of the direct straight route I could walk. I was shocked when he pulled into the driveway of the large new stucco house. As one of the three garage doors lifted, I looked over to the foot path next to his house. It led directly from his street to the next one over, and right passed my house. I was less than a minute walk from home. Driving there would require going out to the main road, around a park and through several other streets to get to.

The Mini was tiny in the garage, unlike the two other cars, a BMW sedan and a Mercedes SUV. We got out and I walked to the garage door.

"Um, see that house," I pointed over the fence to the back of my house. Reid nodded. "That's where I live."

"Really, we're neighbors. You can have a ride to school any time you want."

"It's not that far, it'd be faster to walk," I said, stepping out on to the driveway.

Reid's face changed. He wasn't smiling. "Did you want to leave, I thought we could hang out?"

"What!" I nearly yelled. "No! Shit, I mean I'm not trying to get away."

"Great," he was smiling again. "Come inside. And stop being so nervous."

"I can't help it."

"You said that before. What's the problem?" He stopped and looked me over. "Don't like the English?" he said jokingly.

"No! I mean I do," I was panicking again. "I don't hate the British. I love some of your tv shows."

Reid opened the door leading from the garage to the house, "ah, like what?"

"Um, Doctor Who. And um, Skins. I download them all the time."

"Yeah, I have all those on DVD. Skins is great."

Before we could continue, Reid led me down a hallway to the front entrance and into the open plan living room. Two young men were sitting on the couch, one reading a newspaper, the other cuddled next to him.

"Dad, Robin," Reid said, "this is... a friend from school." The newspaper dropped and I got a full look at the two men. They looked to be in their early twenties. It hadn't occurred to me, but Reid must have been adopted. Reid leaned to me ear and whispered, "I can't believe I didn't even ask you your name."

He was right, and I hadn't offered it. I was so messed up around him that I just assumed he knew it.

The two men got up and walked over. The one with the newspaper put his hand out first, "Mitchell."

I shook his hand and said my own name, "Joel."

The other guy, Robin, put out his hand and when we shook he repeated his name, "Robin."

"Hi." I smiled.

Mitchell looked at me, "you seem nervous?"

"Dad, don't worry, he's been nervous since I met him."

"Well Joel, welcome to our house."

"It's nice and um," I looked around. There were two couches, a coffee table and three boxes piled in the corner. The walls were bare.

"Empty. We didn't bring much. Still getting settled. And we need to pick out paint colors and decide the right look."

"I don't think Joel wants to take interior design, dad."

"Right, of course. Well why don't we leave you to..." Mitchell stopped unsure what to say. I figured he was going to do a dad thing and say something embarrassing. "...hang out. Reid, why don't you show Joel your room."

I couldn't believe it, his father was encouraging his teenage son to take another teenage boy to his room. Then again, I doubt he's gay just because his parents are. Or just because I want him to be.

"Joel, if it's alright with your parents, you're welcome to stay for dinner," Robin said as we turned to go.

"Um, thanks, maybe."

He cut me off, "oh, unless you two want to go to the mall or something. You don't have to eat with us."

"No, it's cool, I mean," I looked at Reid.

"We haven't made plans, what do you think Joel?" Reid interrupted, saying my name for the first time. He said it so softly, like music. He smiled when I didn't answer.

Mitchell jumped in, "Joel, do you live far?"

"Um, just down the footpath out front. The house on the left."

"We're practically neighbors. If you want, we can invite your parents too, welcome them to the neighborhood." Robin said.

"I think they'll want to invite you," I said with a laugh. I wasn't sure if I wanted my parents meeting a gay couple and their son, who I had the hots for.

"We'll still have them over sometime. Wouldn't want them concerned they don't know your friend's parents. Parent worry about things like that."

I nodded.

Reid grabbed my hand and pulled me toward the stairs. "We'll be in my room," he shouted back to his parents. A grand staircase curved up to an open landing on the second floor and down. We took the stairs down to the finished basement.

At the bottom of the stairs, the room opened into a large empty family room that was above ground at the far end with large windows and a sliding door to the backyard. A small dark hallway next to the stairs led to several doors. First we passed a tiny bathroom then continued to the end of the hallway and through a door into a large bedroom.

The room was twice the size of my, with a large walk-in closet and it's own bathroom. Except for the bed, a large flat-panel tv mounted on the wall and rolling cart with an iMac on it, the room contained only four boxes piled near the door. The walls had been painted recently, dark grey, leaving the ceiling white. The floors were bare hardwood, and not the cheap laminated stuff.

"Wow, nice room."

"Thanks," Reid had a huge smile. "I don't have much stuff right now. And all my DVDs are from the UK so they only play on my computer."

"Hey, I'm not complaining, the screen is still bigger than my MacBook. And I don't even have a tv in my room."

"I guess I'm a little spoiled."

"Just a little," I tried to joke. Reid laughed so I think he took it as a joke.

"I hope you weren't bothered by my dads?" He asked slowly, while taking a seat on the bed.

I hovered around the tv, running my finger across it's sleek edge. "No, they seem cool. Really young."

"They're older than they appear," he replied quickly, defensively.

"Are you adopted?" I asked, turning toward him, but not making eye contact.

"No, it's complicated."

Well that was a useful answer. I was asking really personal questions. I just didn't know if I should out myself or not. Reid would be cool with it, I'm sure, but maybe he didn't want a gay friend.

"Come sit down."

Slowly I edged closer to the bed. It was a double size mattress raised up about three feet on a custom frame with drawers underneath. I sat down on the side, dangling my legs over the edge.

"They're good role models," Reid continued.

I didn't know what he was talking about anymore. "Sorry?" I asked, over raising my voice at the end of the word.

"My dads. They make good role models. I hope to have that good a relationship when I find the right bloke."

My heart stopped. He'd said it. I started biting my lip. Oh my gawd, the boy of my dreams was gay. This fantasy was too much.

Reid cleared his throat, "I'm sorry, I didn't mean to drop a bomb on you like that. I realize you're already nervous and the last thing you probably wanted to hear was that I'm gay."

"It's okay," I snapped. "I mean..." I was breathing heavy and I couldn't control myself. My eyes were getting watery and I was shaking.

Reid crawled over and placed a hand on my shoulder, "oh man, it's okay, you don't need to tell me unless you're ready."

"What do you mean?" But before he could answer, I waved him to stop. "How can you tell?"

"That I am gay, well I'm attracted to guys and..."

"No," I said annoyed as he was making it difficult.

Reid leaned in a kissed me on the lips. "That you are gay?" he whispered.

"Oh, boy," when he pulled his lips away from mine I sighed so heavily it was probably a moan. "Do that again."

He did, pushing me flat against the mattress and leaning on top of me. I completely lost track of the time. We must have only made out for several minutes, but it felt like an eternity before he stopped, then it felt like it hadn't been long enough.

"When I walked into English, you couldn't keep your eyes off me. You were practically drooling. And I can read you mind."

I laughed, the fantasy was getting too much, so I didn't need this situation that was really happening to get any weirder. "I don't believe you."

"Well I can prove it. Of course I don't have to read you mind to know you've had a hard on since English." He placed his hand on my crotch and cupped. Then he took my hand with his and held it over his own crotch. He winked. "That's why I outed myself first, I knew you were having trouble saying it. Actually, you're thinking right now that you still haven't said it."

He was right, but it was an obvious conclusion since I hadn't said out loud I was gay. I needed better proof he could read my mind, but then again, he was starting to scare me.

Maybe Reid sensed this or did read my mind at that moment because he laughed, "sorry, it's a trick."

"Oh, that's a relief, I wouldn't want you knowing my deepest secrets."

He kissed me again. "So are you staying for dinner?"

"I'd like to. We just met, and I don't want to leave just yet."

The smile across his face was gorgeous. He blushed. "I should go let my dad know so there's enough for dinner." He kissed me again before getting up and leaving the room.

I suddenly looked around the room. It had been a very unreal day and I needed to pinch myself. In less than two hours I had met the most gorgeous boy ever and he turned out to be gay and, amazingly, he was into me. Well hopefully he was into me, he didn't yet know me enough.

That night we eat pizza and watched a movie while we cuddling on Reid's bed. We agreed to wait and get to know each other before we got too physical. Our waiting period lasted until Saturday afternoon. From the Friday we met onward we were pretty inseparable, but with only one class together, we were a part all morning and most of the afternoon.

For some reason my parents wouldn't let me have a sleep over with Reid. I had not come out to them yet, but when I suddenly brought this new friend home, they seemed to know he was my boyfriend. It took less than a week to agree we were boyfriends. Reid popped the question on the Wednesday.

To reassure my parents, Mitchell and Robin invited them over for a nice dinner two weeks after we'd met. Mitchell and Robin were incredibly supportive, if not slightly casual about allowing Reid and I to be alone and unsupervised in their house. They were not very domestic. Every time I was over for dinner, they would order something in, and Reid didn't eat much. There was barely anything in their kitchen.

So for the dinner with my parents, Mitchell had it catered, but we didn't let my parents know. The meal was amazing, and more amazingly my parents allowed me to have wine with the meal since Reid was allowed to. I was less than six months away from turning eighteen so I didn't see it as being such a big deal. I was really worried my parents were going to make a big deal about how young Mitchell and Robin were, but during the dinner they looked worn down and old, not quite my parents age, but old enough to look almost 40.

I think my parents were more comfortable after meeting Mitchell and Robin, but I still couldn't have a sleep over. This turned into quite an argument about four weeks into the relationship and I blurted out that it didn't matter that I couldn't stay the night because there were other times to be alone.

The moment I let the words out I realized I had screwed myself from ever being with Reid unchaperoned. Instead my parents were calm and understanding. In the end my parents relented, realizing it was too late.

The night after that discussion, I let Reid know the good news.

"Honey," which was what I'd started calling him since his eyes were like sweet honey. "I have some good news."

"Me too."

"Okay then, you first."

Reid smiled and pulled a small box from his pocket. He casually opened it to reveal a beautiful stainless steel ring. I was unable to say a single word. I could feel the tears coming.

"Oh, baby," he said, hugging me.

"It's wonderful. Thank you," I put it on my ring finger.

He smiled, "I love you, but it's not an engagement ring."

"What?" I looked at realized it was on the wedding finger. I switched hands, realizing he'd said the three magic words. "Oh my gawd, I love you too."

"Maybe someday I can get you a proper engagement ring."

"Not if I do it first."

He laughed. "So what's your news?"

"My parents finally said I could sleep over here, but only on the weekends. They weren't going to let it happen until I let slip we were already doing it."

"Ah, I'm sorry you had to go through that, but I don't think you would be able to sleep over. Not yet."

"Why not, your dads are pretty cool?"

"It's not them. They'd be happy to have you over, but it's a bit too soon."

"Is it that a gay couple would be allowing their adopted minor son to have sleep overs in their house, because you know that we're over the age of consent?"

"No, I'm not adopted. Look, now's not the time to talk about it. Someday, okay."

I mumbled.

"Okay?" he asked again.

"Fine. Someday." He kissed me.

"I need to go talk to my parents for a minute, are you going to be alright?"

"Yeah, fine."

Reid left the room and went upstairs. I was surprised he said he wasn't adopted. Except for the night my parents were over, neither Mitchell or Robin ever looked more than 25. Reid was 17 like me so I doubted that his dad had him when he was eight.

I pulled the ring off and examined it. An inscription had been etched on the inside of the ring, "I will love you always, now and forever." I started to cry again, overcome with emotion. The tears were making it hard to see, so when I attempted to put the ring back on my finger, it suddenly disappeared from my hand. I wiped my eyes and looked over the edge of the bed. Certain it had fallen onto the floor, I began to search the floor and then peered under the bed. With the drawers, there was about an inch of clearance under the bed, and I could just make out the ring. I pulled at the drawer to see if I could get underneath it, but the handle didn't budge. I walked around and pulled the other drawer which didn't move either. Examining the drawer closely I realized that the drawers were fake, just handles and grooves to simulate the false fronts.

The nearest real seem was towards the top. The mattress was sunken into the frame, but there was a gap between the top of the bed and the top of the fake drawer of about a foot. Half way up a seem split the wood all the way around the bed. I grabbed the top of the bed and tested if it could move. It shifted slightly but I was apparently on the wrong side. Back on the side where my ring had fallen, I tested the bed top again. This time the entire top section holding the mattress lifted easily, hinged on the opposite side with two hydraulic arms to keep it from dropping.

I knew of beds with storage boxes accessed with the same type of hydraulic lifts but they normally weren't so deep. And this one wasn't being used for storage as it was empty. Instead it was lined in black satin and featured another mattress, covered also with a satin sheet and matching pillows. I climbed in and lay down. It was comfortable, the mattress seemed better than the one above. A satin cord hung from the top and I was able to pull it and lower the lid. The box went nearly completely dark. The numbers on an alarm clock recessed into the headboard glowed very dimly.

The lid lifted suddenly and Reid looked down at me.

"Hey," was all he said, but the expression on his face was less than amused.

"I dropped my ring underneath and the drawers seemed to be fake so I was trying to get at it," I explained quickly.

Reid's head disappeared. Without warning the whole bed tilted up on Reid's end then lowered back down a few seconds later. Reid climbed in and slid the ring on my finger.

"So I guess you're wondering?"

"Um, kinda. If it's a fetish thing you haven't been sharing, I'd understand."

"No, not a fetish. I sleep in here. This why we can't have a sleep over."

"Correction, couldn't. Now I know your kinky little secret," I teased him, giving him a kiss.

"It's not a kinky little secret, unfortunately it's a big secret." he pulled the rope and lowered the lid. Pressing a button by the alarm clock a soft light flicked on. "What does this thing look like?"

"A don't know, a coffin?"

"Yes." Reid kissed me again, possibly for getting the answer right. There were a few immediate questions that were swirling around in my head, I just didn't feel like asking.

Reid helped me out. "Who sleeps in coffins?"

"The dead." I knew the answer but decided to tease him. For some reason I wasn't finding the situation scary, just funny.

"Come on, I know you know the answer."

"Why, because you can read me mind?"

"Yes."

"It's that trick again."

"No, sorry, it's part of the answer."

"That you're a vampire," I finally blurted out.

He didn't say yes. "Can I show you?"

I giggled. I was beginning to think he was role playing. "Of course you should prove it, why ask?"

"Because you need to be ready to see this."

"Argh, show me," I was getting a little impatient.

He kissed me again then opened his mouth. His canine teeth grew longer and his irises became a fiery mix of reds, oranges and yellows. He leaned close and kissed me, holding his lips to my so I could play my tongue along his teeth. They certainly seemed real.

"Joel, I want you to know that I love you very much."

"I love you too."

"We've only been dating for a month and it felt too early to tell you this secret."

I swallowed. My eyes filled with tears again.

"Because this is not something you disclose to a boyfriend unless the relationship is very serious."

"But it is!" I objected.

"I know it is, but sometimes a little time gives you a lot of perspective. And with this we can afford to wait; well could."

"What do you mean by 'could'?" I said, with actual air quotes.

"I was born a vampire. Earlier this year I matured, turning into a full vampire from... well from human. Mitchell is my father, and he passed on the gene to me."

"Mitchell is a vampire?"

"Yes."

"Does Robin know?" I asked seriously.

Reid laughed, which was infectious so I started laughing too.

"Yeah, Robin knows," he finally said.

"Dad is nearly 50 and Robin just celebrated his 38th birthday. We stop aging at 23."

"And how old are you?"

"17. And no, I haven't been 17 for more than a year. But to be serious," he paused and looked me over, casually licking his fangs which did suddenly scare me. "Oh, no babe I'm not going to hurt you, don't think that." He looked back into my eyes, scared.

I swallowed because I had thought that.

"Humans are not allowed to how we exist. When one finds out, there are ways to fix the issue. We would have had plenty of time to work this out had you not found out. I was hoping to deal with this after I turned 23. You would have noticed that I'd stopped aging. If I'd turned you then or after, you would stay 23. If I turn you now, you will stay 17, but I will age to 23."

"That's a lot of talk about turning me. What if don't want to be a vampire?"

"Well the two other options are immediate death, which I won't do, or wiping your memory. And when I say wipe your memory, it would be very hard to successfully wipe only the memories of tonight. It would have to be all or nothing."

"You can't make me forget about you."

"I can, if I have to. Don't make me do it."

"So what are you saying?"

"I'm asking you to make a choice. We can break up and you will be made to forget about me, or you can allow me to turn you."

I didn't know what to say, or how to process the choice.

"Why don't you call your parents and ask to sleep over tonight? We don't have to rush, unless you leave."

"But I'll basically have to decide tonight."

"Pretty much." Reid stood up, pushing the coffin lid up. He reached on top of his headboard and took the cordless phone before lying back down next to me as he pulled the lid shut again.

I called and had a very short conversation with my dad. I heard him cover the phone a speak to my mom then he came back on the phone and gave me permission. I hung up and gave the phone to Reid.

"Look," I started, "I can't see living without you. And I don't know how I would be able to choose to have my memory erased. Although part of me feels challenged by the idea of letting you try because I know I could overcome it."

"You can't, and if you do, you'll go mad."

"I feel like you're only giving me one option."

Reid was crying now. It was hurting him. I knew that he would have to make the decision if I couldn't. If I was finding it hard to choose to breakup, it would be even harder for him to be the one to remember. I tried picturing what he would look like at 23 while I remainder 17, well almost 18.

"I'm sorry if I'm making it seem that choosing immortality is the easy choice, I know it will be a hard decision. Tell me your reservations."

"And if I don't?"

He giggled, "I'll just read you mind?"

"What if I make you choose?"

"I can't make the decision for you..."

"But you would have to if I couldn't settle?"

He cried harder. "If I turned you against your will, you might be unhappy and I couldn't stand losing you if you were miserable."

"Okay, my reservations," I paused. "I'm worried about staying 17 while you get to age to 23. That seems like a bit of a gulf. I mean wouldn't you look a lot like your dad?"

"I guess so. But that's only physical age. Mentality we would be the same. The age difference isn't that significant, and it's common among vampires."

"Reid, you could have let this go earlier, brushed this off as a fetish, but you chose to come clean."

He swallowed hard, "um, you're right."

"So either you secretly want to dump me or...," I left it there, and he didn't respond. I looked around the small coffin. It felt comfortable, cosy and secure, when it could have been claustrophobic and constricting. The last four weeks had been the best in my life. It wasn't something I would trade for anything. Why is it always that I have to make the choice, when I just want the decision made for me?

"Reid, I love you a lot, enough to trust you with my life. I like to think giving you this decision would be right. I don't know what it's like being a vampire, only you do. Make the decision."

The problem was I knew I couldn't live without him. I tried not to make the decision in my mind, he was simply going to read my thoughts.

He smiled showing his fangs. "You choose to give me the power to make the decision."

"Yes."

Reid kissed me on the lips. I could taste his tears. "I love you." His head moved and I soon felt his fangs gently break the skin on my neck. The pain was short, like having a needle inserted to draw blood. The feeling was replaced with euphoria as if the spot Reid sucked was the perfect g-spot. I released a moan. He stopped and I felt his tongue drag across the skin. Lips touched my again but I had closed my eyes. I was too tired to lift the lids. I tasted blood, but it must have been mine. My tongue darted out and licked my lips then I felt skin pressed against my mouth.

Like an instant shot of caffeine, I was awake, my eyes snapped open and I could see Reid's arm at my mouth. I sucked as much of his blood as I could, filling my mouth and swallowing intermittently. He pulled his arm away before I was finish but replaced it with his lips immediately.

I don't know how much time passed, I just enjoyed making out. The last thing I remembered I closed my eyes and felt Reid lay his head on my chest.

The lights were off but I could still make out the details inside the coffin. Reid lay against my chest in a deep sleep, his breathing shallow and steady. Sounds from upstairs were distant yet distinct. Foot steps, the folding of a newspaper and a few scattered words spoken aloud that sounded like a whisper from inside the coffin.

I began to wonder about Mitchell and Robin. We hadn't asked their permission. Reid joked about marriage, which was a serious topic, but I wondered if the commitment we made last night was more momentous. Marriage wasn't forever when compared to immortality. Wow, I thought, deep.

I also didn't know if last night was last night or if I had been asleep for several days. Had I even possibly died?

Reid's breathing changed. He turned his head and looked into my eyes, wet his lips and kissed me. "Good morning. How did you sleep?"

"Dead to the world," I joked, although maybe I had been dead.

"By the way, I can't read your thoughts anymore."

Sadness crept into my mind. I had felt connected to Reid. Then again it was hard not being honest with him. "Am I dead or did I die?"

"No, you evolved, well technically a genetic mutation, but that sounds grim."

"Do your parents know what you did?"

"They might. Since you didn't leave, they'll know something happened. We discussed you before and they knew eventually I would turn you; sooner if you discovered the truth."

"Were you always going to turn me?"

"Yes."

"What if I had said no?"

"Oh, I'm too irresistible and you love me too much," he said with a smile. I didn't know if he was joking, I mean how shallow.

Reid stood up and pushed the lid open. "Come with me, please."

He hopped over the edge of the coffin and into the bathroom. I walked in and he stood me between him and the mirror.

"Okay, I want you to think about your fangs and blood. Try and recall what it tasted like last night."

I shrugged lightly and stared in mirror and created a series of pictures in my head. Suddenly my gums burned and as I flicked my tongue across them to ease the pain, I nicked my tongue on my descending fangs.

With my mouth open wide the mirror reflected my fangs. My eyes took on the fiery glow I had seen in Reid's eyes. He had unsheathed his fangs too. I turned to him and kissed him.

"Keep them out, but close your mouth and eyes, we're going to go have show and tell."

I giggled. I liked giving surprises.

Reid led me upstairs to his parents who I could hear were making out on the couch. He held my hand tightly.

"Dad, Robin, I had to give Joel something last night," he said quite proudly. Offside he whispered, "show them."

I opened my eyes and mouth, proudly showing them I was now a vampire. A smile spread across Mitchell's face and Robin jumped up and gave me a big hug.

"Welcome to the family," Robin said, holding me tight. "Reid is so impatient I'm surprised he waited as long as he did!"

Reid tried to put the blame on me, "Joel did sort of figure it out last night, so I had to turn him."

"Good choice, son," Mitchell stood up too and pushed Robin out of the way to embrace me too. "Joel, you make Reid so incredibly happy. I'm glad he gave you the gift and proud you accepted."

"So am I?" I said with a laugh. I wrapped my arms around Reid and our lips met.

"I think we can finally stop ordering take-out," I heard Robin say to Mitchell. Every time I had been over, they would order dinner, but I never saw them eat. I guess it was done for show.

Reid looked at me and read my face since he couldn't read mind. "Don't worry, you won't have to give up food, but you don't actually need it."

A laugh erupted from my chest, "maybe you can still read me."

He laughed, "only some things."

"Hey, I doubt my parents are going to let me sleep at your house every night, how am I going to sleep without a coffin?"

The sound of a throat clearing came from the couch. Robin was staring at Mitchell while we all waited for him to speak.

"Do your parents come into your room during the night at all?"

"No, they actually respect my privacy."

"Your window faces this house, but theirs' faces the front, right?"

"Yeah, my room is in the basement too. You're not going to suggest building a tunnel?"

Mitchell's smile was wide and had a hint of mischief.

"Seriously?"

"No. But when you go to bed, just slip out and come in through the side door into utility room next to Reid's bedroom. With your new ability to fly you'll be able to get from your window to that door in mere seconds."

"I can fly?" I said, surprised at what Mitchell had revealed. Reid took my hand and we were already floating up to the ceiling. "Cool!"

We continued to float near the ceiling, kissing away. If I hadn't been awake, I would have sworn it had all been a dream.

Second Chance

BY ETHAN KILBURN

"We have to kill him. It's the only way you'll be free."

I looked up at Trevor and gave him my sexy smile, the one that always worked on him. "If you unlock these handcuffs," I paused and rattled the shackles holding me to the bed, "I would be free."

Trevor looked down at me sadly. "You know I can't do that right now. You're too hungry and I don't plan on being your dinner," he sighed and I watched his face fill with sadness. "I'm sorry, it's not that I can't trust you—you know that right—it's the monster inside you I can't trust."

"Trev, you know I love you? I won't bite."

"Don't do this. I do love you but you're not yourself right now. I mean look at yourself."

"Real funny. You know I can't anymore," I looked over to the full-length mirrored doors on our wardrobe. Trevor's back reflected in the glass, but my own reflection was nowhere to be seen.

His eyes were watering again. "I don't like seeing you this way, seeing what he's done to you."

"You can have this too. I want to share this with you," I said, flashing him a smile so he could see my teeth.

"Dylan," he yelled suddenly, "I don't want it! Can't you make your fangs go away, please?"

I licked my tongue passed my sharp extended canines. I was still getting used to them after only three days. "I've tried," I said quietly, "they just won't go back up. I think I need to feed."

"I'll go to the butcher and get you some more blood."

I let out a whine, "that's not going to cut it anymore. Trevor," I said with extra whine, "I need human blood, please."

"No, I'm not going to let you feed before I can save you."

"It's too late, I've changed."

"No, that's where you're wrong, it's not too late, this is what I'm saying. Once we kill William, you'll be human again."

"But I want to stay a vampire."

"Dylan, I'm trying to keep my promise. The night after you first drank his blood you begged me, remember, hmm, you begged me to stop you from becoming a monster."

"Well I've changed my mind. William has given my a gift; he's made me immortal, and made me so damn powerful."

"That's his blood talking. It's taken over you and it's controlling you now. Everything you say, it's the blood talking."

"I still have control over my need. Come close, I'll prove it. I won't bite you, I love you too much."

"No."

"Fine, then leave. If you can't accept what I've become then I can't be with you anymore."

Trevor's eyes filled with more tears, my words had hurt him.

"I won't leave you," he replied using his stubborn determined voice.

I started to cry too, real tears because I felt bad that I'd made him cry. "I'm sorry. This is hard for me. I know I wanted you to stop this, but it feels just so good. I want you to join me and instead you're rejecting me." I stopped and cried some more. "Don't make me choose between staying with you and being a vampire," I finally said.

"I'm not going to change my mind, I just won't become a monster. You have to make that choice. If our love is strong enough, you'll over come this."

"I could say the same thing, Trev. If you love me, you'd accept me."

"Stop. Please, just stop. Make your choice." He sat on the bed turned away from me.

I closed my eyes and thought of losing Trevor, and especially living without him for an eternity. I looked at the sweet boy I'd fallen in love with three years before, and reminisced about sharing every single day since. He hadn't showered and was run down, but he was still beautiful. His messy hair looked good with his real bed head, or in his case couch head, messed look. It was long, but not long enough to cover his soft neck, the one I'd placed many kisses and hickeys on over the years. I could see the faint outline of a vain running beneath the skin. I could smell him from where I lay and he was intoxicating. Tasting his blood would be so much better.

Before I knew what I was doing, I pulled my arms breaking the handcuff chain and lunged at my boyfriend's neck. My reflexes were now quicker than his and before he could react, I had him pinned. I sank my fangs in his jugular, and for the first time I drank real human blood.

Trevor remained calm. He didn't scream or fight back, but he spoke, "make the right choice."

His words stabbed me. I pulled back to look into his eyes. He was trying to hide his fear, but he looked both resigned and willing to sacrifice himself. I licked my lips clean and felt me fangs draw back into my gums.

I didn't know what to say. I don't think he did either. Instead we kissed then cuddled together wrapped tightly in each other's arm until we both fell asleep.

I woke suddenly when I felt the sun rise. Our bedroom already had blackout curtains, but I had sealed them and blocked the window alcove with a large piece of plywood. Sunlight didn't come in through the door so I was safe. But I still felt nervous when I could feel the sun rise over the horizon. I had slept most of the night, when by my new nature I should have been awake, but I still felt a primal need to sleep through the day.

Trevor stirred, probably sensing I was awake.

"Trev, I'm sorry I bit you. I had to feed, and it needed to be human blood. That's not an excuse. I won't do it again. I have made my decision... I made it after I tasted your blood," I paused.

Trevor took the pause as a sign I hadn't chosen him, "I'm sorry you feel this way. You should leave then."

"No, I want to be with you and I can't imagine eternity without you, so I'll settle with growing old with you. Also, if leave right now, I won't survive the sun," I paused, hoping it sounded like a joke. "Now that I've fed you don't need to chain me down, I took enough to get me through until we destroy William. You won't be able to do it alone, you need my help."

His face seemed brighter now that he knew I wanted him.

"You're right, I do need you. I can't take William on myself, and I'm glad you've chosen me. I'm just sorry I didn't see the pain I was causing you, I was more worried you wanted to make me your first kill to finish your transformation."

"Trev, I could never kill you. It doesn't matter how much I need the blood, I need you more. Look, do you have a plan?"

He nodded before shifting in the bed to sit up against the headboard. "Do you think William expects you to come back to him and be with him?"

"I don't know. Why?"

"Well I was thinking you could drag me to his place saying you're ready to make your first kill, but wanted to change me and you need his help. If he wants you for himself, he may want you to kill me."

"He seemed pretty indifferent about you, but he also wasn't throwing himself at me. Now that there's evidence I've bitten you, I could drag you over there crying about nearly killing you and how I couldn't finish. I think he'd push me to finish it. But I also think you would look weak and unlikely to fight back. If I distracted him, you could wake up and kill him."

"Okay," he nodded slightly unsure. "It's your mess and I think you need to clean it up, but then again, I don't want his death to count as your first kill."

"I hadn't thought of that; sort of a way to protect a new vampire from killing their maker to stop the change. So you think it will work?"

"Only plan we've got."

He closed his eyes, probably still weak from the feeding. I nestled in and held him in my arms as I drifted off into my own day long sleep.

Again the path of the sun woke me. I opened my eyes knowing the sun had just disappeared below the horizon. I licked my teeth, but my fangs weren't down. I could feel the hunger building but I knew I could make it through the night.

Trevor rolled over and kissed me, his usual way of waking up. I wondered for a moment if he'd forgotten what I'd become. I hadn't.

"We'd better get ready. Don't shower, in fact I think you shouldn't change either," I said pointing at his ruffled clothes he'd already been wearing for two days.

Trevor only nodded. He rolled out of bed and disappeared through the doorway. I gathered my black hoodie off the floor and pulled on my sunglasses. In the living room I found Trevor gathering several stakes.

"Trev, those don't work."

"Are you sure?"

"Yeah sorry, it's off with his head."

"Well how the hell are we supposed to do."

"A sword or axe... maybe a chain saw?"

"Shit Dylan, do you have a sword lying around?"

"No, but maybe I can use something else."

A few weeks earlier I had bought a curtain hanging kit which was basically a thin steel wire. I pulled the unopened package from the hall closet and cut a length of cable. I formed a large loop and a slipknot then attached the end to our cordless drill.

"Here, if you get this over his head, then hold down on the trigger, the wire will wind up and should do the trick."

"Well I just have to figure out how to get it over his head."

"Don't worry, I'll be able to help with that. Trust me."

"I don't have any other choice at this point. But Dylan," he stopped, holding the drill up to my face, "do not double-cross me or I will use this on you."

I couldn't argue with his angry tone. "I love you," was all I said.

He smiled. "I love you too. Now," he put the drill in his jacket and threaded the wire up the sleeve, "hit me and drag me off to William."

"Hit you?"

"Yes, I think I should have put up a fight when you attacked me. Not only will there be the bite marks, but some bruises."

Without pausing to give it a second thought I throw a punch, my fist smashing into Trevor's face. It knocked him to the ground. He was now out cold. "Oh, cramp." I looked down at my unconscious boyfriend. "I guess that's for the better." I picked him up and examined the bite mark which was already fading, "I'm going to need to make sure the wound is fresh too." I extended my fangs then bit into his neck in the same spot. I sucked up a small amount of his blood to spread on my face making myself messy for effect. I knew I really did it to taste his sweet blood again.

I slid the patio door open and holding Trevor tightly in my arms, launched myself off the balcony. William had a large converted loft in the rougher part of the city. It only took a few minutes to fly there and glide in through the large open window. Of course my landings weren't perfect yet and I stumbled when my feet attempted to make contact with the floor. Instead to avoid crashing I dropped Trevor on the couch as I flew passed.

I managed to slow myself and remained in the air, hovering several feet off the floor. I called to my sire, "William." Tears came to my eyes. "I can't do it... I tried to make my first kill but I can't finish it, I love him too much."

William came over to the edge of the low loft where he had his bedroom and looked at me. I watched him tilt his head as he cast his eyes across Trevor before he suddenly flew down to me, pushing me up against a concrete pillar. He snarled, showing his fangs.

"Why did you come here?"

"Help him. I took too much, I can't kill him. I'll do whatever you want. I'll kill anyone else, just let him live."

"How noble of you. Like I care about a stupid mortal."

"You cared about me?"

"No, I didn't," he exhaled. "If you can't kill him then you're not going to make it as a vampire. I might as well kill you."

"Then do it," I shouted. He eyed me suspiciously then snapped a quick glance at Trevor before settings his eyes back on my. He appeared ready to continue speaking but instead I found myself thrown onto the couch next to Trevor.

William landed on top of me and shoved my face into Trevor's neck. "You need to finish what you started. He'll die either way and you must kill to live."

"I love him. I didn't want to hurt him but I was hungry. I'm just glad I stopped myself before I did kill him." I sobbed, using real tears.

"Silly boy, you've taken too much blood."

"But isn't there a way to save him?"

"You could feed him your blood but he's too weak and won't be able to change. He's gone. Now finish it," he yelled, slapping me across the face. The sting was strong and it made me angry.

"Maybe I should kill you!" I shouted back.

"Good luck silly boy. What do you think this is, some movie where you can fight back and stop the change. It's too late."

I launched myself up at him and throw him across the room. He slowed and hovered in the air, staring down at me, taunting me. I flew up and crashed into him, pushing him up against the wall.

William struggled against the wall baring his fangs. "Okay, do you want to do this like a movie? Then let's see, what's my line. Oh, 'my turn'," and immediately he pushed back forcing me across the room to the opposite wall.

Now I found myself pinned. I looked down at the couch and saw Trevor had opened his eyes; he was slowly pulling out our weapon.

"Dylan, we could continue like this all night, but don't expect me to die."

"Don't be so sure," and again I pushed him. Only I couldn't move, he was stronger.

He rolled his eyes, "why are you resisting the change?"

"I love Trevor and I want to be with him."

"And what, don't tell me, he made you choose between growing old and dying with him, or living alone for an eternity."

"Yeah."

"And like a gutless mortal you choose him. You could have forced him to change," William looked at me with pity. I stole a glance toward Trevor, which William must have caught. He smiled knowingly, "so you two must have a come up with a scheme to kill me," which he said loudly before leaning into my ear and whispering, "if you manage to kill me, you will become mortal again. But just so you know, you will get one more chance to embrace immortality."

"I won't need it," I yelled into his face as I flew him downward into the glass coffee table. It shattered on impact but William was on his feet before the shards had even landed on the floor. Trevor had jumped up from fright, dropping the drill.

"So this was your plan," William surveyed the drill and wire and laughed. In the blink of an eye William grabbed the drill and snapped the tool in half while flinging the wire out the window.

I my searched eyes around the room hoping to spot another weapon, not pausing my stare as my eyes passed over the large shards of glass at William's feet.

"He doesn't seem as close to death as I'd thought," William finally said looking at Trevor. He licked his lips. "Hmm, you have tasted him though. He must have been good; very hard to resist."

Before I could shield Trevor, William had lunged at him, hoisting him up and flying him to his bed. I flew after them and found William lying on top of Trevor on the large bed. Angered I launched at William from behind but as I descended upon him he rolled off Trevor who I slammed into instead. Trevor was knocked unconscious again, his nose bleeding. I gathered him into my arms to protect him and heard William laugh.

Suddenly the mattress began to drop into the floor while the high head-board folded down onto the bed frame. Immediately it went dark.

William's voice was a distant muffle outside the box, "when you're hungry enough, drain the mortal and then I will release you. Don't take too long though, I want my coffin back."

My eyes had adjusted to the complete lack of light and I could see clearly the face of my lover still unconscious. I wasn't hungry, but the fighting had taken a lot out of me and I knew it won't be long. Already my fangs ached.

Trevor's eyes fluttered open and he began to panic. "Trevor, I'm here with you, don't be scared," I said immediately to calm him.

"I can't see. Where am I?"

"We're in William's coffin."

I could hear Trevor's heart beat faster, the sound echoing loudly off the sides of the confined space. I kissed him and wrapped my arms around him. "Don't worry."

He began to reach out and feel the space around him, only able to touch the lid. "It feels big?"

"It's king sized. There's plenty of space and a good amount of oxygen. I can feel air flowing so I don't think it's air tight; William would still need to breathe."

"What's the plan?" he whispered quietly which I could still hear with my enhanced hearing.

"William wants me to drain you before he'll let me out. I wonder if he has another coffin for backup."

"Or guests."

I laughed.

"Dylan?"

"Yes."

"Feed from me now."

"No."

"Please, I think if you take a little now, you'll be able to hold on longer."

"True. Damn, I hate it when you're right."

"Shut up and bite me."

I left the last word to Trevor, moved my head down to his neck and sank my fangs into the side of his neck opposite the first bite. It was the third time I'd tasted his blood and I was beginning to get addicted.

"Okay honey, please stop," Trevor said, giving me a shove. I moved my face to his and pressed my lips to his. He broke the kiss quickly and complained, "clean your lips, would you. I don't need to taste my own blood."

"Why not, you taste so good, the best I've ever had."

"I thought you'd only ever fed off me?"

"Well I've had William's blood."

"That was different, didn't he serve it in a glass mixed with alcohol."

"Yeah, okay I've tasted his and yours, and your blood is better."

"Thanks."

"Trev, I love you." I kissed him again, having licked the remainder of his blood from my lips. "We need a new plan," I said with my lips to his ear in the lowest of voices.

"I know, I'm thinking," he whispered back.

"Well, if you drank my blood, you'll become a vampire, but then once we've gotten out and killed William, I won't be a vampire and neither will you."

"Sounds like a risking plan."

"Got a better one?"

"No, but we're still not doing it."

"The thing is, should something happen to you, say I don't drain you and William decides to snap your neck, if you have my blood in your body, you'll live. We did this your way and it hasn't worked out. Maybe the only solution is for you to accept the gift."

"No," his stubborn voice had returned.

"Enlighten me, what do you have against becoming a vampire?"

"I don't want to kill to live."

"Shit Trev, you're not a vegetarian, you already kill to live. And don't be a hypocrite and claim it's different. You only have to kill one human to change, from then on you only require a small amount from a donor."

Trevor had started to cry.

"I'm curious, if I turned you against your will, would you kill me to cure yourself? Or would you sacrifice yourself?"

"I'd walk into the sun before I'd killed anyone, including you."

"Hon, that doesn't work until after the first kill. It will hurt, but you'd live. Worse, your body will be force you to attack someone in order to survive."

"You don't know how hard it is to resist."

"So don't."

There was a longer tearful pause. "No."

"I can feed you, then our first kill can be William. If killing him doesn't erase our condition then at least we've gotten over our first kill and removed an evil vampire."

There was another long pause. "Maybe," he finally sighed.

I knew I had him, but only just on my side of the fence.

"Dylan, assuming he'll let us out when you've fed me and not drained me like he demanded, I want us to try to kill him without biting him. Biting him should be our last resort."

"O-," I tried to say before he continued.

"If," he said with emphasis, "it doesn't work, just go ahead and drain me. I don't want to end up having to kill."

"Okay." I bit into my wrist and placed it at Trevor's lips before he could change his mind. Amazingly he moved quickly too, grabbing my arm and holding the offering against his mouth as he began to drink my blood. That night I had two martinis mixed with William's blood, which could not have been move than an ounce of blood each, and it had been diluted with vodka. I figured Trevor should take more, I just didn't know how much more. He made the decision for me when he pushed the wound away.

"I think I've had enough."

"How can you tell?"

"I can see you. It's no longer dark in here."

"Really?"

"Yes," he reached up and stroked my face then leaned toward me and kissed me on the lips.

"And how do you feel?"

"Fine. Normal I guess. I bit tired."

"I think it'll still take time for the change to be complete. We'll sleep now." I didn't hear a response. Trevor's breathing was now shallow, he was already asleep.

The rising sun woke me briefly. William must have gone to another resting place.

My eyes opened immediately when the sun set. I turned to Trevor who woke at the same moment. His fangs had grown during the day. Before I could kiss him or point out his extended canines, the lid lifted and the bed began to rise. Without a word, Trevor and I scrambled out of the coffin to confront William.

"I thought I gave you an order. Instead you fed him. Silly boy, you're not getting out of this that easily."

"What do you mean?"

He answered by throwing me across the loft. When I shook my head to clear the fall, I realized I had hit several framed photos on the opposite wall before I slid to the floor. I was now lying in a pile of broken glass and wood. Bits of glass were stabbing my hands and body. One large piece lay against my leg uncomfortably close to my balls.

I looked to the bedroom and saw the back of William advancing on Trevor, who was baring his new fangs. Without debating a plan, I tossed the large shard of glass resting between my legs like a frisbee. It sailed quickly through the air and clear through William's neck.

Surprised and shocked I'd landed a direct hit, I stood up and instinctively launched myself into the air, but stumbled and fell crashing to floor. I looked up at Trevor who held William's head in his arms, a disgusted expression on his face. I continued to watch as Trevor's fangs retracted, and felt my own do the same. I stood up, now feeling pain for the first time since I'd been turned.

"We're human again," I said to Trevor. He licked his teeth and looked sad, dropped the head and ran up to put his arms around me. We held each other crying from the relief it was over.

Finally Trevor pulled back and looked around the large loft. "This place is much nicer than ours. Do you think it's paid for?"

"I don't know. I guess?"

"If we put his body in front of the window, in the morning it should turn to dust."

Wasn't a question, but I answered regardless, "probably."

"You clean up, I'll search for a lease or deed."

Trevor walked down the stairs to an office area and began digging through the desk while I stared after him in surprise.

"I don't get it, Trev. What are you doing?"

"I bet he bought this place outright. If I find the deed we can claim this place. Consolation prize for what he did to us. I'm tired of renting."

He wasn't willing to kill, but stealing from a dead man, or dead vampire, was fine. Go figure. I dragged William's body to the window and ignored the rest of the mess.

"Aha, look. Found it," Trevor said, holding a folder. "Paid for in full with cash through an offshore bank account. Basically his name's barely on the title."

I stood behind him with my arms wrapped around him pretending to read and understand what he was talking about. "Trev?"

"Yeah."

"How did it feel being a vampire?"

"Um," to seemed at a loss for words. Finally after nearly a minute he turned around and hugged me. "I'm sorry for resisting. For a brief few minutes I knew how you felt. I mean I was hungry, but it was the power. My whole body felt so good, it was unbelievable."

"Would you want to be a vampire now after that?"

Trevor smiled, "yes."

I held him and said nothing more. We'd deal with the future tomorrow.

In the morning we watched the sun rise from the roof then waited inside for the sun to come around and shine on William's corpse. We wandered the city enjoying three very good meals and basking in the beautifully sunny day. Before dinner we caught one of the best sunsets we'd ever seen as the sun dipped into the Pacific ocean. We lingered over dinner then finally walked home to our new loft.

"I love you, Trev."

"I love you too."

"There's just something I need to talk to you about, something William said the other night when we tried to destroy him."

"What was that?"

"He said even if I killed him, I'd get one more chance at immortality."

Trevor's eyes lit up. "Really? I wish it were true."

"You do?"

He nodded.

"So do I." I held my mouth open and pushed my fangs down. Trevor did the same, but neither of us could do it. "Maybe not tonight?" I said finally.

Out of the corner of my eye I saw a flash of light then felt something hit my face. Looking up from the ground as someone was kicking me, I watched another guy holding Trevor while a third was throwing punches.

"Stupid fucking faggots," yelled the one kicking me.

I tasted blood on my lips and instinctively licked my lips. My sharp teeth had descended again. When I looked at Trevor, he already had his fangs buried in his puncher's neck. I flew up at the kicker and rammed my foot into his head then launched myself at the guy who'd held Trevor, sinking my sharp teeth into his neck. Before I could finish my first kill, Trevor had moved onto the kicker and was feasting on his blood. Soon I joined him and we drained the guy together.

Trevor stood and surveyed the bodies, licking his lips. "So William was right, we did get a second chance."

"Yes we did."

We kissed, then holding hands we flew home.

As the sun began to rise that morning, we settled into our king sized coffin and had one final kiss good morning.

"So Trev, you fought me long and hard because you didn't want to be a vampire, and yet you killed tonight. What gives?"

"Well those three deserved it, calling us faggots. I hate gay bashers."

"You don't feel bad."

"No," he sighed. "Dylan, I know now what you mean about how good it would feel to be a vampire, but it's more than that. I still feel in control. I was terrified of becoming a monster, but you're right, I just wasn't willing to accept the new you. But not having a reflection, that does worry me."

"Why?"

"What if we've lost our souls?"

"If we didn't have souls, we wouldn't have the ability to love, which is one of the greatest things a human can do. I think I heard about that from the Bible."

"Oh, Dylan, I do love you, and I'll love you forever," he moaned.

I smiled, "I love you too, now and for eternity."

We cuddled together, my arms wrapped around Trevor, safely entombed in our new crypt, and we had an eternity of nights a head of us.